WASHING ASHORE

WASHING ASHORE

A SPARK OF LIFE NOVEL, BOOK THREE

by

GINNA MORAN

SUNNY PALMS PRESS

ISBN 978-1-942073-87-1 (soft cover)
ISBN 978-1-942073-86-4 (ebooks)

Cover design by Silver Starlight Designs
Cover images copyright 123RF

For Inquiries Contact:
Sunny Palms Press
9663 Santa Monica Blvd Suite 1158
Beverly Hills, CA 90210, USA
www.sunnypalmspress.com
www.GinnaMoran.com

For Amy Holliday, one of the most selfless and beautiful souls I know.

CAN'T RESIST THE OCEAN

THE UNFORGIVING CURRENT CHURNS AROUND me, tossing my exhausted body back and forth amongst the waves. Every time I break the surface, another swell washes over me, stealing the breath from my lungs and clouding my vision. Utter darkness, one I haven't seen since my mermaid transformation, settles around me. The black ocean cocoons me in its embrace. Soft light emanates from my chest, but it's neither bright enough nor strong enough to push the night ocean away. All it does is blink in quick successions to the racing rhythm of my heartbeat.

"Carter?" I project the words out into the vast void. Fear grips at my chest, tightening my lungs as they beg for me to gulp in the air I so desperately need. But if I breathe now, I'll drown.

The only cramps threatening me are the ones digging at my side from my struggle to stay afloat. It's been weeks since the last full moon and weeks since I've transformed into a mermaid. I refuse to do so without Carter. I'm not risking the seas without my eternal mate and warrior—the boy the ocean fated me to be with. He's the boy who gave his life to save me from a lifetime of misery enslaved to King Attilonious as his new queen, and the boy I refuse to live without. I vowed my life and gave him the spark he had given me—the one I took fully after his death—the spark that brought him back to life and stripped him of his merman form, at least until the next full moon.

Thoughts of Carter push the panic from my mind, and I freeze in the water and peer through the blurry sea. My hair floats around my face, veiling me like it can somehow protect me from what lurks in the ocean I had suddenly awoken in, disoriented, unsure of how I got here.

And it's not the first time either.

"Ava." The soft voice comes from nowhere and everywhere, wrapping its melodic tenor around me, pulling me away from the spot I sway in the current. "Ava, this way."

I find the strength to move, and I swim, stroking out my arms while kicking my legs. I swim until the edges of my vision turn red, and I'm sure I'll open my mouth at any second to breathe in air that isn't there—not without my gills.

I catch myself in another swell, and it lifts me in the water, sending my stomach to my feet. I don't resist it. Instead, I swim with it, ascending in the dark sea for what feels like forever. A haze of light erupts above me, pale beams from the nearly full moon overhead, shining just for me. They beckon me to the surface that still seems so far away.

Too far away.

I can't hold my breath any longer.

Opening my mouth, ocean water fills my throat and nose, sending fear straight to my heart. I thrash about, choking on the sea. It's like it's begging me to transform, forcing me into it to save myself.

I will for the cramps to seize my legs, for the water to fill my heart and embrace me, but still, I can't transform. Something holds me back. A million things, actually. Fear of the king who stole my human world from me. Fear of the unreliable affinity to the ocean bestowed upon me. Fear of everything the ocean has given me suddenly being stolen away. Fear of losing the few good things in my life I've managed to salvage. All these things prevent me from transforming into what I'm supposed to be.

"Ava," the musical voice says, invading my mind. "Ava, you must not fear. You must accept everything you are if you're to make it in this world. Don't let your fear imprison you." It's like the voice read my thoughts. "You have a duty to fulfill."

I blink in and out of consciousness, trying to determine

where the voice is coming from, but it's impossible as it echoes only in my mind and only for me to hear.

"Please," I say, my thoughts barely audible in my own head. "I'm trying the best I can."

"I know, my daughter. Give it time. You will figure things out."

I stop fighting the current, defeat clinging to me. "I don't have time. Just tell me the answers. Tell me what I have to do."

A quiet calm settles over me. The voice doesn't respond, leaving me feeling utterly alone and scared. This wouldn't be the first time I've drowned, but this time, Carter isn't here to revive me.

Carter.

A dozen images flash through my mind, all moments of our life together. From the first time I saw him standing on the dock in front of the Ocean Jewel, the luxury yacht where we met, to the moments in Pearlestria where we were forced to accept a life against the one we had planned. His shining, ocean eyes, his dark hair, the curve of his muscles I have memorized with my fingers, the softness of his lips—everything about him fills up my very essence with the love we have for each other, turning these dark moments into nothing but light and hope and assurance.

The icy water turns warm around me, and a flash of light glows on the other side of my closed eyelids, turning my vision red. Hands grip under my arms, my body dragged through the surf, and then suddenly, I'm engulfed in balmy night air.

Something thuds hard against my chest, forcing the water in my lungs to expel. I cough and spit, tears burning my eyes worse than the saltwater clouding my vision. Fluttering my eyes open, I peer up into the brilliant night sky. Stars pepper the world in tiny beads of dazzling light, each one shimmering and blinking like they're shining just for me. Pale moonlight sets the foamy waves aglow in a silver sheen. They crash over my weak legs, pulling the sandy beach out from under me, dragging it back into the surf.

Warm arms pull me farther from the crashing waves until my body rests on powdery soft sand. It clings to every inch of me, from my toes to my blond hair, making me sparkle in the white moonlight.

Water drips onto my face, the droplets pelting my forehead before splashing into my eyes. Carter gazes down at me, a mixture of emotions crossing his face—from uncertainty to fear to love to desire—all of them leaving him speechless.

I take a few more breaths, neither of us saying a word, and Carter holds me until my lungs stop burning. His elbow digs into the sand, and he brushes my tangled hair from my face with his other hand.

He closes the distance between us, kissing me gently at first and then deepening the kiss when my body reacts, craving Carter to kiss me so desperately that I'll forget the panic that immobilized me the second I opened my eyes amid the waves.

Carter tenses as I accidentally send him a dozen memories from the minutes I spent in the water along with everything I had felt in the moments before I thought I was going to die again. I don't mean to, because I want to protect him from experiencing such a thing, but they trickle to him anyway.

Ever so slowly, he pulls away. Tears shine in his blue-green eyes, sending sorrow through my own heart that beats in perfect sync with his. He rests his forehead against mine, taking a moment to compose himself while giving me the chance to find my own bearings.

"If you wanted to go for a late night swim, I'd have joined you," he says, forcing a smile, though his eyes line with worry.

I release a shaking laugh, staring down at the tank top and cotton shorts I had worn to bed, falling asleep in Carter's arms like I've been doing every night since we washed ashore on this island.

"I'll definitely invite you next time," I say, releasing a heaving breath. Neither of us says it, but we both know swimming in the dark ocean was something I'd have never planned. The farthest I go into the water now is not even past my waist in the waves. "If I actually wake up before I jump in."

He frowns at my words. The last few times this has happened, I found myself waking up amid the waves with no recollection of what had happened. I assumed my subconscious had been pissed at me for denying myself the ocean, but tonight felt different. It didn't feel like I just sleepwalked to the beach from our tiny bungalow for a dip. I was far enough out that the water was cooler than in the shallows. I was deep, too. I could sense it.

And the voice.

I think the ocean called me to it and got to me when my guard was down. I've been begging for an explanation—why me? What is so special about me that I've been given the gift to be a human without the enchantment of the sea stone ring created by the king? I want to know why both Carter and I are alive, and what I'm exactly supposed to do with myself. I'm not powerful enough to face King Attilonious like I assume the ocean wants. I can't even manage to keep my head above water.

But for some reason unbeknownst to me, here I am, standing—well, laying—on the sandy shore of the Lost Cove where five humans plus my best friend were brought to live in an attempt to spare them from the dire fate of discovering the mermaid secret. And now, I'm just as lost as they are. I'm not safe in the sea or home with my parents. I can't risk someone discovering that Carter and I didn't perish in what the merpeople of Pearlestria have probably declared a legendary love story. One that breaks my heart and makes me laugh. The silly human who was transformed on a whim, who denied the king her loyalty, giving up her chance to rule all the oceans for a boy who loved the land just as much as she did—that is, if we're even allowed to be mentioned.

King Attilonious was always described as a kind and generous king, one who allowed his people the choice of living on the land among humans or staying in the sea. But he was far from kind to me as he manipulated my life. He was unfair and threatening, using everything I loved as a way to get me to comply. He almost succeeded.

I shiver, pushing the thought away. Carter touches my face, and I realize he's staring at me, waiting for me to respond to the quiet questions he won't ask me. He never does. He's always one to wait until I spill my heart out. I hate and love him for that, but if he'd just ask them, it'd be easier for me to say.

"This isn't the first time this has happened," I admit. I haven't told him about the other times because I didn't want him to worry. He worries about me, and everything else for that matter, enough as it is.

"Ava." The sound of his voice swirling through the air tightens my chest.

I reach up and press my finger against his pouty mouth. "I'm fine. I'm sure it's nothing."

He furrows his brows before pulling me into his lap so I have to face him. My legs wrap around his waist, and I rest my arms around his neck, holding his intense gaze. Looking me deep in the eyes, he studies me, trying to find the answers I'm not quick enough to give him.

"So, I guess those few early morning walks you've claimed to go on weren't actual walks," he says, pointing out the fact that I lied. Well, sort of lied. I did have to walk back to our community from the places I woke up on the beach.

I groan, resting my head on his shoulder. "I'm sorry. I didn't want you to worry."

"I'd have been more prepared if you had just told me. I've never been so scared in my life, waking up alone only to feel your panic wash over me in icy waves. I thought the king had found us and someone had dragged you away all while I was sleeping." His arms tighten around me as he relives his own terror, and I now feel especially guilty. But I had no idea I'd find myself fighting the sea in the middle of the night.

I cup his face between my hands. "Hey, it's okay. I'm fine. We're fine. We're safe here."

He exhales a ragged breath. "I know, it's just—"

I interrupt his worry with another kiss. My lips brush against his, tasting the salt of the sea and feeling tiny grains of sand that cling to the both of us. I kiss him until his shoulders relax, and his breathing turns breathless in a good way.

"I don't want you to lose sleep worrying about me. I know you, Carter. You'd stay up all night just to make sure I'm okay. And that's unfair," I whisper into his lips.

"You're my mate. Of course I will," he says. "You're everything to me, Aves."

I smile. "I love you."

I melt in his arms, basking in the love radiating from him. He means every word he says, and it's because of that, I can't help stress about it. Even though he's so beautifully human in this moment, his heart is still purely merman, and he feels everything much more intensely. His life is mine and mine is his. It's something I can't always grasp no matter how much I feel it inside my soul. A merman's bond is life-long and more. Forever. Something I wasn't expecting to have at eighteen, but I'm lucky for it.

"You're not getting off so easily, Aves," he says, smiling the smile he saves just for me. He does it to lessen my annoyance, because he knows the last thing I like is for him to tell me what I already know even if I try to ignore the fact something is wrong with me.

I run my fingers along his shoulder blades. "You sure about that?" I ask, teasingly, hoping the lightness in my voice pushes away the tenseness of uncertainty we're both feeling. I'm all for irresistible distractions.

Carter scoops me up with him from the sand, spinning me around. "I see what you're trying to do."

"Is it working?" We'd stay here all night, but we're quite a ways away from our tiny beachfront community, and I'd hate for anyone to worry.

"You know it is." He kisses me as he strolls in the direction of our new home. Just like in the ocean, Carter is protective over me, always showing affection either through carrying me or holding me close. He doesn't care who's watching, and I do love his attention.

"Good," I whisper. "'Cause I don't want to think about the ocean anymore tonight. I only want to think about you."

He hums deep in his throat, reacting to my touch, and I nestle my head in the crook of his shoulder. My damp hair sticks to me, though the balmy sea air whisks away some of the sand from my skin.

Glancing at the vast ocean lit by the soft moonlight, I see a blink of light in the water. It disappears as quickly as I see it, and I suppress the urge to jump from Carter's arms and back into the sea.

He freezes in the sand, feeling how I stiffen in his arms. "What's wrong?"

I blow air through my lips. "Nothing. I think the ocean got to me. I'm seeing things."

Shifting me in his arms, he peers at the ocean with me, but all I see is the dark water that doesn't glow as brightly in my human form, and the waxing moon, reminding me I can't resist the ocean forever.

"I don't see anything," he says.

"It was probably nothing. It's not like we have to worry, though. This cove is safe."

He kisses the tip of my nose. "I know."

But I know it's not the safety of the cove he's worried about. It's me.

And I'm worried, too.

2

ISLAND LIFE

SUN TRICKLES THROUGH THE CRACKS of our make-shift, palm frond bungalow, which looks like a more sophisticated version of the palm leaf tents I used to make as a child.

Island living—at least secluded island living—is a lot like living in Pearlestria. My new home is bare; there are no electronics or connections to the outside world. Instead of a wall surrounding us, a huge reef extends just past the cove, creating a barrier all the same. It's what keeps us safe along with some other force—the magic of the ocean. Very few merpeople know about the Lost Cove, its secret going back years and years.

According to the longest surviving inhabitant, Sandra, King Attilonious' mate brought a woman here after she canceled her transformation ceremony. Her soon-to-be mate couldn't bear the thought of killing her, asking the king to spare her, but he refused. It was become a mermaid or die. The queen went against the king and used her own magic to create this haven. Sandra said it was why the queen eventually left the king and her daughter, Luna. She doesn't really know the whole truth. The first lost human never confided in anyone, and she died a few years ago when she decided to lose herself to the sea.

Carter's warm hand slides up my side, pulling me from my thoughts of the inhabitants and the former queen. His fingers gently dig into the skin of my stomach, and he curls against me, blowing my blond hair from my neck so he can kiss me in a way that makes it hard to want to get up.

"We missed breakfast," Carter whispers into my ear, sending a shiver over me.

I roll over to face him, the pile of blankets under us shifting with me. It's harder on me to sleep on the sand when I'm not submerged underwater with the buoyancy of the current to lessen my weight. Carter's put down dried leaves to help with the sand, but it still speckles the blankets no matter what we do.

Carter's aqua eyes narrow, intently gazing at me in a way that makes my heart pick up pace. I'm pretty sure he didn't sleep at all, but he'd have had rather let me sleep and miss breakfast than wake me up, especially after last night.

I feel bad that he did, because I can hear his stomach. "You could've woken me up," I say. "I'm getting used to waking with the sun."

"And face the wrath of the beast?" he asks, laughing. "I'd rather starve. Plus, you were saying some interesting stuff in your sleep."

I frown, crinkling my forehead, embarrassment surely turning my cheeks red. "Tell me I gave you some answers and didn't say something mortifying."

"Depends what you'd think would be mortifying."

I glare, pressing my hands against his chest. "Carter."

He leans over and kisses my lips. "Let's call it even for you not telling me about the sleep swimming. I get to keep what you were talking about a secret."

Before I can argue, I catch the sound of a familiar voice growing louder over the rustling of the soft breeze against our makeshift walls. Carter closes his eyes, burying his head into my hair. We both stay absolutely still, just hugging each other. If we're quiet enough, we might get left alone.

"You guys better not be naked when I open your door in three, two—" Giselle shifts a few palm fronds away from the branch-lined entryway into our bungalow, which is the size of a small bedroom. The only furniture we have is a chest where we keep our clothes and a small boulder I perch on when I don't want to sit on the floor.

I smile at my best friend. "Three seconds wouldn't have been enough time to get dressed," I say from my spot on the floor.

She tilts her head back and laughs. "Enough to cover up. You're lucky I didn't come when you guys skipped breakfast."

I groan, sitting up. "Sorry, Gi. I didn't get much sleep last night."

"I caught Ava sleep swimming," Carter adds, remaining on the floor with his hands behind his head.

I cringe and gently knee him in the side. "It's not what it sounds like."

"It's worse," Carter says.

I glower at him.

Giselle's head turns back and forth between us, her gold-flecked eyes wide, nearly bugging from her face. "Whoa, Aves. The last time you sleepwalked was in middle school, and it was only to the guest room because Sapphire opened the window to listen to the waves. But swimming? That's crazy."

"Well, I *am* a mermaid," I say, smirking at the memory she shares with me, one I've forgotten about. Sapphire swore I just stood up all robot-like and left the room the second she had opened the window, but I don't remember doing that. All my friends used to tease me about it until we met Logan in high school, and he once sleepwalked naked across Sapphire's mansion when we all spent the night at her house for her sixteenth birthday.

The memories of my friends pull at my heart. They're probably just as freaked out as our families, wondering what happened to us, and if our missing status is related. I'm happy Giselle is on this boring island with me, but I'm heartbroken she's here because of me—because she tried to help me escape from the king and revealed she knew my mermaid secret.

If it wasn't for Carter's mom, the king would've killed her. I've never been so thankful for the woman who I held responsible for my life in Pearlestria. It was enough that I have finally forgiven Starla for doing what she thought was the right thing with me even though it clearly wasn't.

"...maybe see if it helps." Giselle's voice tugs at my attention. "What do you think, Ava?"

I blink. "What?"

She sighs. "You really didn't get enough sleep, did you?"

Rubbing my palms into my eyes, I force myself to focus. "Sorry, I was just thinking about..." I don't say our friends' names.

Carter hugs me from behind. "I'm sorry, Aves. I know how much you miss home."

Giselle plops down next to me. "Think of it like this, we were already supposed to be moved out, and you know we wouldn't have visited this soon."

I smile at my BFF's words. She always knows how to make the best of things. To me, we're on a boring, secluded island. To her, we're living in paradise free from the worries of our budding adulthood. Her glass is never half-empty, and if it was, she'd just gulp it down and ask for a refill. She would've made a better mermaid than me. I don't mention it, though.

"I know. It's just—we're probably going to be on this is-land until we die," I say. Which is true. As long as King

Attilonious is in control of the ocean, there's no place for us anywhere else in the world.

"Don't be dramatic. We'll be here for a few years tops," Giselle says.

I groan. "Years?"

"Yeah, because that's all the time I'm giving you to figure this crap out." Giselle offers her hand to me and pulls me to my feet. Flinging her arms around me, she hugs me for a moment. "Now, I want you to forget about this and just enjoy the day with me. I volunteered us for fishing duty and even saved you some breakfast to take along."

I grimace. "Fishing duty?" I'd have preferred to pick fruit or gather firewood or something. We're all responsible for pitching in and helping out in the community, but fishing is my least favorite thing to do. I rarely ever eat what we catch unless it's something I like, which never happens. As a mermaid, I can go long periods of time without eating, which has definitely come to my advantage. I really, really miss tacos.

Giselle shrugs her shoulders. "It's a lot more entertaining than anything else. Plus, you're the best one here at fishing. You don't need a line or net or anything if you'd just transform."

I gawk at her for a moment, thinking she's crazy for even suggesting such a thing. I turn to Carter, who still sits quietly on the floor. "It'd be nice if you'd get your tail back already, you know."

His laughter echoes through the air. "The full moon comes in a couple days, and when it does, I swear you won't have to help fish again." If I couldn't see the mer essence glowing in his chest, I wouldn't be sure he would even transform. But the beacon of light glowing just for me proves it. Neither mentions that I ignored Giselle's transformation suggestion.

Giselle gently pushes me. "Nuh uh. You'll both fish and be loved by all—but especially me."

I sigh. "Whatever you say, Gi."

"You have to be kidding me," I say, crossing my arms. "We can't fish like this."

Giselle beams a bright smile. She holds out a hand-carved spear to me, but I don't take it. Raising my eyebrows, I look from my best friend to the lapping water she expects us to spear fish in. Looks like no one's eating fish today if they're relying on us to fish like this.

"Sure we can. We have to. Wes lost the last hook yesterday. He and Bailey are fishing on the other side of the bay so don't stress out. One of us is bound to catch something today." She offers me the spear again, and I take it, swinging it out to pelt her in the leg.

She laughs, swinging hers right back at me, and it takes Carter stepping between us to get us to quit fake sword fighting.

"It's not so bad, Ava," he says, gripping his spear and positioning it like he's going to stake a fish from right here on the shore.

"Says the guy who catches fish with his bare hands." I poke him with the blunt edge of my spear.

Jetting out his hand, he grabs the wood and yanks me right into his arms faster than I can brace myself. I fall into his chest, and he catches me before I topple over on the beach and end up with a mouthful of sand.

Cool water sprays over us as Giselle kicks her bare foot through the surf. "Don't even start, you two. We have work to do, and I'm going to prove to Wes and Bailey I can do this so I don't get stuck gathering crap."

If I didn't know any better, I would think Bailey was some other girl and not my sister with the way she's been avoiding me. After spending a few hours with both me and Carter our first day here, she's basically only ever around during meals, and even then, she rarely sits with us.

Discovering my sister was alive, who I had thought drowned years ago, was the last thing I expected. I'd have never believed she was rescued by a mermaid and dropped off here to live for learning the mermaid secret. I can't imagine what she went through all these years without us, yet I'll never know, because she doesn't confide in me. We're basically strangers who share the same DNA and nothing more.

I hope for that to change one day.

"We'd be an embarrassment if we come back empty handed," Carter says, wading his way into the water. "At least you have an excuse, Gi."

I laugh. "You mean you'd be embarrassed, Carter."

Giselle points her spear at me. "I expect double from you."

Rolling my eyes, I follow Carter into the shallow water of

the bay. Giselle stays by my side and together we wade up to our waists. A few small fish swim around us since the reef is within swimming distance for even Giselle. We all stand together a few feet apart and just watch the crystal clear water.

Every time a small swell rocks us, the fish dart away, making this task pointless. Carter sinks under and peers around. He stays beneath the surface for an excruciatingly long time, long enough that I think he might've transformed without me. Giselle looks from me to Carter's blurry form, and I shrug.

He pops up empty handed with a look of clear frustration crossing his face as he glares at the water. Shaking his head, he splashes me with sea spray.

"We should swim to the reef," he says, hopping up with a small swell. "I've never speared fish from the shore and might have better luck where there are more fish."

"I'm down with that," Giselle says.

I grimace. "Do I have a choice?"

"Sure, you can either swim with legs or a tail. Your choice," Giselle says.

"Legs it is," I mutter.

The swim to the reef is better than I could imagine. I haven't swam much without my tail, but with how calm the ocean is today and how beautiful our surroundings are, it does feel more like vacation than our new way of living.

The reef teems with life; all sorts of fish swim about or hide in the coral and sea plants. A few good sized gray snappers hunt for their next meal, and Carter already sets his gaze on one. This section around the reef is shallow this time of day, and I can touch the ocean floor without swimming.

I sink under the surface, my vision blurring, but I keep my eyes open anyway. My blond hair floats around my face, veiling the world around me. I extend my hands out in front of me, just swirling them through the water, and a silver fish with a deeply forked tail comes right up to me and swims around my fingers.

A spear cuts right through the water, impaling the fish. I accidentally suck in a gulp of saltwater in surprise. Shooting to the surface, I cough and spit, shoving my wet hair from my face.

"What the hell?" I ask, glaring at Carter, who drops the now dead fish into the bag Giselle holds open. "I can't believe you did that." I shouldn't be surprised. It's not the first time Carter killed a fish right in front of me. I'm just lucky he doesn't start deboning it right in the water to eat in this very spot.

"I know you love all the fish and would rather make all of them your pets, Ava, but we're here for food not to make fishy friends." Like Carter even needs to remind me. I'm more annoyed I didn't get a warning.

"Still not cool," I say, splashing him in the face with water.

He closes the distance between us, wrapping his arms around my waist. His head tilts to the side when I pout my bottom lip out. He kisses it. I don't kiss him back though. Not because I don't want to but because I like to drive him crazy.

"Give the guy a break," Giselle says from her spot a few feet away. "He's trying to feed our poor, starving community."

I roll my eyes. "No one is starving."

"Well, we will be," she quips.

"Forgive me?" Carter asks, a smile on his lips. He knows I've already forgiven him, but he's totally milking the fact that Giselle has picked his side.

"You know I have."

Carter and Giselle take turns trying to catch fish, but the more they move through the water, the more the fish dart away. At this rate, we'll be out here all day with not enough fish to feed everyone dinner.

I blow out a frustrated breath. "Maybe we should relocate."

"All the fish have swam to the other side of the reef," Carter says.

Giselle peers through the crystal clear water, toward the barrier that protects the island. "Then maybe we should, too. It won't hurt if we stay close."

Swimming closer to the barrier, Carter floats above it to look over. "It dips down pretty quickly, but I'm a great diver. I think we can manage to get at least a few more."

I stare between the two of them. "Are you two serious? There's a lot of water within the barrier to relocate to."

"That'll take time," Giselle says. "Don't be scared, Ava. A mermaid isn't going to just materialize and drag us into the abyss. You can see them coming."

She makes a good point, and clearly, they look like they'll

cross over whether or not I'll agree. The last thing I want is to watch from the safety of this spot. If anything, I can be the lookout.

I sigh. "Okay, fine. But we're not staying long. If you can't catch another fish in ten minutes, we'll do things my way."

"Deal," both Giselle and Carter say in unison.

Carter swims over the reef first since he's closest, and he treads in the water too deep to touch his feet to the bottom but not deep enough where I can't see it. Giselle crosses over next, a grin lighting her face like we're trespassing somewhere awesome. She swims a few feet away from Carter and dives under.

A small swell pushes me forward a foot, and I kick my legs, swimming to Carter. He wraps his arms around me, his stomach pressing against mine. I kiss him softly and then turn my head to look at Giselle.

Fear shocks me in my heart when I don't spot her right away.

"Where is she?" I ask, spinning in Carter's arms.

A wave of water splashes my face, and Giselle breaks through the surface a dozen feet away. I don't have time to release a breath of relief. From behind her, a swell rises, crashing over all three of us. The last thing I hear is Giselle's scream before we all sink under.

3

SUBMIT TO THE SEA

A STRONG CURRENT PULLS ME away from Carter, and I let it drag me a few feet into the open water. Through my blurry vision, I spot my mate half a dozen feet away. He's already back to the surface. It's not the first time he's swum in rough waters. He makes staying afloat look effortless, and I can't help just staying underwater in my spot.

He dips back under, spinning to face me. Closing the distance, he locks his fingers on my arm and pulls me back to the surface. I gasp in a deep breath, my mind kicking into action. Something feels strange. It's like I can't keep focus, not with the water encompassing me, inviting me to submerge myself again.

"Ava," Carter says. "I can't see Giselle."

Carter's words blow the fog from my mind, and I swim a few feet away from him to where I last saw Giselle before the wave separated us. A voice echoes through the air, drawing my attention to the open water. Giselle fights a current, trying her best to swim back toward the reef.

Carter swims forward without me, cutting through the water quickly even in his human form. He's not even within twenty feet of her before she sinks back under again. He dives down, now too far for me to keep my eyes on his figure. I can still see the flash of his spark, the one that always allows me to find him, light up the water even with the bright sun overhead.

He resurfaces, taking another breath, and dives back under. I swim after him, fear pushing me to keep going. We're traveling too far from the reef. If we can't make it back, we'll risk our lives in the open water or risk drowning.

A few bubbles erupt on the surface, and I head in their direction. Neither Carter nor Giselle comes back up, and I dive under and peer around. Bubbles blur the water, and I can't see either of them. I can't believe this is happening. I can't believe I'm about to lose both my mate and my best friend to the ocean that has protected me in the times I've needed it to. The ocean that chose me to be a mermaid.

Tingles crawl up my legs, starting from my toes and working their way to my torso. It's an all too familiar sensation, one I haven't felt since the last full moon where I transformed back into a mermaid to nearly lose everything at the hands of King Attilonious.

Pain washes over me, cramps causing me to arch my back before bending forward. I moan, resisting the change. Nothing—not the constant sound of the sea, the allure of the waves begging me to swim under, nothing—has triggered the transformation, and I thought maybe it wouldn't happen again until Carter transformed under the full moon.

And I'm terrified of what's happening. The king stole my sea stone ring, and I knew I was living on borrowed human time.

Cramps seize through me again in an intense wave unlike anything I've felt before. I bend forward, nearly submerging my head completely under, feeling like my bones are breaking and my skin is tearing away.

"Ava! Help!" Giselle's voice cuts through the air. "Something's out here. It keeps pulling me—"

Water splashes as her words cut off, and she's pulled under again. I resist the change, forcing the pain pulsating through me away and swim forward. My life feels like it's spinning out of control.

Hands lock onto my legs, pulling my head under, and I thrash until I realize it's Carter. He's close enough to see clearly, and I pull us both up to the surface.

"Someone's got Giselle," I say to Carter. "They'll drown her."

Her voice rips through the air again. It's like she's being

toyed with, tortured by only being able to stay up long enough to gasp a breath before being pulled under. Tears burn my eyes, blending with the seawater that keeps rising to splash me in the face.

"I can't get to her, Aves. Every time I get within reach, I'm washed back to you," he says, kicking to keep us both afloat.

Another series of cramps jet through me, and I yell out, dipping under. Carter hooks his hands under my arms and pulls me up. Before he has a chance to say anything, a look of panic crosses his face as he realizes what's happening.

All I can think about is I'm changing and my best friend is drowning, and in a few moments, the merperson after her will come after me next, and there won't be anything Carter can do. He's stuck in his human form until the full moon. Though he still wears his sea stone ring, and he'd give it to me, we now have to face what we've been avoiding since we washed ashore on this island. What will we do once the full moon rises and triggers his transformation again? We'll be doomed to split our time away from each other if we want to be on land, or we'd just have to submit to the sea.

Giselle's screams echo through the air again, clenching my heart, and as much as I want to resist and fight the pull of the sea, I can't. I might be our only fighting chance, and there's no way I'm letting someone steal away my best friend again.

Convulsions rip through me again, and Carter helps me strip from my bikini bottoms before my legs fuse together and tear them away. Tears burn in my eyes, a sob taking hold of me.

My lungs burn with every gasp of breath, but I don't want to go under. I don't want this to be happening at all.

"Ava, calm down," Carter says. "You have to calm down and dive."

"Not without you," I say, my voice shaking. I'm afraid to face the ocean alone.

Carter tightens his hold on me and dives, dragging me under with him, not giving me a choice in the matter—like I ever had one at all. His fingers cup my cheeks, combing my floating hair from my face. His blue-green eyes sparkle the same turquoise as the ocean, and he squints at me while holding his breath. It's like the first time I transformed into a mermaid all over again. I can almost hear him whisper for me to just breathe.

I inhale the ocean water, letting it push through my gills to ease the ache running through me. It's only when I relax that Carter let's go of me and swims back to the surface for a breath of fresh air.

I don't break the surface though. I swim forward, flicking my tail to force my way through the current that has separated me from my best friend. My vision clears, and I let the ocean fill me, washing away the lingering fear of what lies in the sea's depths. I expect to see an army of the fiercest merpeople warriors or even the king, but no one is in the water apart from Giselle.

She floats a few feet below the surface, her bronze hair covering her face. She doesn't move, and the ocean just suspends her in a haze of sand and bubbles. Swimming as fast as I can, I close the distance between us and hook my arm around her to pull her to the surface.

She automatically gasps in breath and starts flailing. I squeeze her tighter, keeping the both of us above the water.

"Let go of me!" she screams, smacking her hands against me like I'll drag her back under.

"Gi, it's me," I say, using my arm to block her from hitting my face. "Stop. You're okay. I have you."

Pushing the sopping wet hair from her face, I meet her gold-speckled eyes. She releases a long sob, bawling her eyes out as I hold her. I flick my tail, propelling us back toward the reef. Carter meets me with serious eyes, but I don't say anything to him. I can't think about the fact that I'm a mermaid or that my best friend nearly drowned. All I can think about is getting the two most important people in my life back to shore where it's safe, where the ocean or anything in it can't hurt them.

With my free hand, I reach out and lock my fingers with Carter's. I tug him closer, and he swims right next to me. A swell rises in the water, pushing us back over the reef and into the shallow water where both Carter and Giselle can stand.

I still don't let go of either of them.

"We're all okay," Carter muses out loud, like his words will somehow make this whole situation better.

Giselle nods, releasing a shudder as she turns her gaze back to the open ocean. "Remind me to never go over the reef again," she says, her chest still heaving from fear.

"What happened out there anyway?" Carter asks. "Was it a—"

Giselle shakes her head before he can even get his question out. "No. It was just some freaky current."

Carter glances at me. "Did you see anyone?"

"No, but something wasn't right. And now look at me," I say, my voice cracking. "What am I going to do?"

"This is all my fault," Carter says.

"Uh-uh. It's mine, too. We should've listened to you, Aves," Giselle says.

I blink my oncoming tears away. "I—" I snap my mouth shut, unable to find anything else to say. It is what it is. This is who I am no matter how much I want to deny it. It's Pearlestria all over again, but instead of a mermaid colony, I'm stuck swimming in a bay and around the shallow shores of the island. I might be free of the king, but I'm still imprisoned in the sea.

"Don't panic, Ava," Carter says. "You can have my ring. It's going to be okay."

"It's not. The full moon is coming," I say.

He squeezes my hand. "We'll figure it out."

But I'm not so sure we will. My dreams of us living on the land, even if it's limited to this island, slip through my fingers to get lost on the waves. The king has won. He not only stole my human life from me, but he stole the land, too.

Without saying a word, I swim the three of us through the bay to the shore near our small community. Carter helps Giselle to the beach while I remain in the waves. I'm afraid to face the others in the community.

Bailey comes rushing from the shelters. She waves her hands wildly, pointing in my direction, and I can't stop the sinking feeling in my stomach. I can't hear what she says over the hum of the waves, but it's enough to make Carter run his hand over his head to his neck. He shifts on his feet, and Giselle hugs herself.

The heaviness in my heart threatens to drag me under, and I let it. I know I should wait for Carter to return to me, to bring me his ring, but I just want a moment to myself to think things through, to get used to the idea that'll I'll be staying in the water more than on the land.

Without waiting, I dive down and head to the deepest part of the bay, the part where only the fish can bother me.

I settle in the sand, leaning back on my elbows, and stare up at the glittering surface. Sunlight ripples over the waves, reminding me of all the times I sat on the sea floor in Pearlestria and dreamed of the land.

It's not until this moment, with the peacefulness of the calm bay surrounding me, that I realize I've missed being in the waves. I've missed the freeing feeling of swimming in the water without worry. Sitting here alone allows me to think. Maybe things won't be as bad as I thought. I've dealt before. I can deal again.

Memories from last night trickle into my mind and how I heard a voice through the water. I thought it was my imagination, but what if it was the ocean communicating with me? She said I had to let go of my fear.

And I'm ready to let it go. I can't live my life in constant turmoil. Happiness isn't out of my reach, even if I can't go to shore with Carter. This life is still better than the life the king wanted me to have. At least here, I can have both worlds.

The single thought sends cramps rushing through me. Surprise propels me from the floor, and I rub my hands over my tail as my scales smooth out into skin before it splits, and I gape at my legs. My chest lightens, my gills no longer letting me breathe underwater, but I don't swim up toward the surface.

Instead, I close my eyes and will myself to transform back into a mermaid.

It works, and I didn't even need to breathe air.

Faster than ever, I take on my mermaid form and push water through my gills. Excitement replaces my fear, and in this moment, I realize how much I've missed being a mermaid. It's like it was a part of me I had forgotten about. Without the worry of discovery or the worry of being trapped in the sea, I can actually enjoy what I am.

A shadow overhead blocks the light trickling to me. One of the two small row boats we use to go around the island floats above me. It rocks back and forth on the surface, and then a figure jumps over the side, sending glittering bubbles through the water.

Carter dives down toward me, following the pull he feels from the bond we share as mates. I peer at him for only a second before I push from the sea floor and swim up to meet him.

He couldn't possibly make it down to me as a human no matter how hard he tries. But he will try. I know him.

Grimacing, I meet Carter's curious expression underwater. He tilts his head to the side, getting close enough to my face to see me clearly. Bubbles shimmer from his nose as he lets out a tiny breath in front of me, but he doesn't motion for me to head to the surface.

Closing the distance between us completely, he brushes his lips across mine, shifting his hands up to my face to hold himself to me. A dozen images flash through my mind from Carter's, all images that radiate with the love he has for me, and I yearn to hear his voice in my mind. It's been too long.

A sudden wave of emotions crashes over me, coming directly from Carter. He misses being a merman seeing me as I am right now. Unlike me, it's always been a part of him, even if he did claim the land as his home. I'm sure our official coupling shifted something inside him, and it hurts him I'm in a form he cannot take, one he probably feels the most powerful in.

I flick my tail and propel us to the surface. Carter gasps against my mouth, his warm breath making me want to steal it from him with another kiss, which he eagerly accepts. We could survive on our kisses and love if we tried. I'm tempted to do so.

After another long kiss, Carter eases back but doesn't let go of my face. I fan my tail enough to keep us treading water so he doesn't have to. His legs brush against my tail, and it's one of the few times I've felt him as a human against my mermaid form.

"Giselle's going to be fine, you know," he says instead of saying what I know must be on his mind. "And so are you. Have you...?" His voice trails off.

I don't have to read his thoughts to know he's wondering whether or not I've tried to transform back into my human form.

"I think I want to stay here for a while," I say instead of answering. I'm afraid to admit how alluring the sea is. Not only to him but to myself. I'm afraid because the ocean was more welcoming than I care to admit. I guess losing my old human life in Azure Waters has changed me. I just didn't know how much until now.

Carter presses his lips together into a line. "Okay, if that's what you want. I can wait on the shore."

It's tempting to let him go so I can sink back to the bottom of the bay. But the sadness in his eyes pulls at my heart. "Stay with me?" I ask. Just because Carter can't transform, doesn't mean he can't still be with me.

He smiles. "I'd like that." Reaching down, he caresses the small ridge on my back and pulls me closer by the backside of my tail. "I've missed this, you know. Just you and me in the water."

"Is that so?" I ask, peppering him with salty kisses.

"More than you know."

"Then let's swim."

4

NO ESCAPE

CARTER SITS ON A ROCK AMID the waves. White foam bubbles around me, and I sway back and forth in the current, holding onto his legs. We're down the shore from the bay, far enough away from our little community not to be bothered.

In this section, the reef rests closer to shore, but the distance is far enough from home that no one really comes here unless they plan on walking the shore for a few hours. In my mermaid form, I could swim around the island in that time, and Carter could do it even faster.

I dip under the water and let the wave suck me a few feet

from Carter before it pushes me back toward him. The sun hangs low in the sky, turning the blue color yellow. The expansive ocean disappears into the horizon, and I imagine swimming freely like we used to do in Azure Waters.

Carter's gaze never wavers away from me, and I arch to dive backward, sending a wave of ocean water over him. Smiling, I pop back to the surface to see water dripping from Carter's grinning face. He shakes his head, sending water droplets cascading through the air, and then he holds open his arms for me.

I swim forward, and he pulls me up onto the rock next to him, adjusting me so my tail rests on his legs and slaps against the rising tide. His fingers send tingles over me, his touch exploring my smooth scales shimmering like diamonds in the setting sun.

Carter twines his fingers with mine, sliding them back and forth against the webbing that stops just below my knuckles. Unsaid words hang between us, threatening to ruin what feels like a perfect moment after a scary and strange day.

We haven't talked about what happened earlier, and I almost don't want to go back to our community so I don't have to think about it. But Giselle would be furious if I abandoned her overnight without a word. She'd assume the worst, and I couldn't put her through that.

"Why do I have the feeling you don't want to go back?" Carter asks, finally speaking what's weighing on his mind.

I shrug. "Because you know me so well." Resting my head on his shoulder, I watch the foamy waves curl and splash toward the beach. "I just—I'm afraid."

He sucks in his bottom lip, looking so kissable. "Me too."

Those weren't the words I was expecting him to say, and I shift to look him straight in the eyes. "You are?"

A sad smile crosses his face, and he pulls me closer against him. "You know, I never imagined my life would turn out this way."

Transforming into a mermaid definitely wasn't a part of my five year plan, but I don't have to tell Carter that. Instead, I ask, "And what did you imagine?"

It's something I've never asked him, and the fact that I have to tightens my chest with guilt. I fail more often than not when it comes to thinking about something besides my own ruined life. But Carter's life has been ruined, too.

"Before or after I met you?" he asks, reaching down to cup water in his hand to sprinkle across my tail.

"Before."

He doesn't respond right away, almost as if he doesn't really want to answer my question. It takes him a minute of looking at the sun fading completely into the horizon for him to answer. "I was working on the Ocean Jewel to save up to start a watersports store. I had imagined living on a beach somewhere, maybe in a small apartment above my shop and then I'd offer lessons or whatever, but then I met you."

"And I had to go and mess up everything," I say.

He wags his head and then leans over and kisses my temple. "You made it better."

"Yeah, right."

Chuckling, he kisses the bridge of my nose. "Seriously, Ava. Meeting you was an unexpected good surprise. You know I don't like to believe in fate, but I do believe it was more than a coincidence that I met you. It's like your soul called to me." He turns his face away. "This sounds so lame now that I'm saying it out loud."

I grin, because he's right. It sounds cheesy as hell, but it doesn't change that I love every single second of his admission. And in his admission, that's where I can see our differences. Carter doesn't like the idea of having some force mess with his life. It's why he fought to have me continue my human life as it was. I don't blame him for thinking that way, either. I hate the idea that things happen for a reason without giving us a choice in the matter, but just because I hate it, doesn't mean I don't believe it.

Out of all the humans in the world, I just happened to meet one who was born a merman in the ocean I had once feared. And Carter isn't just some ordinary merman. He's been gifted with speed, strength, courage, and an unending devotion to me I can't even grasp. He's a born protector of our people, one who would serve the king well, but instead, he's here with me. He's my warrior. The ocean picked me for him when I fell off the yacht.

It was more than an accident. It was destiny. I know that now. But why? It's something I've yet to find out.

"So, why are you afraid," I ask, redirecting the subject away from all the what-if possibilities that were never meant to happen, of the life we were never meant to have no matter how much we wanted it.

"Why are you?" he asks.

I fake glare at him. "Not fair."

"Ava," he says.

"Carter." I pout my bottom lip for a second. He brushes the pad of his thumb across it to hold my chin so I don't look away, but he doesn't let me in on what he's thinking. I pull his hand away and grasp both of his between mine. "You can be incredibly frustrating. I feel like the worst mate because you're always worrying about me and how I'm doing. But you know what? I'm worried about you. I want to know what you're afraid of for once without you being concerned about my fears."

He tilts his head up and meets my gaze, a strange look crossing his face. His expression is a mixture of curiosity, surprise, and even joy. His mouth is gaping but also half smiling, and his eyes blink a few times. I've caught him off guard, and he's not sure what to make of me.

"So spill," I say, nudging him with my shoulder. A wave collides into the rock beneath us, soaking us in tropical water.

He sucks in his top lip in consideration. "Okay, fine, but let me tell you something first. I sometimes feel like it's me who is the worst mate. Like I'm undeserving of your love, which you give so much of to me. I feel like it's my fault we're in this mess and that I've failed you."

"You didn't fail me. Carter. Never think that," I say. "You

gave up your life and family for me to make sure I didn't end up with a monster. You could've just left me and moved on, living the way you wanted on the land."

"I'd have never—"

I hold my hand up. "And that means the world to me. It means everything. I might not be living with Giselle in some beachfront condo about to go to college, but that doesn't even matter to me anymore. What matters is we're both alive and away from King Attilonious and we're figuring all this out together. And you know what else? I thank the unpredictable ocean every day you were the one who saved me."

"God, I love you, Ava," he says. "No matter what form you're in, I love you."

I gently kiss him. "Is this what you're afraid of?" I ask, waving my hand over my tail. "That I'm going to stay like this?"

"It sounds bad when it comes from you," he says. "But that's not all of it. I'm afraid the sea got to you. I'm afraid even though we're not in Pearlestria that you don't have a choice, that we never had one to begin with."

I think over his fears. They're the same ones I thought about earlier when my transformation was triggered, but I'm not afraid now. I know I can. Because the ocean was right. Fear has been imprisoning me, stopping me from accepting that I am who I am, and there's nothing to be done to change it—not that I want to now.

"I think you're wrong. We do have a choice, but we just weren't seeing the options." I release Carter's hands and jump back into the waves, ducking my head under. Closing my eyes, I will my transformation to take hold of me and turn back into the human I was born as. It happens so suddenly, I accidentally try to breathe underwater. Kicking to the surface, I cough and spit, and Carter reaches down and pulls me up by my wrists, taking in my half-naked human form.

Weeks ago, I'd have blushed. I'd have panicked about the possibility of being seen by someone. But no one is here. Only the brave would swim out to this rock during the high tide in a churning sea.

"And the ocean didn't get to me, Carter," I add, sitting on his lap. "It's had me all along."

Breaking the surface, I spit out a mouthful of water like a fountain over Carter's head. He laughs, pulling my bikini bottoms from the pocket of his board shorts and tosses them to me. The weight of the world seems less heavy now that Carter and I have spoken our fears to each other.

I slip into my bottoms, using Carter to keep me from being sucked back into the wave. When I'm dressed, I hop into his arms and he charges through the waves all the way to the dry sand. He sets me on the beach, flopping down next to me and cradles me against his sandy body, just holding me like we haven't spent most of the day alone together in the water.

"I thought you guys got washed out to sea," Giselle says, getting up from her spot leaning against a palm tree. It's dark enough I didn't even notice her there, and I wonder how long she's been waiting for us.

"Sorry, Gi. I didn't think we'd be gone this long," I say, getting off Carter's lap and back to my feet.

She stands in front of me. "I was worried you wouldn't be able to come back to shore."

I wrap my arms around her. "I'd have figured out a way. I wouldn't abandon you."

"Good, because if you haven't heard—"

Carter clears his throat, cutting her off. "I haven't told her yet."

My forehead crinkles. "Told me what? Is this about the conversation you had with my sister?"

Giselle lifts her chin, straightening her shoulders. "Yes and no."

I study her for a moment and then glance at Carter. Someone better start talking soon. "One of you spill."

"There's a reason no one goes on the other side of the reef," Carter says, finally speaking up.

"Obviously," I say.

"The island doesn't only protect us from the king, Aves. It also stops humans from leaving. There's no way I'll ever make it off this island alive. This is it for me." For the first time since our arrival, Giselle sounds hopeless.

Her words lace around me, squeezing me tight enough to leave me breathless. It's like I'm suddenly floating amid the dark ocean with no sense of direction to the surface. Every ounce of hope for a future back in the human world swirls down an imaginary drain. All three of us have been treating this place like a pit stop, not our final destination, but now that I know the reality of it, I can't stop the ache clenching my heart.

"No," I whisper.

Giselle shrugs. "Look at it this way. At least it's better than the alternative. I'd much rather be living in boring, blissful paradise than to not live at all."

"Doesn't make it suck any less. We don't belong here."

"Technically, it's only you and Carter who don't belong here. This is my life sentence. Not yours. You can leave at anytime." She doesn't say it in a mean way but just a way that states the facts. "The king isn't the only thing protecting the mermaid secret. The ocean does a great job at doing that, too. But at least here, we're given a chance to live."

I'm stunned speechless. I had no idea the inhabitants of the Lost Cove never left the island because they couldn't. I had assumed they were too scared to risk their lives in the human world. Even being land locked couldn't protect them if the king was determined enough. The full moon only keeps merpeople in the water for a short time out of a whole month if they choose to remain on land.

My gaze flicks from Giselle to Carter. "No wonder I feel like some people are uncomfortable with us here." No one has ever downright said it, but I can tell a few of the inhabitants distrust me and Carter. They avoid us unless forced to be pleasant otherwise. Even Bailey. I hate to think it, but she clearly holds something against me. And now I know it's probably because I'm not a prisoner here. I stay by my own freewill. Well, I stay because I'm not ready to face what lurks in the deep water.

Carter wraps his arms around me from behind, resting his head on my shoulder. "Don't stress over it, Ava. We have enough to worry about as it is. A few people's opinions don't change the fact that we're in just as much, if not even more, danger than they are."

He's right about it, but it's like my mind just expands to let in all the extra worry freely. I hate that I'm as different on this island as I was in Pearlestria. I miss Azure Waters more than ever. It is the only place I feel I belong.

I slump my shoulders. "I guess you're right. But it still doesn't mean I want to endure any more community time than I have to, especially since I know what's up. Why don't we make things a little easier and pack a dinner and head down the beach to have a bonfire, just the three of us?"

Giselle claps her hands in her regular excited fashion, the heaviness of the conversation now tossed to the sea with everything else we can't change in the moment. "God, yes. I'll pass on awkward community dinner every day of the week if I could."

"Totally," I say.

"Now, if only the ocean would send a hot guy my way, I'd be set." She laughs at her own thought, tilting her head back.

I beam her a smile, my heart already feeling lighter. "I'll put in a good word."

"You can do that?"

Carter laughs. "You never know."

5

WASHING ASHORE

OH, NO.

Not again.

Opening my eyes, I stare into vast, utter darkness. The churning ocean sends me adrift in a current so strong I can't even manage to swim out of it. My heart pounds in my ears, the only sound I hear through the muted sea that steals all my senses away.

I kick my legs, trying to swim to the surface to gasp for air, but when I get close enough to see the nearly full moon, I'm dragged down farther.

"Why am I here?" I ask, sending the thought out to whoever is willing to hear it but afraid of who might respond. Panic threatens to consume me. With every passing second, my lungs burn more and more.

I will myself to transform into my mermaid form, imagining submitting to the ocean that clearly wants my attention, so much so it risks drowning me. But nothing happens. My body agrees with what my heart wants, which is to make my way to the surface to swim back to shore, wherever that may be.

"Please," I say, "answer me. Tell me what you want."

Exhaustion washes over me, and I give up trying to swim to the surface just out of my reach. Silence wraps around me, squeezing me as tightly as the darkness of the water, and I almost feel as if I don't exist at all. I would believe it if it weren't for the excruciating pain I fight against to stop myself from swallowing a mouthful of the ocean.

"Please," I beg again.

The temperature of the ocean shifts from cool to warm, and a swell pushes me up through the water. "You must not give up, my daughter. You still cling to your fears. You still resist."

"I'm not resisting," I whisper. "I accept who I am."

"You don't."

I fade in and out of consciousness, the foreign thoughts, swirling through my mind, almost mocking me. Another strong current pushes me, and I tumble through the wave, letting it take me with it.

Like the flip of a switch, the world suddenly turns on as my head breaks through the surface. I automatically gasp, filling my lungs with balmy night air. A sudden bright light cuts through the darkness, igniting the night, and my knees hit the soft yet solid ground. Another wave tosses me right back to shore, the ocean rejecting me.

I roll over and push to my hands and knees, coughing and spitting the sea foam coating my face. My whole body hurts like I've spent hours at the gym, and I fall forward and rest my cheek on the sand.

Glowing light turns my eyelids red, and warm hands dig under my arms and pull me farther from the waves crashing over me. Through my bleary eyes, I gaze at a figure shadowed in the firelight coming from the torch staked right into the beach.

"Ava, what are you doing?" a familiar voice asks.

I blink the salty water from my eyes and meet Bailey's questioning gaze. I half expected for her to be Carter, but he's nowhere to be found. Instead, I face my sister who carries an empty bag on her shoulder.

I groan, sitting up. "Swimming." More like drowning. That's all I remember. Waking up in the sea before it spit me out instead of sinking me to its depths.

"In your pajamas?" she asks, kneeling next to me in the sand. "And you're hurt." She leans down and inspects my legs. Now that she's mentioned it, they do sting. Blood trickles from the scrapes on my legs and into the sand. They're nothing to worry about, because I heal much faster than a human, but I'm still surprised by them.

"I'll be fine. What are you doing out here anyway?" I peer around. We're probably a good mile from our community. I've ended up near this exact spot before—one of the few things I do remember from the other times. "This isn't exactly close to home."

Stars shine brightly overhead like silver glitter tossed onto midnight fabric, and the moon sets the beach aglow in soft light. My sister's sky blue eyes shine in the firelight from her torch, and it looks like she might consider getting up and walking away instead of talking to me. Clearly, eight years away from each other has turned us into awkward strangers. She never wants anything to do with me though the ocean reunited us after it tore us apart.

She shifts and stands up, towering over me. "There was supposed to be a drop-off of supplies, but it didn't make it ashore."

"Oh." I had no idea someone dropped off supplies. I had assumed everything we had here was stuff that usually washed ashore. All the clothes and basic necessities we have came from Carter's mom, and she's not to come back. The less merpeople who visit, the safer it is.

"I'm not too worried about it. It's not the first time. I was just really looking forward to replenishing the supplies. As you know, we've lost our last fishing hook," she says. "Food might get a little light around here without them."

Offering out her hand, Bailey helps me to my feet. My

knees shake for a moment, and it takes me walking a few feet to find it in me not to limp the whole way back to our community. Bailey yanks the torch from the ground, and I stroll along next to her, keeping my eyes trained on the foamy waves that seem a lot less threatening from my spot on the beach.

"I can catch fish," I say after a quiet moment.

I had resisted transforming into a mermaid until it was triggered today because I was afraid to do it without Carter, afraid to face that we might have to share a ring to go ashore, but now that I know something's changed in me after denying the king my eternity, I'll transform to help out the best I can. Even with how much I despise fishing. If it came down to people eating or starving, I'll catch the damn fish. It might make things a little less uncomfortable for me in the community anyway.

She doesn't respond right away, just keeps strolling along, keeping all her thoughts to herself. Without her leading the conversation, finding anything to talk about with Bailey feels like I'm reaching into a deep hole and unable to grab things from the bottom. It's frustrating.

"I don't mind transforming into a mermaid if it helps," I add so she knows I don't mean I'll be on the shore to spearfish like today.

She glances at me in her peripheral vision, swinging the bag from her hand in one arm while keeping the torch steady in the other. "That'll be extremely helpful. Thank you."

The polite small talk is killing me. It's tempting to jump

back into the water and just swim the rest of the way. She's my sister for crying out loud. It shouldn't be this hard.

"Is this how it's always going to be between us?" I ask instead of responding with more excruciating pleasantries. "I've spent the last eight years of my life missing you every day. I've dreamed of what it would've been like had we chosen to stay in the sand that day and how our lives would be. I was so happy to find out you were alive, even if we're both stuck on this crappy island."

"I'm the one who is stuck here, not you, Ava," Bailey says. I guess my suspicions were right all along.

I blink the surprise from my eyes. "Do you have any idea what I've been through?"

"Do you have any idea what *I've* been through? What it was like for me?" she questions.

I throw my hands up. "If you'd just talk to me like we're sisters and not like we're strangers then maybe I would."

She waves the torch in front of her. "Don't you get it? We're not sisters anymore."

"What's that supposed to mean?"

"We're not even the same species."

Her words burrow deep into my soul, hurting me in a way I never thought she'd ever hurt me. I'm beyond hurt. I'm devastated.

The ocean might not have killed us, but it ruined us. The sister I looked up to as a child lost herself among the waves like I lost my human self. I hate to admit it, but whatever hope I had for us as a family has been snuffed out like the torch she holds hitting the waves.

Tears well in my eyes, my heart aching, and I don't bother arguing with her. Whatever grudge she holds against me runs far deeper than even the ocean. She made up her mind about me the moment she realized I wasn't a human. That I wasn't brought to shore over the same secret that brought her here. For her, washing ashore was a curse. For me, it was a blessing.

Dashing away, I leave her behind. I can't stand to be around her for another second because now I can see the reason for her shutting me out. I can feel it flowing through my veins. I run along the shore out of the reach of the waves. Bailey doesn't call out to me or try to stop me. She just lets me go.

Sea spray coats my face, cooling my skin in the breeze, and I don't stop running until I see the faint glow of the fire burning from the clusters of palm frond shelters. A figure sits in the sand, and I head straight for him. Carter faces the ocean, staring off into the distance. He's so focused he doesn't hear me coming over the hum of the waves.

He startles when I fall next to him and embrace him, burying my face in the damp cotton of his black shirt.

"You were too far. I couldn't reach you," he says, breathing into the nook of my neck. "I didn't mean to doze off. I hate this, Aves."

I sniffle, feeling his emotions wash over me. "I'm fine, Carter. I don't think the ocean wants me to drown. It's trying to tell me something."

"You know, I never looked forward to a full moon before," he says. "At least if I can transform, I can protect you like I should."

"Don't blame yourself. It's been a long day for the both of us." I kiss him, holding onto him in the sand. "I just want to go back to our little house and forget about everything."

He shifts back to look at me, noticing the tear stains cutting through the sand sticking to my face. His eyes travel from mine to the blood dried on my knees. "What happened?"

I shrug, not wanting to talk about it, so I kiss him again and show him the memory instead—from the moment I remember in the ocean to my sister pulling me from the sea.

"She hates me," I whisper.

He pushes my sandy hair from my face. "I'm sorry, Ava. We'll get this figured out, okay?"

I nod without saying anything.

I'm not so sure that we can.

You still cling to your fears. You still resist.

The words haunt me, though I can't remember what they sounded like in my mind. The harder I try to think about last night, the foggier things become. I barely remember seeing Bailey on the shore or the conversation we had. All I know is whatever familial bond we had was severed the moment she realized I was a mermaid. Seems cruel of the ocean to reunite me with Bailey only to make sure I know I'm no longer the person I once was. I thought I accepted that. I thought I accepted this is my life now—whatever home I left in Azure Waters is gone.

But I guess I haven't accepted this at all. Maybe the ocean is right. I'm still resisting. But why shouldn't I? This is my life. I have to fight for it like I've been fighting all along.

Tears sting my eyes, thinking about my parents and the grief I'm putting them through. Even if I manage to safely get away from this island. I can't go home, and especially not without Giselle and Bailey. But I doubt Bailey would even consider coming with me. She doesn't trust me at all.

"Ava?" a masculine voice asks from behind me.

I shift in the sand, turning away from the lapping waves. "What's up?"

Wes stands ten feet away without a shirt, his long hair, which he usually wears down, twisted into a knot on the back of his head. Sand clings to his legs like it clings to everything else, and he crosses his arms over his broad chest, staring at me for a second before closing the distance between us.

He shocks me by sitting down. "I'm surprised to see you away from Carter."

I hold my expression calm, even though I want to frown. I haven't talked to the others much, and definitely not to Wes except to offer him a friendly hello when we gather for meal times. Giselle usually does all the talking. She's basically inserted herself in the community like she belongs here—which she technically does. And now that I know what my sister truly thinks, I'll be pulling away even more. I'm basically isolated with Carter just like in Pearlestria. At least this time, Giselle hangs out with me, too.

"I'm surprised to see you away from my si—Bailey," I say. I've never actually seen Wes and Bailey kiss, or even hold hands for that matter, but they're always together. They even share a place.

He holds a serious expression, matching mine, and digs his bare feet into the sand until they're completely covered. "She wanted me to see if you were still willing to—um, go fishing."

I turn away. She couldn't even face me herself to ask. "Why wouldn't I be?"

"She thought after last—"

I hold up my hand, cutting him off. "I'm not going to punish this community because my sister—or anyone else for that matter—hates me."

"She doesn't hate you, she just—"

I release a frustrated growl, and he snaps his mouth closed. "If she wants to explain herself, she can, but I—"

It's his turn to cut me off. "Hey, don't kill the messenger. And if it makes you feel any better, if you were my sister and just washed ashore, I'd be so happy you were here. Hell, I am happy you're here. Carter and Giselle, too. The more the merrier in my book. Maybe one day we can turn this place into a civilized world or something."

His words surprise me, fizzling out my anger. "I'm sorry. I just had a rough night. A rough few months, really."

"I can relate. I've been on this island going on eleven years."

"So, you were here when my sister arrived," I ask.

"With a welcome packet and everything. You know she thought you drowned? She hated it was her who was rescued. She does love you, even if she's having a hard time right now," he says.

I kind of doubt it. I don't mention it, though. With his words, her weirdness toward me makes better sense. She thought I died, but then she discovered I hadn't and have been living the life we were both supposed to and still managed to mess it up and end up here, as a mermaid no less. I think I'd be pissed off at me, too. But I'd never disown Bailey and say she wasn't my sister.

"You mean she doesn't always act like this?" I ask.

He tilts his head back and releases a loud laugh. "Definitely not. She's the most caring of the bunch. Selfless. She's risked her life countless times for us over the years, even crossed the reef once to rescue Reyna when she tried to leave in one of our boats after her arrival. She'd do it for any one of us." I search my mind for knowledge on Reyna and remember Giselle telling me her sad story. She didn't happen upon a mermaid. Her own brother, who chose the merman life, decided he wanted his sister to join and tried to set her up with a friend from the Caribbean colony, who flashed his fins, expecting her to just join them. Her brother was gone for over five years, and Reyna married during that time, so of course she wasn't going to willingly leave her husband. To escape death by the hands of the jerk she rejected, she wound up here after her brother's mate saved her from that fate.

"Not for me," I say, pushing Reyna's heartbreaking story away.

"Well, you *can* change into a mermaid."

A laugh bubbles in my throat, the sound surprising me when it comes out. I'm kind of annoyed by it. I shouldn't be laughing. I came on this beach to sulk and feel sorry for myself.

"So, what do you say? Do that mermaid thing of yours and catch us some lunch and dinner?" he asks like I was ever going to say no.

I nod. "I'll go find Carter now."

Wes helps me to my feet and dusts the sand off his shorts. "Everyone will appreciate it, Ava." Turning away from me, he strolls in the direction of our bungalows.

"Hey, Wes?" I ask.

He looks over his shoulder.

"Will you do me a favor and tell Bailey I'm sorry."

"Sure thing. I'll tell her to chill out, too. We're lucky to have you here, and I mean it," he says.

For the first time in weeks, someone's finally made me feel like I belong here.

Maybe I do.

6

POWER

GISELLE'S LAUGHTER ECHOES THROUGH THE air, a sound so musical and carefree, it brings a huge smile to my face. She clings onto my back, holding on for dear life as I cut through the water fast enough to make her scream.

"Get ready to hold your breath," I say. The moment I hear Giselle's inhale, I flick my tail, sending us into the air before I dive underwater. I swim past a school of tiny silver fish too small to eat and travel along the reef outside the bay.

Sunlight sparkles across the surface like a glittering mirror, and I speed toward it and breach, flipping backward, taking Giselle with me. She releases my shoulders the moment we hit the water and swims up to take a breath of air. She treads in place, floating with a swell, and I watch as she lets it take her toward the shore. I don't let her get far. Popping up next to her, I spit water over her head and laugh.

She splashes water into my face. "That was way more fun than my trip here with Carter's mom."

"Probably because you thought you were going to die," I say, trying not to frown at the memory.

"And to think I used to be so jealous that Sapphire got to swim with the dolphins in Hawaii. My best friend is a mermaid! A mermaid!" She says it like she's just letting the information sink in. It probably helps we're enjoying ourselves during somewhat lighter circumstances. No one's trying to kill us, and I'm not being imprisoned by the ocean.

I flick water at her. "Shhh, you're giving away my secret."

She laughs, rolling her eyes, and then swims closer and locks her fingers onto my shoulders. "Imagine how I felt when I couldn't say that out loud?"

"It probably wasn't as hard on you as it was me." I swim forward, making her squeal, and cut through the current straight to shore.

The waves drag us both forward, and we skid to a stop in water shallow enough that I can't dip my head under unless I flatten myself against the sand. Giselle gets to her feet and stares down at me as I lie in the sand, feeling the warm sun on my scales. It's a lot more comfortable than perching on the rocks off shore.

"I thought you decided to abandon me for a girl's day," Carter says. He stands in front of me with dry sand sticking to his muscular legs. Giselle insisted I drop him off here first so she wouldn't have to wait alone.

Using my upper body strength, I drag myself closer and struggle to flip over so I can sit up and face the waves. I don't know why I do it, why I remain in my mermaid form when it'd be easier to transform back, but there's something freeing about sitting on the beach as a mermaid without having to worry about who sees me.

"We almost did," Giselle says. "You can't hog all of Ava's mermaid time, you know."

Carter sits in the sand next to me, stroking his fingers along my tail like he can't resist touching me. Who knows? Maybe he can't. "I can see that now. Just don't give the whole island ideas, okay? We don't need Darren asking for a ride up the shore all the time."

Giselle tilts her head back and laughs. Darren is the oldest inhabitant in our community and claims to have been here for twenty years, which is crazy to think about, considering he hasn't even been here the longest.

"Definitely not happening," I say, smacking my tail on the lapping waves. "You should've seen him earlier when I brought the fish. He kept making jokes that I'd be the best fishing buddy he's ever had and even told Carter he should take the day off so he could help me instead."

Giselle cracks up even harder. "He didn't!"

"I told him you were just as talented," I say, flicking water at Giselle.

"Ava!"

After I had brought back enough fish for lunch and dinner, I was completely surprised how excited and welcoming everyone was to me. Sure, I might have sort of bought their friendliness in the form of fish, but the atmosphere had definitely changed. I suspect Wes might've had something to do with it as well.

"What? He's a nice man, and he did technically wash ashore," I say with a laugh.

She drops a handful of wet sand on my head. "Like fifty million years ago."

Her response gets a chuckle out of Carter. She scoops a handful of sand up and drops it on his head, too. Before Carter can do anything to retaliate, Giselle dashes away, heading farther down the beach.

"Come on, Ava," she calls. "Lose the tail so we can have some human fun."

I dig my hands into the sand, attempting to pull myself forward, but I'm too far away from the buoyancy of the water to swim back into the wave. Giselle releases a loud laugh toward the sky, and I fall back in the sand, splaying out. Warmth flourishes in my cheeks as embarrassment clings to me.

Staring at my tail, I will it to transform into legs so I don't have to ask for help getting back in the water. Nothing happens. An ounce of fear trickles through me, and I continue to glare at my caudal fin slapping against the lazy surf barely caressing the tip of my tail.

"Are you kidding me?" I ask, poking my finger into my scales. "I can't change."

Carter chuckles next to me. "Let me help you back into the water."

I wave my hand at him. "I can do this."

"Don't be stubborn, Aves," Giselle calls, kicking sand up as she walks closer. "Let the guy help your beached ass."

Maybe I want to be stubborn. Carter would do everything for me if I allowed him to, and it's something I don't want. I don't want to be coddled. I like doing things for myself. It makes me feel better, like I can do this on my own.

Carter ignores my protests and reaches down to pull me into his arms. It annoys me more than it should, and I flick my tail, throwing him off balance. We both fall to the sand. Giselle laughs again, and I burn her a heated look, my eyes narrowed and my lips pursed. It wouldn't be so funny if she was in my position.

A small wave rolls over my tail, sparkling in the sunlight. I swing out my arm and slap my hand against it. The sudden movement causes a swell to rise up where the ocean drags the wave back, and it crashes forward. Water cascades over my head, lifting me from the sand. I flip to my stomach, riding the wave back until I'm no longer stuck.

Water fills my lungs, and I swim deeper, my tail no longer hitting the bottom. I spin in a quick circle. If I could hug the ocean, I would. It's the first time its bent to my will since the last full moon, and the rush of power fills me with something light, something magical. It's like I've cracked the wall of my imaginary tank to set myself free.

I don't stay under for long. I let the cramps seize my tail and wait a moment for my lungs to start burning before I kick to the surface. I spit out seawater and spin to face the shore. Surprise peaks my brows when I see the change in the surf. Large swells pulverize the beach. Giselle stands near the tree line, her hair dripping wet, and a startled expression widening her eyes.

Carter swims through the rising swells in my direction, diving under before the waves can collide into him and send him back to shore. I meet him halfway, letting him wrap his arms around me. We float up and down, lifted with every wave, and it takes a look into his blue-green eyes to realize this isn't some natural occurrence. It's reminiscent of the king's power.

"What's happening?" I ask.

"Relax, Ava. It's okay," he says.

The rough waters threaten to rip us apart, but Carter's strong grip keeps me against him. Lifting his hand, he presses his fingers against my chest over the spark flickering in sync with his. It's enough to suppress my oncoming panic, and I exhale a long breath. The waves settle, leaving us standing waist deep in the now tranquil ocean.

Scrunching my brows together, I look around again. "Was that—?"

"Yeah," he says. "That was all you."

Carter embraces me as I hold myself, letting it all sink in. I knew I was connected to the ocean on a deeper level, that somewhere, buried within me was an ability that could protect me when I needed it to, but I wasn't expecting it could also attempt to wreck things on my behalf. All I wanted was to return to the ocean on my own. I didn't want to nearly wipe Giselle and Carter out with a swell.

"Whoa," is all I can say.

Carter hands me my bikini bottoms, letting me brace myself against him to get dressed, and together we head to shore to meet Giselle. She hesitates a moment, turning her eyes on the now lapping waves like they'll somehow surprise her and drag her out to sea. I pout my bottom lip, breaking away from Carter to run to my best friend.

"I'm so sorry, Gi," I say. "I could've hurt you."

She pulls back and holds me in her gaze. "Hey, you don't need to apologize. That was actually pretty awesome. If only I had my surfboard."

I smile at her glass-always-half-full mentality. "Only you would think that."

"I'm being serious," she says. "My best friend rocks."

I don't feel like I rock. I feel like if something so small could set off threatening waves that I'm a disaster waiting to happen. One look at Carter tells me he's thinking the same thing I am.

I grimace. "No one would agree with you, Gi. Can you imagine how Bailey would act if she knew?"

"She'll be ecstatic," Giselle says.

"Where have you been? You know she holds a grudge against me because I'm a mermaid," I say.

"But that's because she doesn't know how amazing you are." Giselle reaches up and shakes my shoulders. "You can control the ocean. Do you know what that means?"

I suck in my bottom lip and don't answer. I can't see where she's going with this.

"I don't think it's going to be that simple," Carter says, interrupting.

"Of course it's that simple," Giselle says. "If she can control the waves here on shore, she can control the ones on the other side of the reef."

Everything sinks in. Giselle thinks because I got the waves to rise to shore to help me get back into the water I somehow possess the ability to stop whatever magical force traps her on this island. She thinks I'll be able to get her off.

"Giselle," I say, cutting off her thoughts. I can't give her hope if I don't have it. "Carter's right. This was a rare occurrence. I can't just tell the ocean to quit trapping everyone here. It doesn't work like that."

She pushes strands of drying hair from her face. "Maybe with practice."

"And then what? We all just go home and pretend none of this ever happened?" I ask. "Because I think you're forgetting the reason we're here in the first place."

"I'm not afraid of the king, Aves. He might rule the ocean

and tries to rule the merpeople, but he can't rule us," she says.

But he can. He does.

Sadness washes over me. Giselle will never understand. She wasn't there to face the king. She's not a mermaid and doesn't have to deal with the fear that comes with our secret. She might be my best friend, but maybe my sister was right last night. We're not the same species. It does make a difference in the grand scheme of things.

Carter comes up behind me and rests his chin on my shoulder, hugging me from behind without a word. My emotions run hot, flowing from me to him, and without having to tell me, he senses the despair washing over me, putting a wedge between the humanity I cherish so dearly and who I've become.

"You're right, Gi," I say even though I don't believe in the words. "Just don't expect things to happen overnight."

She nods her head. "Of course I don't."

I force myself to smile. "Good, because I don't want to disappoint you."

"You could never," she says.

"She's right," Carter adds. "But I still don't think you should tell anyone. Ava's under enough pressure as it is."

Giselle leans forward and wraps her arms around both me and Carter, squishing me between them. "Totally understand. I'll do whatever I can to help, okay?"

"Okay," I say.

"Now, come on. Let's stop thinking about the ocean and enjoy the land," she says.

But I'm not sure I can enjoy it in this moment, not when I can't stop thinking about the sea or how I could very well ruin everything here. For the first time since I've arrived, I'm not scared of what hides in the ocean.

I'm afraid of me.

7

DISASTER WAITING TO HAPPEN

"DON'T STRESS, AVES," GISELLE SAYS. She points at our small community. "Everything looks fine."

From my place holding Giselle in the bay, I can see everyone gathered around the fire as they prepare dinner. The sun hangs low in the sky, and I know I should just hurry and pick up Carter from where I left him on the beach to return back and enjoy a quiet dinner, but the more I look at the others, the less I want to return to shore.

Flicking my fin, I propel us until we're close enough that she can swim to shore on her own. She pushes away from my back and swims in front of me to tread water. My gaze flicks away from her and to the beach where I catch sight of Bailey coming out of her shelter with Wes behind her. Our gazes lock for a quick second before she turns away to say something to Darren, who slices some fruit at a table made from a cut down tree.

"Don't be mad at me, okay," I say to Giselle instead of responding to her comment. "But I think I'm going to stay in the water for a while longer."

She frowns. "But why?"

I shrug. "I don't know. It helps me think."

"You need to stop thinking," she argues.

I roll my eyes. "I'm not abandoning you, if that's what's on your mind."

"What about Carter? You know it'll bother him if you decide not to come back to shore with him," she says.

I lift an eyebrow. She says it like I don't understand my mate and what he's going through. Of course I know what he's going through. I can feel his emotions through our bond. He used to hide them from me, but ever since our coupling, I have complete access to them. And now, the last thing I need is for Giselle to use Carter to make me reconsider my need for space.

"Don't worry about us, okay? I don't want you to wait up, either," I say.

Before Giselle can argue, I sink under the water and remain there until she gives up on waiting for me to break the surface again. She spins and swims in the direction of the shore. I only pop back up to ensure she makes it to the sand. Without another glance, I dive and swim out of the bay and along the shore a few miles from our community. I let my bond pull me directly to Carter.

Our gazes lock the second I surface. He stands amid the waves, letting them flow around him. The sun fades behind me, the water darkening enough to set my nighttime vision aglow. Carter looks even sexier with the way the shadows define his tight abs and the hard muscles of his chest and arms.

He wades in, dipping down until the water reaches his neck. I close the distance between us, locking my hands around his and pull him deeper until my tail no longer sweeps against the soft sand. We hold each other amid the rocking sea, letting it drift us farther away from shore.

"I'd give anything to transform and go for a real swim with you," Carter says. He leans forward and brushes his lips against mine, breathing his warm breath against me.

"Soon." It'll only be a few days before the full moon rises and forces Carter to transform again into the merman he was born as. "We'll be back to normal soon."

His longing encompasses me. "I can't wait."

We just hold each other for a while, kissing, feeling our bodies against each other—me as a mermaid and Carter as a human. He doesn't ask me why I'm not quick to hurry back, and I think he already knows the answer. If only we could sink to the bottom of the bay together and feel like it's just the two of us in the world, things might not feel so heavy. I miss the days before I was dragged to Pearlestria, when we could explore the ocean on our own terms without having to be confined.

Dipping under, I transform into my human self and pop back up to clear my lungs of seawater. Carter doesn't wait to pull me in the direction of the shore. I put on my bottoms and emerge from the water with him, and together we lie in the sand and watch twilight fade into night. Stars sparkle overhead, shining brighter than I've seen them since we lie in the dark without the glow of a fire.

"You were amazing today," Carter says, drawing away from his inner thoughts. "I know you're worried about what all this means, but what you did—it was incredible."

"More like terrifying. I'm out of control all over again. But instead of accidentally revealing myself to Giselle, I might send the whole island underwater." I sigh, rubbing my fingers against my temples.

Carter leans on his elbow. The rising moon gives us enough light that I can see his eyes shining. "You just need practice. Things won't be overwhelming once you hone your skills. I'll help you the best I can."

"I'm afraid to even try," I argue.

He brushes strands of hair from my face. "Don't be afraid of what you're capable of, Ava. It'll just make it harder to figure things out."

His words resonate with me, stirring the memory of the voice I heard when I awoke in the ocean—the one telling me I was still afraid and resisting. Maybe it wasn't referencing my transformation at all. Maybe it was referencing me.

I close the distance and kiss Carter, sliding my hands over his taut shoulders to caress the muscles on his back. He slides his tongue into my mouth, kissing me deeply, like kissing me will ease the anxiety threatening to wash me out to sea. And it does. When I can concentrate on just Carter and the feelings we share, I don't think about what else is happening. I don't need to be in the ocean to feel as if it's just the two of us in the world after all. Because lying on this beach under the pale moonlight in the powdery sand away from the community gives me exactly that. A life where I don't have to worry about anything except the feeling of his skin against mine, the way his sweet lips taste, how he makes me feel like I'm not a disaster waiting to happen.

"Can we stay here tonight?" I ask, whispering into his mouth.

He hugs me tighter. "If that's what you want."

I nod. "More than anything."

"Ava," a voice whispers.

Snapping my eyes open, I glance around the dark beach. The hum of the ocean echoes in my ears, suddenly loud on this quiet night. Carter sleeps soundlessly next to me in the sand, and I maneuver his arm off me to sit up. We both fell asleep right on the beach where we've spent nearly half the night talking and sharing memories with each other through our kisses.

"Ava, your fear will keep you lost forever. You must let it go." The voice comes from everywhere and nowhere, drifting into my mind.

I don't respond. Instead, I push to my feet. Sand sprinkles from my tangled hair, and I dust myself off and stroll straight to the edge of the water where the surf pushes and pulls against the sand. The foamy waves glow in the light, and the white moon above creates a glittering trail I can imagine walking on, letting it take me into the black horizon.

Water rolls around my ankles, cooler than the balmy air, and I crouch down to run my fingers across the frothy surface. I scoop up a handful of water, holding it in my palm, and watch the pale light of the moon bounce off it. It looks magical in this moment, unmoving in my hand, like the glass surface of a mirror.

Flicking my fingers, I toss the water back into the waves. The surface explodes in a large splash like I threw a boulder into it. The sudden sound startles me, and I jump back and fall into the sand. A swell rises, spilling onto my legs. I don't even have a chance to move as it hits me in the chest, knocking me flat on my back. It steals my breath away like it steals the sand right out from under me, dragging me from shore.

I thrash for a moment, trying to break free of the strong current, but it's useless. I'm being swept away, and there's nothing I can do about it.

Ocean water burns my eyes. I try to focus on which direction leads to the surface. Sand clouds everything around me, and unless I can transform into a mermaid, there is no way for my vision to adjust to the fullest ability. The water isn't completely dark, an inner light still manages to glow within every tiny bubble, but it's not clear enough to see.

I roll through the wave, concentrating on pinpointing the light of the moon. If I can spot it, I'll know exactly which direction to head. But it's like the night sky swallowed it whole. After another few seconds, my lungs burn, begging to take a breath that'll only cause me to drown if I don't transform.

Calming my nerves, I concentrate on changing, but in the moment I need to, it doesn't happen. I groan, hearing my muted voice hum through the water to my ears. I didn't have any problems transforming all day, but now something stops me. It's like the ocean wants me to be weak while I'm held in its clutches.

"Please, let me go. I can't transform." I send the thought into the water like it'll somehow make a difference.

I'm greeted with silence.

"Why did you draw me to you if you won't let me transform? Why are you punishing me?" Fear trickles through my mind when I'm greeted by more silence.

I'm sure I heard the voice on the shore. But now, as I hover in the dark abyss, I'm starting to think that maybe I've been imagining it all along. That it's all in my head.

My chest heaves, my body reacting to the lack of oxygen. I inhale salty water, unable to keep my mouth closed any longer. Panic seizes me, and I kick my legs, thrashing against the current that wants me to drown.

Exhaustion rolls over me. Shadows crowd the edges of my

already dark and blurry vision as I drift in and out of consciousness.

"Ava, let go of the fear," the quiet voice whispers in my mind.

I don't respond to the nagging voice. I can't. All I can do is wait until I lose myself completely.

I close my eyes, my body too tired to fight any longer, and the ocean settles around me. Light breaks through from the surface, and I realize I'm hovering only a few feet below it. I rise with another wave, bubbles clinging to me, and without even having to move, I float up and cut through to fresh air.

Water spews from my nose and mouth, my lungs expelling it not unlike when I transform from a mermaid to a human, but this time it's more forceful and out of my control. I cough and spit, splashing until I'm upright.

I heave a few deep breaths, just letting the air in and out of my lungs. Water drips from my hair onto my forehead, and I wipe it away with the back of my hand. Spinning around, I gaze at the vast ocean and then turn toward the moonlit shores.

"Ava!" Carter's voice echoes through the silent night.

I follow the sound of his voice and spot his spark through the water as he swims in my direction. My legs and arms ache with fatigue, but I manage to stay afloat until Carter pulls me into his arms and does the rest of the work for me.

He carries me to shore, pelting me with cool water drops from his dark hair. Within his usual bright eyes lies a sorrow comparable to the hours after he admitted to me I had drowned in the ocean, and he saved my life by transforming me into a mermaid.

Strolling all the way to the tree line that leads inland, Carter sits as far away from the ocean as he can get without actually going into the tropical forest. He cradles me in his arms, brushing his lips across my forehead a dozen times without a word. I laugh when he showers my cheeks with a handful more and then kisses my lips, sending a dozen images into my mind—but they're not the usual ones I expect from him. He shares with me the fear he had from the moment a wave woke him up to the moment he tried to get into the water only to be stopped by another wave that refused to allow him into the surf. His fear's enough to send tears spilling onto my cheeks.

"I'm sorry," I whisper. "I heard a voice, and things got out of control."

"You didn't sleepwalk?" he asks.

"I—" I don't really know. "I don't think I did, but now it's all blurry in my mind. Do you think I caused the waves?" I've never manifested power in my human form, but I know the waves that dragged me from shore were not a natural occurrence. "What if it wasn't me? What if it was someone else?"

He kisses my hair, thinking over my questions. "I know what you are capable of, and that was definitely you, Aves."

I release a shuddering breath. "I'm scared, Carter. I don't want this."

Gently pinching my chin in his fingers, he forces me to look at him. "It's because it's new. The full moon rising is increasing your instability, but don't let that freak you out. We'll practice more. You'll get it under control." He runs his finger along my cheek. "And when you do, who knows? Maybe Giselle is right. Maybe this island living doesn't have to be forever. We can protect each other. Maybe make a new haven elsewhere."

"But the king," I say.

"Screw Attilonious, Ava. He doesn't scare me, but you know what? I think you scare him. He was so scared of you that he went against his own laws. He tried to force you into coupling with him. A merperson never finds a new mate if something happens to theirs. It's unheard of, yet he tried to do it."

I shiver at the thought. "That's why he won't waste time if he ever realizes I'm alive. He'll murder me."

"I'd never let that happen, understand?" he says, holding me close. "I'd die for you."

A pit settles in my stomach. Carter did die for me, and I never—and I mean never—want to go through that ever again. Just thinking about it sends my heart racing, my palms sweating, and my breath quaking.

"Never again, Carter," I say quietly. "I'd rather stay lost on this island forever than risk losing you."

"You won't lose me. You know how I know?" he asks.

I just snuggle my face against his damp chest without answering.

"Because you're the most powerful, beautiful mermaid I know." He runs his fingers over the spark in my chest. "I can feel it right here." Moving his hand, he places it over his own heart. "And here."

"You really think this is only temporary?" I ask.

He nods. "I know so. Attilonious might try to rule the sea, but he can't rule us."

Deep down, I know he's right.

8

CHOOSING THE OCEAN

"AVES! THANK GOD YOU'RE BACK," Giselle yells from her place in the sand just outside the palm frond shelters. She hops to her feet and sprints toward me, nearly knocking me over with a huge hug. "I thought I might've lost you to the waves forever."

I push her back a little so I can look into her golden amber eyes. "I promised I'd never do that, but Carter and I have been talking and—"

"Don't you dare say what I think you're going to say," she says, wagging her head back and forth hard enough that strands of her bronze hair hit me in the face.

"Hear me out." After last night, all I can think about is the risk I'll cause everyone. It was like the ocean entranced me and bent to my will by accident. Like with the rocky waves yesterday, things could get worse and worse. "I accidentally caused some rough water last night while I was in my human form. I feel out of control enough as it is, but it's like the ocean is messing with my head when I'm most vulnerable. I don't want to put anyone at risk. We'll just sleep elsewhere, okay? Maybe even in the water when Carter can transform."

She scrunches her face, her lips puckering up to her nose and her eyebrows lowering on her forehead. Her expression speaks volumes. "Why does it feel like you're choosing the ocean over the land now?"

I huff a breath. "I'm not. I promise. I just don't want anything to happen. What would you do if you were me and could possibly wipe out our island?"

Her gaze drops to the sand. "Do what I can to make sure it doesn't happen. But it doesn't make me less sad."

I hug her again. "Same. But you know what? You can have me all day today, okay?"

"What about Carter?"

I peer over my shoulder at him as he talks to Wes, giving me the space he knew I needed to talk to Giselle. He offers me a smile, though his eyes don't crinkle in the corners with the happiness I wish he could carry around all the time.

"Carter will be fine. He'll be busy getting things ready for us," I say.

She beams a smile, shaking my shoulders. "Can we go for a swim? I mean, can you take me for a swim?"

I laugh. "Whatever you want."

"Okay, all powerful mermaid, show me what you got," Giselle says, standing in waist deep water next to me while I float on my back.

"You didn't just seriously ask me to try to control the sea, did you?" I stare up at the crystalline sky instead of Giselle.

Smacking her hand on the water, she creates a small wave that splashes me in the face. "I'm not asking you to create a tidal wave. Just show me something cool. You gotta practice, Aves. I wasn't kidding about using you as my ticket out of here."

I roll my eyes. "I will practice. Just not with you."

Her eyes narrow, and she slaps the water again. "I'm your best friend. Carter isn't the only one who can help you. Please, just try something small."

"No, Gi," I say. "Maybe after I get better control."

"Don't let the ocean scare you," she argues. "Eight years was enough time."

"I'm not afraid of the ocean." Not in the sense she's implying. I'm afraid of what the ocean can do under my control, considering I don't have much of it.

"Liar," she says.

Annoyance washes over me. I know she wants to be helpful. She wants to be here for me. But that's my problem. I don't want to mess things up because she's here with me.

"Why does everyone keep saying I'm afraid?" I ask.

"Because you are."

"I am not!" I lift and smack my tail against the water, sending a current over the surface. The water quivers, rolling away from me and toward the shore. Giselle claps her hands when the surf rolls all the way up the sand like the high tide, before dragging itself in our direction, pulling us along with it until we're in water deep enough that I can float upright without hitting my tail on the sea floor.

Another wave swells, lifting us higher, and Giselle screams out in both excitement and fear. I lock my fingers onto her, stopping her from getting caught in the current I created, and I flick my tail a few times to take us closer to the shore.

A scream rips through the air, drawing my attention away from Giselle. It came from the bay. Fear rushes through me, and I meet Giselle's now wide eyes for a moment. Without a word, she locks her fingers to my shoulders and inhales a deep breath before I dive under and swim in the direction of the scream.

With Giselle, swimming takes a few minutes longer because I have to surface every thirty seconds for her to breathe unlike with Carter who can hold his breath for minutes. I swim us along the reef, scaring fish out of the way, and rise up at the edge of the bay to get a good look around.

The waves rock us back and forth in the water, unusually rough in the bay, and I know I'm the reason for this. Another scream rips through the air, and I focus my attention on the rowboat across the bay in the spot my sister and Wes favor fishing.

The boat floats on the water in the direction of the reef leading to the open sea. Two figures struggle to paddle to get the boat under control, but it's like the ocean is determined to drag them beyond the border that means certain death.

"Oh, my God," Giselle says. "It's Bailey and Wes."

"This is why I didn't want to mess with my affinity, Gi," I say, panic welling in my chest.

"I'm sorry. Last time the waves didn't reach here. I thought we were far enough away."

Even if I swim my fastest, I'll never reach the boat in time. I clench my teeth, willing the current to stop, to calm down so they don't cross the barrier, but nothing works. If anything, the waves grow higher, pushing their boat even harder.

A few voices yell from the shore, but no one rushes out to try to help. Bailey jumps from the boat first, sinking under the wave, and soon Wes follows. The boat drifts out to sea without them, but the rough waves make it hard for them to swim.

Without thinking, I dart forward, cutting through the bay as fast as I can. Giselle squeezes against me, pressing her cheek into my back, and I make her wait an extra twenty seconds to break through the surface to get air.

My heart seizes the closer I get. Both Bailey and Wes struggle to stay afloat and fight against the sea to remain in the bay. The current sucks Wes under, and he smashes against the reef.

Bailey screams as a swell lifts her up and over it, forcing her into the ocean that will kill her even for an accidental escape. Blood stains the clear sea red, sending my heart into my stomach. Wes is tossed around since he's been knocked unconscious. I've lost sight of Bailey altogether.

"Swim a bit from the reef and leave me," Giselle says into my ear. "I'm a great swimmer. I'll make it back to shore."

The last thing I want to do is to leave Giselle to fend for herself, but I know it'll be hard to help three people. Two will be pushing it. Giselle loosens her grip like if I don't swim her away from the reef she'll let go of me right here. It's enough to make me switch course.

"You can do this, Aves," Giselle says. "Remember you're the one in control." Giselle releases me, dipping under, but she pops back up and strokes her arms while kicking to swim to the shore. My nerves calm knowing, she'll be fine. My emotions shifting from fear to relief triggers something in the water, and the rocky waves settle until the bay turns as calm as an untouched lake.

Another scream rips through the air, and I catch sight of Bailey trying to reach the reef to hold onto it. She can't swim over it on her own as a swell pushes and pulls against it. I narrow my gaze on her, looking past the tiny bubbles settling within the sea, and spot Wes' body on the other side of the reef from Bailey. He floats face down, unmoving. Bailey yells, trying everything she can to cross back over to reach him, but the ocean stops her.

I dive down, navigating the bottom to the shallow water near the reef. I reach Wes first and flip him over and hold him upright. Blood drips down a gash on his forehead, staining the front of my pale pink bikini top.

"Ava!" Bailey screams.

Water sprays through the air as my sister sinks under. Without Wes being conscious to hold onto me, it makes it harder to swim to my sister. He'll die if I leave him, but my sister will die if I don't. She'll also kill me if I choose her over Wes.

"What do I do?" I ask out loud, like someone will give me the answer. *Control the water. You can control it. Make it listen.*

With one hand on Wes' chest and my other reaching out toward my sister, I imagine the sea coming to me. I concentrate with my entire being, pulling the sea, forcing it to create my own personal current.

The water churns around me, stirring up sand and catching tiny reef fish in my small whirlpool that travels around me. Wes coughs from my arms, throwing up water, and then he gasps for breath. I not only summoned the sea around me, I managed to pull it right from his lungs, allowing him to breathe.

I listen for my sister but can only hear the ragged breath of Wes inhaling and exhaling. His eyes remain closed, though. Swimming forward, I grab at the water with my hands, pulling more and more to me, dragging a new current from the open sea.

I manage to bring the rowboat back over the reef, and I lift

Wes over my head and push him into it, letting the boat drift into the bay. Diving down, I jet through a tunnel in the reef to the other side of the barrier and glance around the clear water.

Bailey flails about, spinning and flipping just under the surface. Every time she gets close to breaking through, she sinks deeper and deeper.

"Release her," I say, sending my thoughts into the sea. My voice resonates in my mind, and a trickle of fear swells in my chest. If there are any merpeople nearby, it's possible they've heard my command. But I can't think about that now. I need to get to my sister and get us back to where it's safe.

Bailey floats toward the surface, kicking her legs. The ocean no longer holds her under, and I watch the surface explode in glittering bubbles when she breaks through. Closing the distance, I swim under her and pop up a foot away from her. She screams out, slapping me in the face, and I use my arm to shield myself.

"It's me!" I yell. "It's okay. I'm here. You're safe."

For the first time since our one and only hug moments after I arrived here, Bailey embraces me. Her arms lock around my neck, and she sobs in my shoulder, burying her face against my neck as I tread us in place.

I swim us from the spot without going under and let her cling onto me all the way to the rowboat. Wes is still unconscious and bleeding, but his chest rises and falls as he breathes. I just hope he can recover. If something more happens to him—if something more happens to anyone—I don't know how I'll live with myself. The guilt and grief would be enough to send me into the sea and away from humans forever, even if it means my own life would be at risk.

Bailey climbs into the boat and pulls her wet shirt over her head. She presses the fabric against the gash on Wes' forehead while whispering something in his ear I can't hear.

I'd give anything to have been gifted with a healing ability like Carter's mom and grandma. I'd trade my ability to walk on land for it. But my thoughts are pointless, because the ocean might be powerful, but it seems I've already used my one miracle on Carter. There's nothing I can do for Wes except hope for the best.

"Get Sandra!" Bailey yells from the boat when we're within reach of the shore.

I dip underwater and will my transformation to take place. Cramps wash over me but disappear within seconds. I break through the surface and expel the ocean from my lungs in time to touch my feet to the sandy floor.

Darren and Giselle rush into the water and pull the boat into the sand. I stumble onto the shore and help the two of them get Wes out. More blood drips onto me, and I look like I've just survived a shark attack.

Sandra rushes from the palm tree shelters with Reyna behind her, and the two of them help Darren with Wes as Giselle helps Bailey from the boat, supporting her while they follow the others.

"Ava!" Carter's voice echoes through the air, and I catch

sight of him running from down the shore where he was working on setting up a new shelter for us away from everything. He probably felt my fear and ran the whole way back here.

Instead of running to him, I just fall back in the sand and stare up at the bright sun through the tall palm trees. The blood in the sand spreads out with every wave, staining the shore around me in its crimson color. I'm too exhausted to do anything about it. All I want to do is close my eyes and fall asleep. Maybe if I do, all of this will have been a dream. Wes wouldn't be hurt. I wouldn't be drowning in my own guilt. And Bailey wouldn't have another reason to hate me.

"Oh, God, you're hurt," Carter says, falling to his knees next to me.

He brushes his fingers over my skin, using a handful of seawater to clean off my chest. He searches for wounds that aren't there, and I reach out and lock my hand around his wrist and just hold his hand between mine over my heart while I compose myself enough to talk.

"I'm fine," I finally manage to whisper. "This isn't my blood."

"What happened? Who's hurt? Is it Giselle?" His wide eyes search my face for answers when I'm not quick enough to tell him no.

I shake my head. "It's Wes." My voice trembles as the words escape. "This is all my fault."

Carter pulls me into his lap. He wraps his arms around me and kisses my hair. A wave washes over us, rinsing the blood away, and drags it into the bay where it disappears in the water. I sniffle through each breath, my heart aching as much as the rest of me. If Carter wasn't holding me, if he wasn't whispering in my ear that everything will be okay, I'd surely fall apart.

My heart clenches when I hear my sister sobbing from within her bungalow. "I need to see Bailey," I whisper. I'd much prefer to run away and never look back, but I have to face what I've done head on.

Carter only nods and lifts me up without setting me on my feet. "Don't tell her, Aves. It'll make things worse for everyone. This wasn't really your fault."

"She deserves to know," I say.

He shakes his head. "Not right now. She has enough to worry about. We'll reassess things later."

I bury my face in his shoulder, knowing he's right. If I told Bailey I was responsible for this, she might try to murder me. I'd probably try to murder me.

Taking a deep breath, I say, "Okay. You're right."

Carter takes me to the entrance of Bailey's bungalow, and we peek in and see her kneeling on one side of Wes with Sandra on the other. Reyna, Darren, and Giselle sit out of the way and just watch Sandra stitch up the gash on Wes' forehead with a pretty pathetic first aid kit.

"Anything we can do?" Carter asks without ducking down to take us inside the already crowded shelter.

Bailey looks up at me with watery eyes but doesn't say any-thing. Sandra finishes her last suture and pours fresh water over her work before drying it and taping gauze to Wes' forehead.

She meets our gazes. "If he doesn't wake up soon, he's not going to make it. We don't have the medical equipment to take care of him."

I suck in a breath. "Oh, God." The words only come out as a whisper.

What have I done?

9

LOST FOREVER

THE GLOW OF FIRELIGHT CASTS the shadows of the palm trees behind me across the sand. They stretch out to the foamy waves, making bar-like patterns—a reminder of how the island holds everyone apart from me as its prisoner.

"Walk me back?" Giselle asks, plopping down next to me by the fire.

She's been here since this afternoon after she told me there wasn't any change with Wes. If there's no sign of improvement by tomorrow, then all hope for his recovery will be washed out to sea. I shiver at the thought.

"Mind if Carter walks you?" I glance at Carter, who stands quietly by a large palm, his back pressed against it.

He's been reserved most of the day. I can't tell if it's because the full moon rises tomorrow or if it's because I've shut him out. I don't want to hear him tell me one more time that everything's going to be okay when it's not.

Giselle squeezes my shoulder. "You sure? Maybe I can just stay the night here."

I thrash my hair back and forth, the blond strands slapping my cheeks. "No way are you staying here."

"Then come with me. Bailey asked about you," she says.

"I can't face her, Gi. I can't even look any of them in the eyes. No wonder they don't like me. I'm a monster." I push to my feet and spin to turn away. Sorrow washes over me in waves strong enough to drag me out to sea where I belong.

"Aves, you're not a monster," Giselle argues. "Monsters don't feel guilt."

"But they do hurt others. Now please, just let Carter walk you back. I'll see you in the morning, okay?"

Carter shifts from his spot, lighting a torch in the fire. His gaze locks onto mine. His sad eyes shine in the firelight, and he clenches his jaw like he's holding back from saying something.

I don't give either of them a chance to argue with me. I strip off my shirt and shorts and drop them in the sand. Leaving my bikini bottoms close by them, I rush into the waves. Giselle's voice cuts off the moment I dive under, kicking far enough out that I can transform without getting stuck in the shallow water.

I know abandoning Carter and Giselle hurts them—it hurts me—but I just need to swim and not think about anything. I need to face the fact that maybe the ocean isn't my friend after all. It might've saved me from King Attilonious' clutches, but it's no better than him, forcing me here to wait for Carter to transform, forcing me to see all the possible damage I can cause humans by accident. It's like it gave me the ability to be a human, but also wants me to see that just because I can be one doesn't mean I am one.

Swimming in a few quick circles through the glowing waves, I flick my tail and pop back up high enough to see the beach without expelling water from my lungs. Carter holds the torch, meandering next to Giselle. They're deep in conversation, probably planning some mermaid intervention. It takes Carter looking in my direction to make me dip back under. Our bond allows him to find me anywhere, but with him in human form and me as a mermaid, I can go places he can't follow.

And I do just that.

I swim in the opposite direction to where the island jets from the ocean to create cliffs, and I maneuver through the black rocks to the base of the cliffs where the whitecaps smack against the rocks. This spot is only accessible by sea without rappelling from the cliff tops, and I haven't been here before, but I knew it was here from a swim with Carter. We just got close enough to check them out.

Pulling myself up onto a rock, I sit with my tail pulled to my chest, my whole body out of the water. The glowing ocean expands for miles like the sun shines from underneath the surface instead of from above it where the nearly full moon casts a beam of shimmering light in a moonlit pathway leading out to sea.

The balmy air dries my hair and skin, and I listen to the sound of the waves around me. Out here, nothing seems suffocating. I can breathe in and out without my chest aching, without the spark in my heart flickering a million beats a minute. But out here, I feel so utterly alone in the world, and I already feel lonely enough even with the others around. I might have been an outsider within my group of friends back in Azure Waters, but I was never treated like one. What I wouldn't give to swim away from here—even if only for a day—to go back home where I've always felt I belonged, even now if I don't.

"Your fear will keep you lost forever, my daughter," a soft voice says into my mind.

I jerk my head up and peer at the sea. "I'm getting really sick of you. Just leave me alone!" I yell, my voice cutting over the sound of the waves.

The voice doesn't respond.

Searching the sea, I look for signs of life, of a mermaid who could be taking pleasure in making me look crazy—or maybe I am crazy. Maybe the sea has really gotten to me, crawled not only into my heart but into my head.

I might have the ability to control the water, but the ocean clearly still controls me. How King Attilonious does it, I have no idea. It's not like I can swim up to him and ask why these things are happening and what I'm supposed to do about it.

Just because I can control the ocean doesn't mean I should. I'm not trying to protect a kingdom. I'm not even trying to protect the lost ones. I have no true purpose. I can't face the king and get my life back. I can't even help Wes. All I'm good at is causing one disaster after another. The ocean claims my fear will keep me lost forever but maybe it's what I deserve.

I slap my tail against the surf, and a swell curves high above me, knocking me hard against the rocks before dragging me across them and into the sea. I grind my teeth as pain cuts across my back and tail, and if I could see, I'd probably glimpse blood tinting the water.

Another wave crashes into me, forcing me to cling onto one of the rocks so I'm not thrown into the side of the cliff. Regret washes over me. I shouldn't have come here. Now, I might end up injured like Wes in a place no one can help me—though I doubt anyone would try apart from Carter.

The moment his name enters my mind, I unleash a wave of panic thinking about what I'm putting him through this second. What if he tries to swim out here? I wouldn't put it past him.

Sucking water into my lungs, I push it out through my gills to relax. I stop fighting the current and allow it to drag me from the rocks far enough into the sea that I manage to swim through the narrow channels and back into the deep water.

I swallow my fear, and the water stops pushing me around as if it's intertwined with my every feeling. Drifting on a current of my own making, I let it take me back to the shore. A flash of light glows in the darkness, a single torch on the beach, but the light of the fire can't compete with the light shining from Carter's chest.

He drops the torch in the waves, pulls off his shirt to discard it on shore, and runs deeper into the water. He swims in long, even strokes, surfacing only once for air until he reaches me. His strong arms pull me to him, and he presses his lips to mine, sending a dozen memories to me—the ones he always sends that remind me of our happiest moments together.

"Are you okay?" he whispers in between kisses. He can't see me through the darkness like he could if he were a merman. If he could, he'd probably freak out over the cuts and bruises from the rocks.

I shake my head. "No."

He kisses me again, holding me to him. His legs brush against the sore scales on my tail, and I keep my face buried in his neck so he doesn't see me grimace.

"The ocean spoke to me again," I say, knowing full well that it sounds crazy coming from my mouth.

Carter cups my face. "You've been under a lot of stress, Aves."

I pull away. "I'm serious, Carter. We don't belong here. I think it's why things are getting worse and worse with the full moon nearing."

"Of course we belong here," he says. "And even if we didn't, I can't leave until the full moon."

"That's tomorrow."

"So, you want to leave? What about Giselle?" he asks.

I lift and drop my shoulders. "I don't know. All I know is we can't stay here forever. I'm afraid if we do someone else will—" The words stick to my tongue. Wes is not dead yet. Not if I can help it.

With the thought, hope lights within me like a spark in the water—like the spark that gave me life, that bound me to Carter. Wes doesn't need the human world after all. He needs a mermaid, one who can heal him.

And I know where to find one.

I bring my gaze up to Carter's. "Actually, I know exactly where we're going to go."

He stares at me intently, already knowing what I'm thinking before the words slip from my mouth. "Ava, that's too dangerous."

"We don't have a choice. Your mom is one of the only merpeople who knows about this place. She can help Wes."

"You sure about all this?" he asks, pressing his forehead against mine.

I kiss him. "Never more sure of anything."

10

A FLAME AMID THE DARKNESS

"I CAN'T DO THIS," I say, yanking away from Carter to head back in the direction of our new shelter a good two miles away from the bay.

I thought I could face Bailey, face Wes, but I don't have it in me. What if I can't come through with bringing Carter's mom back? Or what if she can't heal him? I'm afraid to get my sister's hopes up just to have them fizzle out. I don't even want to get my own hopes up.

"Yes, you can," Carter says, grabbing me by the shoulder to spin me back around. "I'll be here for you the whole time."

"Can't you tell them for me?" I know if I bat my eyelashes hard enough and pout my lip, he won't be able to resist my pleas.

"Ava." Uh-oh. He's using his please-don't-use-my-affection-to-get-what-you-want voice.

I pout my lip farther out. "Please."

He closes his eyes for a second, still holding onto my arm. "No."

I sigh, scrunching my nose.

He releases a chuckle and kisses the frown off my face. "You make resisting you incredibly hard, but I do think this is something you need to do."

I sigh again. "Fine."

Carter leads the way, nearly dragging me down the beach. I kick up sand with every step. The closer we get to the community, the more anxiety grips at my chest. It's the same feeling I used to get looking at the ocean. But now, I feel like death is lurking on the other side of the palm frond walls. But not my death.

I suck in a few quick breaths, my hands shaking enough that Carter pulls me to a stop to wrap his arms around me. I think he's about to change his mind about making me confront my sister, because I'm sure he can feel what I'm feeling, but a murmur of voices cut through my heavy breathing and then someone calls my name.

"Ava, you're here," Giselle says, rushing from the spot where she was hanging wet clothes to dry.

I half hug myself. "Any change?"

Her smile falters, and she shakes her head. "No."

Tears well in my eyes, and I turn to Carter. "Maybe I should go alone now instead of waiting for you."

His tense jaw and furrowed brows shoot the idea down before he can even open his mouth. "It'll take a day of me swimming to get to San Francisco, and you don't know how to navigate the ocean. You'll get lost or worse."

He's right. I can barely navigate the shallows near Azure Waters. I have no idea where we are, only that we're in the Pacific Ocean because that's where Pearlestria was and we only drifted on the sea for a few hours. At least if Carter stayed here, I'd know how to come back...I think.

"What if we wait too long?" I ask.

"Too long for what?" The voice comes from behind me, and I turn to catch sight of Bailey hovering in front of her shelter. I'm sure she's heard the entire conversation and only asks to find out exactly what I'm planning to do.

I straighten my shoulders. "I don't want to get your hopes up, Bailey," I say, because I'm afraid of hurting her more than I already have. "But I've decided to leave the island to get help from a healer—Carter's mom to be more specific."

Her eyes widen. "You'll do that for Wes?"

I nod. "I'd do it for anyone here." Her eyes soften, and I remember Wes' words about how selfless he thought Bailey was and how he thought she'd risk her life for anyone here. Maybe Bailey and I are more alike than I thought. "I just can't stand around and do nothing when I can leave."

Bailey closes the distance between us, stepping in front of a suddenly quiet Giselle and Carter, and wraps me in a hug. It feels more than a thank you hug, like Bailey is finally starting to think I'm not a monster after all, even if I don't necessarily agree with her. Wes wouldn't be in this position if it wasn't for me.

"You have no idea what this means to me, Avie," she says, surprising me by using my childhood nickname, the one only my parents and Giselle's mom use now. "Wes is—" She sucks in a deep, shuddering breath. "Wes is everything to me."

Carter clears his throat, drawing both our attention to him. "We'll leave first thing when the moon sets."

I twist my lips to the side. "We can leave when the moon rises."

"It's too dangerous. We need to be able to leave the sea if we have to," he argues. "You know how the full moon affects us. Everyone will be out swimming away from the colonies."

I open my mouth to respond, but Bailey nods her head.

"He's right," she says. "And I'm sure Wes wouldn't want you to risk unnecessary danger when he's stable. Who knows? He could wake up at any second, and then you wouldn't have to go."

I guess I'm outnumbered. It doesn't make me feel any better, though. We could already be in San Francisco come morning and back here tomorrow night. But that's not even what I'm most concerned about. I'm afraid to stay here for the moon's pull. I'm afraid of what it'll do to me. What it will do to this island.

"We can only hope," Giselle says, speaking up.

But that's the problem. I'm feeling all sorts of hopeless.

"You have to keep practicing," Carter says, running his arms up mine as he holds me amid the waves. "We're putting ourselves at risk, and we need to do everything we can to protect ourselves, including having you grasp how to use even an ounce of your power."

"You don't think I know this?" I ask. We're as far away as I can possibly be from the others on the island. Carter insisted we spend our day doing something productive to us, and I couldn't exactly tell that gorgeous face of his no.

"Then stop resisting. You're fighting your instincts. I can feel it," he says.

I huff and try to summon water up to splash him, but my water affinity is still a hit or miss no matter how hard I try to keep it in control. Negative emotions leave it volatile while my positive emotions barely keep water from seeping through my fingers.

Spending nearly all day wading among the waves—sometimes in quiet contemplation and other times kicking and screaming in frustration—hasn't helped much. And Carter's as lost as I am, standing behind me like he can get the ocean to obey me if he intimidates it enough.

"I'm trying not to, but I have a lot on my mind," I say.

"Just take a breath," he says.

I do as he says, inhaling a long breath of the briny air. It settles in my chest, helping ease some of the tension roiling through my body. And then there's the sudden distracting pull of the soon-to-be rising full moon that'll finally unite Carter with me as a merman.

The longer I stand amid the waves, the more I start to feel the pull of the sea. It'll be too strong for me to resist soon, even if I'm able to remain on land without the sea stone ring.

"Can we stop?" I tilt my head toward the sky. "I can't concentrate on the water anymore, not when I can't stop thinking about—" I spin around and press my body against Carter's, brushing my lips to his to send him a dozen images of us together in our true forms.

Warm arms wrap around me, and Carter kisses me more deeply. He lifts me into his arms, and I hook my legs around his waist. My kiss makes him antsy, and he releases a low moan that vibrates over my lips, sending tingles down my spine.

"It's almost time," Carter says, breaking away from me. "I haven't felt the pull so strongly before."

"It's because it's like you're a new merman." Before I saved Carter's life, he could hold off for a couple of hours before going into the water. The pull was there, but it didn't make him sick like it did me. The pull always made me feel like I would die if I didn't succumb to it because I was new. It's weird that the roles have been reversed.

"Why am I so nervous?" he asks, mostly to himself. He

rests his head in the crook of my neck.

I respond anyway. "Because this time is different. The circumstances are different." I hold him tighter, my lips lingering near his ear. "I'll hold your hand if you want."

He chuckles and hums against my damp skin. "You know I always want that."

I release a laugh. "Good."

We stand together and watch the sun dip into the horizon, leaving a golden sky in its wake. Oranges and reds bounce off the fluffy clouds, and I soak in the mesmerizing warmth of the twilight. The moon will rise from behind us, and I can already sense the pull that makes me take an automatic step forward. Tonight, I'm not resisting it.

Carter's eyes trail from my face to my cerulean bikini, one that matches my soon-to-be fin, as he stands me on my feet. Strolling together hand in hand, we head deeper into the waves. A million thoughts flash through my mind. I can't believe that come morning, instead of heading back to shore we'll be leaving straight out to sea and to San Francisco.

The thought weighs heavy in my mind, because just going to Carter's parents' apartment puts us at risk. Starla, Carter's mom, told us she couldn't tell Mateo about us. He has no idea about the island, and I don't know what kind of damage this sort of secret would have on their relationship. The bond between mates is eternal, but I never really considered what happens when something threatens it—like with what happened between the queen and king. She gave up her bond—though I have no idea how real it was to begin with. Maybe he used her like he tried to use me.

"What's wrong, Aves?" Carter asks, bobbing in the waves next to me.

I blink the tears from my eyes before they can fall. "I'm fine. I was just thinking."

"About tomorrow?"

I shrug. "About everything."

Leaning forward, he kisses my head. "Let me take your mind off of things for now."

His lips travel from my forehead to brush against my cheek and then to my lips. His arms, so strong and muscular, hold me against him, gently traveling down my back and to my hips where he plays with the strings of my bottoms.

The waves roll higher around us as Carter gently guides me deeper and away from shore. He sends image after image of us together through his mind before showering me with a wave of pure desire and need, one that leaves me breathless.

Carter strips from his board shorts and tucks them into the bag slung across his broad back while I cling onto him. My bottoms go next, but all we do is continue to kiss, strolling into the water until we're no longer able to touch, just treading together in the sea.

The current drifts around us, swirling my long hair out behind me. I refuse to let go of Carter, and he dives under the water, taking me with him and swims until we're a dozen feet below the surface as night grabs hold and the sea calls to us.

His hands release my waist to clasp my hand, and then his fingers tighten their grip. Closing my eyes, I will my transformation to take hold, allowing the cramps to rush from my toes to my spine. My dorsal fin pushes against the strap of my bikini, and my pectoral fins on my arms glitter through the water, catching on the light of the spark in Carter's chest.

My vision adjusts, lightening the dark water even more, and I take in a deep breath of the ocean to fill my lungs with what it needs to breathe. Bubbles and sand swirl through the ocean with the current, turning the world into a brilliant, magical place I've never been so happy to share with Carter.

His eyes remain closed, tiny bubbles clinging to his face, and he slowly starts to transform. Before, his transformation used to take seconds, but now, it's taking the same amount of time it took me to go through my first transformation.

Blue-green scales sprout on his legs, crawling from his ankles to his thighs, and he arches as his dorsal fin protrudes from his back. I swim closer, bringing up my free hand to his face and graze my fingers along his strong jaw.

"You're almost done," I say, projecting my thoughts into his mind.

His eyes flutter open, their jewel-like color dazzling me like the first time I saw him as a merman. A smile lights his face, and then a second later his legs fuse completely, and he opens his mouth and sucks in the ocean water.

He pulls me close enough that our noses touch, and then he kisses me like the dozens of times before, holding me in a way I can feel his entire body against mine, where it feels like we're almost one.

"I forgot how much I missed your voice in my head," he says, sending his thoughts to me. Flicking his tail, he tugs me with him, swimming a few dozen feet in a matter of seconds. "And swimming like this. Feeling how perfect you fit against me."

I smile as he basks in everything he loved about the ocean. In this moment, nothing else really matters. It reminds me of all the times we swam alone without a care, focusing on us and losing ourselves together in the sea.

I trail my fingers down his sides, running them over the ridge between his torso and tail. He sucks in his bottom lip, letting me explore his merman form, memorizing every glittering scale, creating a map of his body for me to hold in my mind like I've done with his human form a dozen times.

When he can't take it anymore, he swims quick laps around me, twirling me in a current of his making before pulling me back into his arms to kiss me. I can tell he's anxious to swim, to feel how powerful he is in this form among the waves. I ease away and spin him around to lock my arms to his chest to press myself to his back.

"Know what I missed?" I ask, kissing the nook of his neck. "Swimming with you like this."

He flicks his tail, propelling us forward so the world blurs around us. Carter darts along the shallows, dipping low to run his fingers over the sea grass, stirring up sand. We can't go as deep here as we did in Azure Waters, since the reef traps us, but it's better than nothing.

Once we make it around the island, Carter slows down and dips to the bottom of the bay just outside our community. Manta rays congregate above us, gliding through the water like gentle underwater butterflies. It's an enchanting sight to see since I've never seen one in the day around here. Swimming up and away from Carter, I float along with the majestic animal, smiling when its mouth widens like it's grinning at me.

"It's so cute," I say to Carter.

His hands lock around the base of my tail and he gently tugs me down. A frown puckers his eyebrows, causing me to grimace.

I reach out and touch his face. "What is it?"

"I forgot how seeing animals up close like this makes you so happy, and I can't even show you all there is out there on our own terms without having to constantly worry." His voice is barely a whisper in my mind as he motions toward the reef, but I know he's referring to the ocean beyond it.

His sudden sadness ignites anger in me, not at him, but at all the circumstances that have led to this moment. I knew being here would wear on him, but it's happening more quickly than I anticipated. It's such a cruel fate that we're supposed to spend our lives here. I refuse to accept it. I won't. I just hope tomorrow goes smoothly. If Carter can see it's a big ocean and that we're not as trapped as we think, maybe things can start to change.

"I hate this," I say, slicing my hand through the water. A strong current erupts in the bay, sending the manta rays swimming away from us, unhappy with the sudden swell in the calm water. "It's Pearlestria all over again. The king shouldn't have this kind of control over us anymore."

The churning current rocks us back and forth, and Carter swims forward to grab onto my hands to keep us from separating. But I can't calm down. I can't do anything except imagine pummeling the king with the waves, treating him the way he treated me, hurting him the way he hurt me, stealing what he loves the way he stole from me.

"Ava, calm down before you wipe out the community," Carter says, pulling me against him. His arms wrap around me, encasing me in his love. Our chests glow, warmth traveling from his heart to mine until the water mellows and he doesn't have to fight to keep us from washing away on the swells.

Fanning my tail, I propel him up to the surface so I can take a few calming breaths of sea air. He hovers in front of me, still holding me, and I tilt my head back and stare at the glittering sky to get my racing heart to slow and to clear my head.

"I'm sorry." My voice echoes through the quiet air. "Tonight wasn't supposed to be like this. I should enjoy being with you instead of getting mad at things I can't change."

"This is my fault." Carter brushes wet strands of hair from my face. "I pushed you too hard today."

"But it's not. It's my fault. We'd have never been in this position if it weren't for my recklessness and my stubbornness."

He kisses the words from my lips like he can't stand to hear me say them out loud. "Stop, Ava," Carter says into my mind instead of speaking. "There's nothing we can do tonight."

"You mustn't fear, my daughter." The familiar, haunting voice sneaks into my mind, pushing Carter's voice away.

I yank back and stare around with startled eyes. "Did you hear that?" I ask Carter.

His brows scrunch. "Hear what?"

"The voice."

He turns to peer around the water, but it looks the same as it did a moment ago. "I don't hear anything," he finally says.

"I'm not dreaming, right?" I ask, pinching myself for good measure.

"No, I—"

"You mustn't fear and remain lost. It's time to prepare. It's time to get ready for what lies ahead," the voice says into my mind again, forcing Carter's voice away once more.

"I'm not afraid!" I call out through the air.

"You are," it says. "Your fear imprisons you. Come to me, my daughter."

"Where are you?" I ask. A wave rises and curls before crashing to the now rocky surface of the bay.

I pull away, breaking free from Carter. His voice echoes through the balmy air, and I can't focus on what he's saying. I think it's my name, but all I want to do is find where the voice is coming from. I want to confront whoever it is.

"Push the fear away. Be the brave girl I've chosen," the

voice says.

Anger washes through me in hot waves, and I swear the water heats around us, sending steaming bubbles to the surface. I smack the water again, sending a swell crashing toward the shore. I can't help it. The voice is more haunting than ever, and all I want is it to either be straight with me or leave me alone.

"Tell me where you are!" I scream. "Stop playing these games."

I swim a few dozen feet toward the reef, daring the being behind the voice to reveal herself. The full moon hangs overhead, lighting a path for me. One I can't resist following even though I have no idea where it'll take me. I can't see beyond the horizon. Staying here in the bay, on this island, isn't giving me the answers I need.

"Ava, stop." Carter's voice erupts in my mind, and I flinch at the sudden fear in his voice. "Ava, please."

"Don't be afraid, Carter," I say, projecting my voice into his mind.

Swimming faster, I head right for the tunnel in the reef that'll take me to the open sea. I've been beyond it twice now, and if I can just go out again, maybe I'll get the answers, because whoever speaks to me isn't within the protection of the reef.

Hands lock around my waist, stopping me in place, and I thrash in the water. "Ava, please. Talk to me. Tell me what's going on."

The ocean churns around us, and I suddenly feel suffocated

and claustrophobic. The bay feels ten times smaller now that I have the open sea in sight.

"I can't stay here," I manage to say, calming myself enough so I don't send us crashing into the reef.

"It's dangerous out there right now, Aves," Carter says. "Morning will be here soon enough."

I close my eyes and let water push through my gills. "I don't care. I need to go."

His forehead presses against mine. "You know the risks we'll face. If King Attilonious discovers us—"

"I'm willing to risk it," I say. "Please, just trust me. You don't hear what I do. I need answers."

"What do you mean?" he asks.

"I won't find them here," I say, ignoring his question. I'm afraid if we don't hurry that whoever wants me to find them will leave, and I'll stay lost. "But don't worry. I'll protect you."

"Hey, I'm supposed to be the one protecting you." His thought is lighter, more like him than the sudden uncertainty that was gripping his emotions moments ago. "And if you feel we must leave the reef now, then okay. I trust you."

"Just outside. We won't go far."

Carter turns his back on me, letting me cling to his shoulders. He swims us to the reef and toward the tunnel too narrow for us to fit through together. I flick my tail, cutting ahead of him to go through first. Tiny tropical fish scatter, swimming out of my way, and I follow the soft light of the moon shining on the other side of the narrow tunnel.

The moment I'm through, a strange wave of joy swirls through my heart, and I bolt away without even waiting for Carter. I can't help it. It's like moving from a bath tub into an Olympic-sized swimming pool, and I want to test myself to see how far I can go.

"I'm here," I call out through the sea. "Please, show yourself."

No one responds, so I keep swimming. The ocean wraps me in comfort instead of fear, and even outside of the protective barrier, I feel safe. I feel like I can do anything.

The water sparkles in front of me, glittering above the drop-off that'll take me deeper into the ocean to unknown waters I've never had the chance to explore. Without hesitating, I dive down, loving that the bottom doesn't sneak up on me like it does in the bay. A swordfish darts through the water, its full length as long as I am, and I swim next to it, matching its pace.

A shadow falls over me, and I flip in the water, swimming with my face toward the surface and catch sight of Carter swimming right along with me but with caution unlike my new carefree attitude. He doesn't dip down to hold onto me as always, letting me lead the way.

I break away from the swordfish and race up toward Carter, latching my hands around him until he follows me toward the surface. Together, we breach out of the water, cool air circling around us, the moonlight shimmering off our pearlescent skin. My hands break back through the surface, and I dive down again a few feet.

And then I see it.

A glowing light flickers below me, freezing me in place. Carter swims circles around me, and I push him back before he can lock his hands on me to pull me away with him.

The light intensifies, growing brighter and brighter, rising from the deep, and I push my fear away. I want so much to swim as fast as I can back to the safety of the island, but something stops me.

"What is it, Ava?" Carter asks.

I extend my arm out and point to the light, like a flame burning underwater, as it floats in our direction. It's not unlike Carter's spark, the one he gave to me to bring me back to life as a mermaid after I drowned.

"Do you see it?" I ask.

Carter pulls me to him, wrapping his arms around me. "I don't see anything." His fear creeps into me, but I resist letting him pull me away.

I rip free of him and swim forward. Carter's voice echoes in my mind, and his fingers lock around my caudal fin, but I wave my hand, sending a swell directly at him, breaking him free of me.

Jetting forward, I descend deeper, following the light. Neither fear nor worry grips at me, just the strong urge to see what it is, to touch it. It's like I'm stuck in a gravitational pull and can't get myself away.

"Do not fear, my daughter," the familiar, feminine voice says.

The spark radiates with a light that reminds me of the sun shining from the surface. It's as small as the palm of my hand, just floating in front of me, and I reach out and touch it. Heat travels through my fingers and into my arm, coursing through my entire body, setting me aglow with the light.

"Ava!" Carter's voice cuts through my mind, but I can't see him past the light.

My heart quickens, the light becoming all consuming, shining so brightly I can't see anything else. It's like all I am is light, a flame amid the darkness.

Suddenly, the light disappears, and I'm left floating in the churning sea.

11

ANOTHER LIFE

MY MIND FOGS WITH HUNDREDS of memories that don't belong to me.

Small pieces of a mermaid's life scatter across my vision like a puzzle to be assembled without a guide. I glimpse rainbow light, like the sun shining into a crystal prism, the light coming from silver scales so breathtaking they look ethereal.

Tendrils of midnight hair curtain my face, hiding me from a world I'm excited yet afraid to enter, though I know it's not me. I see a diamond the size of my palm, weighing heavily in my hand. It reminds me of the one in King Attilonious' staff, the same staff he channels his ocean magic through. But this one is different. It doesn't belong to him but to the mermaid filling up my mind. All these tiny pieces of someone else's life shift and move through me not unlike when Carter revealed his whole life to me through his kisses.

But the life flashing before my eyes isn't just any ordinary person's—it's the life belonging to Celestiana, the missing queen who abandoned her kingdom for the land. The queen thought dead by the king after he could no longer find her essence through their eternal bond. A bond she broke to create the island of the lost to protect the humans fated to death by a mighty king who would destroy the land to keep the merpeople hidden.

More memories flood my mind. An old human man and older mermaid with a merbaby girl swimming in the waves—grandparents with their granddaughter. It's a moment from the queen's childhood. Her love of the land sparking from her grandmer, who loved a human without bonding with him. I see a young mermaid playing in the water just offshore, younger than me. She waves at the land, and I bask in the love radiating from her. It's different. Deeper. It's not just love. The mermaid is in love. Another image swirls through my mind. Pearlestria and all the merpeople. Sparkling bubbles. A merman. The king. Enchantment and respect replacing the love within me.

"Ava," a soft voice calls, pulling me from the memories. "Ava, come back to me."

Slowly opening my eyes, I peek through my lashes at the

bright sun overhead. Salty air expands my lungs with every deep breath I take, and the soft sand beneath me begs for me to close my eyes again to fall asleep.

I stretch my arms over my head, yawning, trying to fight the exhaustion consuming my body, which happens after a night of swimming. A soft thud sounds near my ear, and color-ful light blinds me as I stare at the multi-faceted surface of a huge diamond on a chain—the gem shaped like half a heart, the same one from the foreign memory in my head.

Jolting upright, I glance in front of me at the cerulean sky merging with the crystalline ocean in the horizon. Puffs of white clouds litter the atmosphere and reflect onto the water. A sud-den peace blankets the panic rising in my chest, and a warm hand squeezes my fingers, drawing my attention away from the sea filled with unraveling secrets.

"Ava," Carter says. "Thank God."

"What happened?" I ask, flicking wet sand from my tail.

Carter leans back on his arms, stretching his tail out so the next wave can roll over him. "You tell me. I couldn't swim through the current you created until you fell unconscious. I spent most of the night holding you until the moon set."

"I'm sorry," I say quietly. "Something came over me."

Carter shifts, wrapping an arm around me to pull me clos-er. I lean into him, meeting his lips to mine, and show him the memories flooding through my mind. I can't stop them as they pour from me to him in a confusing wave that makes him jerk away from me to stare at me with startled eyes.

He flicks his gaze to the sand and scoops up the diamond in his hand like he's seeing it for the first time. "Not something. Someone. Ava, this belonged to the queen."

Searching through the memories that were bestowed upon me, I know he's right. An image flashes through my mind, the queen floating in front of a mirror with the stone weighing over the spark in her heart. Another image shimmers into my mind, one of her and King Attilonious, hand in hand, hovering on a platform like the one he had set up for my coupling ceremony to Carter, which he turned into a nightmare coronation to swear my loyalty to him. The king looks younger, black hair like the queen, but her eyes mirror the sea while his eyes mirror the night.

They kiss each other, the fascination the queen has for him rolling over me. The sparks from their chests travel up to each half of their diamond, lighting the sea in a glow like the full moon before returning back to their chests, bonding them with magic. It's something that didn't happen at my failed coronation the king tried to force upon me. And I'm glad for it, because in this moment, holding the queen's half of the stone, I realize that he wouldn't have shared his magic with me like he did with Celestiana. He'd have taken mine altogether. But I don't have to worry about that now. I have the queen's heart, her essence, her everything in this diamond the ocean gave me.

It'll protect me.

But just because I have the essence of the ocean embodied in my hand, doesn't mean I'm strong enough or powerful enough to face the king yet. I will be, though. And when I am, I'll get my life back. I'll give Carter his life back and all the others on this island.

Carter gently digs his fingers into my side, and I turn and catch him watching me as I try to pull myself from my thoughts. He's giving me time to process without badgering me, something he's always been good at.

I dangle the chain with the diamond. "This belongs to me now. Help me put it on?"

Carter takes it from me, and I lift my long hair so he can clasp it around my neck. It thuds against my chest, sending beams of light sparkling across the surf and both our glittering tails like specks of a rainbow.

"This is all so surreal," he says, breathing on my neck. "That stone is for royalty, Ava. It's half of a matching set. You don't think it means you're meant—"

"I'm meant for you, Carter. Don't you even think for a second I'm supposed to be with King Attilonious."

He smirks. "That's not what I was going to say. I definitely know you're my soul mate. I promised you forever. What I was going to say is that maybe this is some sort of sign."

"I'm tired of signs. I'm tired of trying to figure things out on our own. I'm tired of thinking about all of this, really. I just want to go to San Francisco, get your mom, and then figure this out later. Who knows, maybe she'll have some answers."

"Okay," he says.

Carter shimmies from his spot on the sand until a wave lifts him so he can propel us both back into the water from the shore. He reaches up and hooks his arm around my waist, pulling me into the sea with him and diving down.

I inhale a long breath of water into my lungs and push it out through my gills. The gemstone around my neck glitters in the water, each facet projecting white light through the sea. Carter hovers in front of me, stroking his fingers on the surface of the diamond like it'll somehow give us a plan.

He darts us along the reef until we reach the calm bay in front of our community. We pop to the surface, and I catch sight of Giselle sitting on the sand alone near the water. I lift my hand up and wave, and she blows me a kiss, waiting for us to dive under.

"So, you're absolutely certain about this?" Carter asks, staring at the open sea before us.

"I'm not afraid anymore, Carter." I reach up and run my fingers over the diamond around my neck. The spark in my chest sends beams of light scattering across his chest and through the water around us. "This will keep us safe."

It's not until this moment I finally understand what my dreams have been telling me all along. I don't know if it was the queen or the ocean speaking to me, telling me not to fear, to accept who I am, and to prepare or else I'd be lost forever, but whoever it was had answered my question all along.

It wasn't my fear of transforming I had to overcome. It was the fear of the open sea, of the world that lies hidden among the waves. It wasn't my mermaid form I had to accept. I had to accept I was given these abilities, given this life, for a reason. With these things, I can now prepare myself for what is to come. Because I'm not supposed to hide here in the Lost Cove. If I do, I'll be lost forever. Giselle and the others will be lost forever, too.

Carter studies the stone for a moment longer before he motions for me to hold onto his back so he can lead the way. With a flick of his tail, we surge forward. He breaches out of the water and over the huge reef in an elegant arc that puts us in the open sea.

I expect a dozen negative emotions to grip at my chest, to squeeze my heart and warn me what I'm doing is dangerous, but all I feel is hope. I now feel like I'm finally making my way home.

12

RETURN TO SHORE

"CARTER, YOU'RE GOING TO WEAR yourself down," I say into his mind, resting my chin on his shoulder.

I've been swimming off and on since we left the Lost Cove, but the light now fades from above, and the only signs of life come from the shadow of a vessel on the surface. I'm afraid if he continues at this pace, he'll do more damage than good.

"I don't want to stop until we get there," he says, his voice sounding as tired as I'm sure he feels.

"Then let me swim us. I know I'm not as fast, but I can handle it."

He slows, relenting to my suggestion. We switch places with him wrapping his arms around my ribs instead of on my shoulders like I usually position myself. I twine my fingers with his, letting him hold me, and then flick my tail, jolting us forward.

It's a lot more awkward than I expected it to be. Carter makes it look so effortless with me on his back. But his body is more rigid compared to mine, heavier even in the water, and it takes me a good mile before I get used to pulling him along.

I'm half as fast, but Carter doesn't complain. All he does is rest against me, his heart beating on my back. I close my eyes, letting my body take over so my mind can wander to the task at hand. Carter's parents live close enough to the beach that we can walk to their apartment.

I refuse to even think about Carter's dad and what will surely be a surprised reaction, discovering we didn't drown in the sea together after I returned the spark to Carter when the king stole his life away.

Carter brushes his lips on my neck, drawing my attention out of my mind and to him. I'm glad for it. I hate thinking about that night—the night that changed everything.

I open my eyes, glancing at the wide ocean in front of us. A school of Pacific bluefin tuna swim around us, darting out of the way before I can get too close. Some of the fish are as long as we are, and swimming among them freaks me out just a little.

"I never thought I'd say this, but the ocean is feeling kind of crowded," I say, thinking my words to Carter.

Bubbles erupt at my ear, tickling the side of my face. It's rare for him to laugh out loud underwater, but I'm glad he does, because it makes my heavy heart feel a little lighter. As much as I try to push the doubt away, it still clings to me with every breath of ocean I take. I'm afraid Starla can't or won't help us. I'm afraid Wes' condition will change while we're gone. But at least I'm not afraid of the water. It's comforting as it surrounds us, reminding me I'm where I should be—at least in this moment.

With a strong flick of his tail, Carter propels us faster and then leans his weight heavy on my shoulders, pushing me down to dive. He navigates our way out of the school from below and then shoots us toward the surface when we're in front of it. I expect him to stop swimming and let me take over, but he just continues to hold me to him, our fingers still intertwined, and pushes us forward at his usual fast pace.

"Carter," I complain. "What did I tell you?"

"I'm good, Aves. I got the break I needed. It's only two more hours until we reach the San Francisco Bay."

I scrunch my nose even though he can't see it. "You're coddling me."

"And?" Carter's laughter fills my mind. I shift, spinning in his arms and lock my fingers around the back of his neck so I can face him. His fingers press into my sides, stirring tingles through me. I lean up and suck his bottom lip into my mouth. We kiss while he navigates the sea like he's made the trip a million times, his body taking over while his mind stays with me, imagining all the things we love about each other.

"Continue to kiss me like this, and we might never make it back to the water once we leave the bay," Carter says, letting me go to swim a few quick circles around me. He catches me as his current spins me and locks me in his arms again, pressing his chest to mine.

I kiss him once more. "You're making it incredibly hard to focus on what we need to do."

He turns his face away before I kiss him again. "We can't have that now, can we?"

"Are you trying to resist me?" I ask.

He grins. "Now, you're the one making it hard to focus."

Carter swims me forward through the shallows to the beach closest to his parents' apartment. We hover for a few minutes in the waves, like neither of us is ready to leave the sea to face what we need to do. We're both aware of the danger that comes with revealing ourselves, but we have to trust that Mateo is as loyal to Carter and me as he is to the king. I know he doesn't want to see his son hurt, but he's the one who convinced me to give in to the king. He stood by and did nothing during my coronation except look at me with pity. All along, I had a distrust of Carter's mom, but the more I think about Mateo, the more I worry.

"You're having doubts," Carter says, waiting for me to transform first.

"It's just—your dad," I say. "Your mom wasn't going to tell him about us for a reason."

Carter brushes his fingers through my floating hair. "Don't worry about him, Aves. He will understand."

"And what if he wants me to return to Pearlestria so you can get your life back? What if he blames me for the position we're in?"

Carter shrugs. "He'd never ask me to give up my mate. He considers you his daughter."

I can only hope that's still the case.

Kissing Carter once more, I take a moment to transform back into my human self. Carter hands me my bikini bottoms and helps me put them on. I hold my breath and remain in place in his arms, waiting for him to transform next. He closes his eyes, leans forward to press his forehead to mine.

Nothing happens. He doesn't transform.

And I can't wait much longer. Without his voice in my head, I can't hear his thoughts. He just shakes his head and points to the surface. Propelling up, we break through together, and I gasp a breath of cool air into my lungs. It's been a while since I've felt a crisp night with how humid the Lost Cove is with its never-changing weather.

I shiver in Carter's arms, adjusting to what feels like freezing waters, and he rubs his hands up and down my arms.

"I guess I'm not used to changing back," he says, letting me steal as much of his body heat as I can.

"It's okay. I'll wait here."

Sinking back under, Carter swims a few circles around me. I watch the flicker of his spark light up the tiny whirlpool around me. The bay's dark enough that no one will spot me here, and I can't see any activity on the shore where we're supposed to emerge.

Another minute later, Carter pops back to the surface and spits out water next to me. I blink, staring at the fins still shimmering on his arms. Fear nudges my mind as I take in Carter still in his merman form.

"Something's wrong," I say.

Carter presses his lips into a thin line. "I can't transform."

My forehead scrunches, and I pull his hand from the water and look at his sea stone ring. "Try again."

He releases a small sigh. "Ava, it's not that I'm not trying. I can't. Look at my ring again."

I study the stone in the dark night and realize something's different about it. The sea that used to swirl through the tiny gem has disappeared. It's now just a colorless stone on a piece of silver. The magic that allowed Carter to transform from a merman to a human before is now gone.

"This can't be," I say. "How is it possible?"

He holds me tight. "I don't know."

Pulling back, I glance between him and the nearby beach. "I'll go to shore alone."

"Ava," he argues.

"Carter, we didn't come all this way for nothing. Your mom might know something we don't. I'll be okay."

His eyes line with a sadness I haven't seen in them before. This is the first time I'm going to land without him being able to follow, and it reminds me of all the times he used to go to land without me. I wish with everything in me he didn't feel like I did in those moments. I know what it's like to be bound to the sea, and it's a terrible, heartbreaking feeling not being able to follow your mate.

I run my fingers through the short tendrils of wet hair hanging on his head. "I'll be back as fast as I can, okay? Just wait here."

He nods because he doesn't have a choice. I'm going to shore. Not only does Wes need our help, but now so does Carter.

Carter leans forward, pressing his lips to mine, and sends a dozen images into my head. He reminds me how to get to his parents' apartment, taking me down the least busy streets through his mind.

Without a towel to dry off, this will be one of the most uncomfortable night walks of my life, especially since I now have to do it alone. I don't even have shoes. The only thing I have going for me is that Mateo and Starla live near the beach. Otherwise, I'd draw attention to myself, strolling through the city covered in sand and drying seawater.

"Be careful," Carter says. "I don't know what I'd do if something happened to you, Aves."

I kiss him once more. "Nothing will happen. I know how to protect myself if it came down to it."

Carter nods without a word and swims me as far as he can to the beach. I search the shore for a moment, finding it deserted and dark, and then swim away from Carter and let a small swell carry me to the sand.

I remain on my hands and knees, adjusting to how solid the ground feels compared to the open ocean. The sound of the waves hums in my ears, and I consider lying in the sand, but a siren in the distance makes me push to my feet. I slide into wet shorts from the bag Carter brought and head toward the path that'll take me to the nearest street.

With my hands dangling at my sides, I strut down the sidewalk ignoring an unwanted catcall from a passing car. Luckily, I can shake off the few curious gazes and not let them get to me. If I wasn't a mermaid on a mission, I'd feel all sorts of self-conscious. But now? I just need to hurry.

Starla and Mateo's apartment complex looks exactly how I remember it. A sprawling lawn with flowerbeds decorates the outside of the small complex, and the three-story, U-shaped building surrounds a gated-in swimming pool. Each door faces the courtyard with Carter's parents' ground floor apartment in the center.

I stroll around the pool to their apartment. Unlike the last time, the window and door is closed, the lights all off. Taking a deep breath, I raise my hand and knock on the screen door a few times, hoping they're sleeping and not gone.

After my third set of knocks, I step back and cross my arms. No one answers, which means they're definitely not home.

"The Stevens' left yesterday and haven't been back yet.

They usually take a trip to see family once a month," a voice says from overhead.

Cigarette smoke trickles to me, and I crinkle my nose before I look up. Starla's neighbor, an old man who I remember Carter calling Mr. Mooney, stands outside his apartment door, blowing the smoke from a cigarette into the night. He must've come out of his apartment seconds ago because I didn't see him on my walk around the pool.

Straightening my shoulders, I force myself to smile. "Hey, Mr. Mooney. I don't know if you remember me, but I'm—"

"Mateo's daughter-in-law. I remember you," the old man says, offering me a warm smile. His eyes flick over my tangled, now dry hair to my bare feet. "Your father-in-law never shuts up about you. How's Carter? He hasn't been around in a while."

I release a small breath in relief. This could've gone terribly wrong if Mateo had told Mr. Mooney that Carter had died. His father, everyone apart from Starla, thinks we drowned in the ocean after I transformed Carter into a human again to save his life.

"Carter's great. Spending a lot of time on the ocean with me," I say. Technically, he's *in* the ocean, but Mr. Mooney doesn't need to know that. "We've actually just docked in the bay. Starla and Mateo said they'd be back, but I guess they're running late. We don't get the best cell reception on the yacht." The lie comes so easily I wish it was true.

Mr. Mooney studies me for a second. "I have a spare key in

case of emergencies. I'm sure your in-laws would give me hell if I didn't give it to you to wait inside."

"That would be great," I say. Carter might start to worry if I stay here long, but I can't just leave if his parents might come back.

"Let me get my keys." The old man snuffs out his cigarette and tosses the butt in a small coffee can by his door.

Mr. Mooney heads inside. The screen closes with a bang, and I listen as keys clank against each other. He returns in under a minute and drops the apartment key to me with a smile on his face.

"Tell Carter to come by sometime to say hello, will ya?" he asks.

I force my head to nod. "Of course." Holding up the key, I wave it back and forth. "And thanks for this."

Leaving Mr. Mooney, I enter Carter's parents' apartment. I peer around at the white and blue décor, the hints of the ocean woven throughout the paintings and knick-knacks lying around.

I flick on a light before shutting and locking the door behind me, feeling odd standing in the quaint living room alone, but its familiarity wraps me in a comforting blanket. The familiarity comes from the memories Carter shared with me and not my own, but it doesn't make a difference to me.

My footsteps mute on the soft carpet, and I head toward the kitchen first. It's been weeks since I've eaten anything that wasn't caught or grown on the island, and I can't stop myself from flinging open the fridge to peer inside.

My heart slides into my stomach. It has been completely cleared out and turned off. The cupboard isn't any better. The only things that remain in the pantry are some spices, a few jars of jam and peanut butter, and a box of spaghetti noodles.

I swipe the jar of peanut butter and pull a plastic spoon from the cabinet with disposable plates and cutlery—things that have never even been opened. Something is utterly wrong. Who cleans out their fridge and pantry if they don't plan on being away a while? But where would they go? Mr. Mooney expects them to be back, but after looking around, I'm not so sure. At least not anytime soon.

While scooping spoonfuls of peanut butter in my mouth, I stroll down the dark hallway that leads to two bedrooms and a single bathroom. This is the first time I'll ever see things for myself apart from Carter's memories, and I can't help how excited I am entering the room Carter grew up in—the room that hasn't changed even though he moved away a year ago to work on the Ocean Jewel luxury yacht.

The scent of sunscreen and the sea clings to the entire room, and I can't stop myself from flopping onto his double bed. The sheets smell like fresh laundry, like Starla might've washed them before she left, and I bury my face in his pillow. I could fall asleep if I allowed myself to, because it's been so long since I've laid in an actual bed.

I breathe in and out a few times and finally drag myself away. Looking in Carter's closet, I spot a waterproof bag and pull it out. I also grab one of his shirts and slide into it. It's long enough to be a dress so I tie a knot in the back to cinch it. I can't help myself, and Carter won't mind.

Moving to his parents' bedroom next, I peer at Starla's half of the closet. I feel weird going through her things, but I want some sandals or flip flops to take back with me. I pick out a few sundresses while I'm at it and shove them in the bag, and then I load it with a few necessities, including a hairbrush and a towel, things that are sorely lacking on the island.

I crinkle my nose, looking around for anything else I can take. I catch sight of Starla's purse hanging on a hook by the door, and I dig through it and find a twenty dollar bill in her wallet. Using a pen I found next to it, I write a quick note on the back of a receipt and apologize for taking what I did. I doubt Starla would care, but it makes me feel better.

When I'm through, I head to the front door. I sniff the air to see if Mr. Mooney is back outside. The air smells clean, so I jog around the pool and out the entrance without returning the key to the apartment.

I pass by a twenty-four hour grocery store on my way back to the beach, and I can't stop myself from going inside. If I have to go back to the Lost Cove without Starla, the last thing I'm going to do is return empty handed. I grab a first aid kit, a travel-sized bottle of sunscreen, and some over-the-counter medicine. I wish I had more money and there was a way to load up and swim with a suitcase, but it's not really possible. The Lost Cove is too far from here.

Up ahead, just a block from where I'll turn to enter the beach, a crowd of people hang out on a gated off patio of a bar. Music hums through the air, a few girls laugh, clutching glasses of clear liquid, and a few bar-goers stare in my direction. I hadn't come down this street on the way to the apartment, but my detour at the store had me going a different way back.

"Looks like someone was kicked out," a guy says to me as I pass by. He stands near a table with another man and two girls, and they all share a laugh at my expense.

I roll my eyes and continue walking toward the path that'll drop me directly into the sand. The Golden Gate Bridge glows in the distance and city lights pepper the dark night like tiny stars brought to earth.

Laughter sounds out from the stairs above me, and I grimace, seeing the group of people that were at the bar.

"Hey," the same guy calls out. "You plan on sleeping on the beach or something?"

I don't respond but instead stare at the dark waves, looking for Carter's spark. I see it just past the night swells as he waits for me to return.

"Too good to answer me?" the guy asks, forcing me to stop in my tracks. I'm afraid he'll continue to follow me, which will prevent me from returning to the sea.

He jogs down the stairs, leaving his group of friends at the top, and they just laugh when I glare up at them.

"I'm sorry, but I'm busy," I say as the guy approaches. I don't wait to let him close the distance though. Instead, I kick sand up and head toward the roaring surf.

"You don't look busy. You look like you have nowhere to go."

"And why does that concern you?" I ask, spinning around to face him.

His eyes flick from mine to the bag on my shoulder before stopping at the diamond on my neck. It would pass as costume jewelry from the sheer size of it, not to mention I don't exactly scream wealth at the moment.

"It doesn't, but my girlfriend likes your necklace, and I have cash. You look like you need some. You wouldn't have to sleep on the beach then." Without hesitating, he reaches into his back pocket and pulls out his wallet. He wavers on his feet, clearly drunk.

I purse my lips at the three twenty dollar bills he holds out to me. "Thanks for your concern and all, but I'm not sleeping on the beach, and I don't need your money." Without waiting for him to respond, I turn away and stroll into the water, hoping it'll get him to leave me alone since he's wearing dress pants and shoes.

A bony hand locks onto my shoulder and tugs me back. I stumble and fall into the sand with the guy looming over me. Anger splashes over me in a waterfall of heat, and I glare, scooping up a handful of sand. I throw it in his eyes without hesitating.

He yells out, and voices sound from the stairs. His three companions rush toward us on the beach, and panic squeezes my chest, stealing my breath away. The guy takes their arrival in stride, acting as if they'll back him up, and he reaches down and locks his hand around my ankle to pull me toward him.

"Come on, Donnie. Leave her alone. I don't want the necklace that bad," one of the girl's, a pretty redhead in a tight black dress, says. "I only wanted you to make an offer."

The guy, Donnie, shakes his head, refusing to let my ankle go.

I scream, my voice ripping through the air, and I throw more sand. It doesn't stop him from bending down and locking his fingers around the diamond on my neck. The second his fingers touch it, a wave swells next to us, causing his companions to yell out. I reach out and dig my nails into the skin of his wrist, stopping him from breaking the chain from my neck. The wave crashes over us, knocking the guy away and off his feet.

I sit in my spot, now soaking wet, and watch the sea drag him underwater. Carter's spark glows through the surf nearby, circling the man, and for the first time ever, I imagine Carter doing something unthinkable on my behalf.

The redhead, who I assume is Donnie's girlfriend, runs into the waves. His voice echoes out as he pops to the surface long enough to be pulled back under—not by a wave or the current but by Carter.

Another wave swells, slamming into the girl before she can get in past her knees, sending her to the shore. The others start screaming for help, and I know if they continue, they'll bring attention to us if they haven't already.

Pushing to my feet, I run through the waves and make my way to where I see Carter circling, pulling the guy under every time he pops back up for air. I wish I could scream his name, tell him to stop, but I can't. Instead, I slap my hand on the water, sending a current strong enough to push Carter away.

His rage and fear floods through me, and I know he's doing this because he's feeling the despair that comes with his inability to leave the water to protect me. As merpeople, we're fiercely protective, putting each other first. I just know Carter will regret his actions once his mind clears.

The voices of the panicking humans disappear when I dive under and swim in the direction of Donnie. It'd be easier to transform, but then I'm pretty sure we'd have to take four people back with us to the Lost Cove, and that's the last thing I want to do. All I want is to get out of here and figure out what to do next.

Before I can get within reach of the now drowning drunk, Carter locks his strong hands around my waist and pulls me under. My eyes blur in the saltwater, and I can't tell him to let me go, so I press my hands into his chest and push him until he releases me.

I swim underwater to where Donnie floats amid the sea and grab him by the back of his button-up and yank him to the surface. He spits and coughs, his wild eyes meeting mine, but he doesn't fight me. He tries his best to swim with me as I help him back to shore until our feet touch the sandy ground.

He falls to his knees, and his friends rush to him to pull him out of the waves. The redhead rushes over to me, trying to see if I'm okay. I walk backwards to keep space between us because I want her nowhere near me.

"Stay away," I say. "Your boyfriend is a psycho."

She ignores my words and says, "I'm sorry. He gets a little carried away when he drinks."

I grimace. That was far from getting carried away. "He's lucky, you know. I could've let him die out there."

"Let me help you. My apartment is just around the corner. You can take a shower and warm up there. I won't let Donnie come either," she says, surprising me. "We'll order some take-out. Whatever you want." I can't tell if she's being nice because she wants to be or because she's worried I'll get the police involved.

I shake my head, my wet hair slapping against my cheeks. "Thanks but no. I'm on my way home."

Reaching down, I pick up my discarded belongings and swing the waterproof bag over my shoulder. I might regret doing this, but I'm so over the land in this moment that all I can think about is jumping back into the sea.

And that's what I do.

I stroll a few feet away from her and head straight into the water, not caring that she calls out her protests. She doesn't follow me in, though. I gaze over my shoulder once, smiling at the four people staring at me, and then I duck under the waves and swim a few feet until Carter drags me away from the surface completely, probably leaving the group with confusion that'll last them the rest of their lives.

The second my lungs burn, I tug off my bikini bottoms and transform, leaving on the T-shirt I stole from Carter's room. His lips meet mine, his thoughts rushing at me faster than I can comprehend, and all I do is hug him, pressing my body against his, and wait for him to calm down.

"Carter," I say, finally getting a word in. "What you did back there..." My voice trails off.

"I was so close to coming to shore to reveal myself," he says.

"You could've killed that guy."

"I wanted to."

I frown, pressing my forehead to his. "And that scares me. I know you want to protect me, that you'll do whatever you can to protect me, but I don't ever want you doing that. It's not you. We're not those people. That's something the king would do."

"Ava." His voice is a small whisper in my mind. "I'm sorry. You were so scared, and I just couldn't handle it. I can't handle it."

"But you have to trust that I can," I say.

He closes his eyes, pushing water through his gills. I hate seeing Carter like this—lost and uncertain. I hate seeing him feel like he's no longer good enough for me because he can't go on land.

"And we have bigger problems to worry about than some

stupid drunk wanting my necklace," I add, holding his face between my hands.

He stiffens in my arms. "My parents weren't home?"

I shake my head, my hair veiling my face in the water. "No, and it looks like they're not going to be home anytime soon. I think the king—" I don't want to even project the words to Carter.

"You think he's the reason my ring's not working?"

I squeeze my eyes shut. "I think he called everyone back into the sea."

13

PROTECTED

"NO," CARTER SAYS. "THERE'S NO way we're going back there."

We sit on some large rocks offshore just outside of the San Francisco Bay. A lighthouse shines in the distance, but no one will see us this time of night from our position facing away from the shore.

"But, Carter. Wes needs help. And what do you expect to do? Just stay in our protective little bay all the time? That's like putting you in a tank."

"Going to Pearlestria is suicide, Ava. I don't care if you

think that necklace will keep us safe. I don't want to risk it—not for someone we barely know." He rubs his hands up his face and into his hair, pushing the strands out of his eyes. He sounds more exhausted than anything, and I'm sure the journey has worn him out. It's why we sit here sharing the rest of the jar of peanut butter I stole from Starla's.

"He's like that because of me," I say. "I can't go back there without help, Carter. I can't face my sister."

"Then we'll risk it out here and stay far away from any of the colonies," he says.

I huff. Anger rushes through me hot and fast, and it's sudden enough that Carter snaps his head in my direction. This is the second time tonight I've been mad at him, and I don't know if it's the sea or his inability to transform that's getting between us, but I don't like feeling like this. I don't like that he's the reason I feel this way.

Without saying a word, Carter jumps back into the water and swims a few small circles not far from where I remain. The cloudy current he creates collides into the rock, knocking me back, and I flip over the edge and land in the water. Another wave catches me and pushes me into the rock where I hit my shoulder, sending pain through me.

I don't even have a chance to cry. Carter pulls me into his arms and away from the current of his creation and swims us back a dozen feet.

"Ava, I'm sorry. I didn't mean—God." His guilt pours over me in cold streams. His eyes glass over under the light of the moon, and he runs his fingers along the red mark forming on my arm that will surely bruise.

"It was an accident," I say. "I'll live."

"I'm failing you." Carter's words surprise me.

I purse my lips and cup his face to look into his jewel-like eyes. His brows hang low, and a crease pinches his forehead. His emotions are all over the place, batting me with grief, worry, guilt, sadness, and his ever-present love. All of his feelings are because of me. I'm the one doing this to him.

"Why would you say that?" I ask.

"Because I'm a coward. I should be on your side. I should want to help you no matter what. I should be able to protect you no matter what. But I—" He sighs and stops talking, just hangs his head while ocean water mists his face.

"You're the bravest person I know," I say. "You've done nothing but fight for me and protect me. You saved me not only from death but from the king."

"You think I'm brave? You're the brave one, Ava. You fell into my arms in stride, fighting the fear of the ocean, and then the fear of losing your human life. You've held strong to what you've wanted instead of just accepting this was how things were going to be. You stood up to the king, fought the king, and even after everything he's put us through, you're still willing to go back and risk facing him again. And for what? A human. I do what I do for you, Ava. But you, you do things for anyone." He rests his head on my forehead, our lips hovering close enough to kiss.

I smile, hearing his thoughts of me put into words. Thoughts I never considered to be true about me. I've always considered myself selfish and Carter as selfless, but in the end, we've been doing the best we can in the uncontrollable circumstances of our lives together.

"I don't even know how to respond to that," I say. "I think you have me confused with someone else. Maybe the sea is getting to your head. I'm pretty sure I want to do this for me."

He laughs, tilting forward even more until his voice hums against my lips. "If it was for you, then you'd listen to me and go back to the Lost Cove. We'd have never left in the first place."

"So, you know I'm not going to listen to you," I say.

"You might be the bravest person I know, but you're also stubborn as hell, Aves." His lips disappear as he presses them together. "And I want you to know I'm still not on board bu—"

I frown. "Carter, I don't want to fight."

"Just hear me out."

I snap my mouth closed.

"I'm willing to make a compromise," he says. "We'll go back to Pearlestria, but we're not going past the wall. If my mom is there, she'll come to us. If she's not, then I'm sorry. There's nothing else we can do for Wes. I'm not getting anyone else tangled in our life."

Hope swells in my chest, and I lean forward and kiss him like he's told me he figured out a way for us all to go home. He holds me tightly as we tread in the water. A dozen warm, inviting emotions swirl between us, and for the first time in days I have hope.

Carter pulls me down with him, and we sink under the waves crashing against the rocks. The moon shimmers across the water above us, and Carter swims us into a dense kelp forest. It's closer to Pearlestria than it is to the Lost Cove, but they're both west of us now.

"I need to rest a while longer, Ava," Carter says into my mind. "I'm not taking us into dangerous waters when I'm not in the best condition."

I relent to his needs and curl against him on the sand amid the kelp forest that'll protect us. He slaps his tail along the bottom a few times, and I listen to his muted heartbeat as he drifts off.

I can't sleep, though. I'm too wound up. I shift in Carter's arms, digging my chin into his chest.

A leopard shark swims nearby, and I suck a breath of water into my mouth to push it out through my gills. The shark jets by close enough to touch, but all I do is watch it weave through the kelp until it disappears. I just stare at the ocean life, the fish and crustaceans, navigating through the glowing forest. At least I don't have to worry about any of them bothering us.

I shift again in Carter's arms, and this time he opens his eyes to look at me. Running his fingers through my floating hair, he pushes it out of my face so he can peer into my eyes. The sea gently swirls around us, making the kelp sway, but Carter's heavy enough that neither of us moves.

"What's wrong, Ava?" Carter asks into my mind.

I turn away from his eyes and press my cheek against his chest. "I can't sleep. I'm too nervous."

"Would it make you feel better if I stayed awake until you do?" he asks.

It would, but I don't want to ask that of him. He shouldn't have to suffer through exhaustion because I'm worried about a million things despite knowing the diamond hanging over my chest protects me.

"No," I say.

He pouts his bottom lip out, shifts up, and pulls me onto his lap, cradling me. I laugh as he rocks me back and forth, and he plants his lips to mine, kissing me deeply like his kiss can somehow push away all the dark feelings competing with the dark water.

Trailing my fingers over his shoulders, I trace the curve of his taut muscles down his back. He moans into my lips, the vibrations cutting through the water. It stirs desire in me, and I press against him, pushing him back in the sand. I lie on top of him, resting my body against his. Running his fingers down the fin on my back to my tail, he locks them onto the ridge that separates my tail from my torso. His lips travel along my jaw, and he releases tiny bubbles from his mouth as he makes his way to my neck.

In a quick motion, he flips me off him and onto my back. Sand swirls around us, glittering in the pale moonlight shining down from the surface. Carter sends a dozen memories to me, reminding me of his favorite moments of us together, including some that ignite a fire in my stomach in a good way.

His spark blinks rapidly in his chest, bouncing light off my necklace and through the water. He rests his elbows on both sides of my head, kissing me deep enough that I smack my tail on the ocean floor sending a ripple through the water, making the sea life scatter.

The shadow of an early morning vessel about to fish the kelp forest draws my attention away from Carter, and I freeze mid-kiss. While our sparks protect us from being discovered, I still get nervous seeing humans above us. Carter presses me into the sea floor, resting his cheek against mine like I somehow need to be shielded from the rest of the world in my moment of nervousness.

"You okay?" Carter asks into my mind after a moment.

"I'm just a little on edge is all," I say. "It's weird being out in the open like this. The boat overhead doesn't help."

"How about I keep a lookout, and you try to get some sleep? You'll feel better after you get some rest." He rolls off me and sits in the sand next to me. Pulling me halfway onto him, he brushes his fingers through my floating hair, letting me use him as a pillow.

"I don't think I can. Why don't you try to distract me again?" I ask, reaching up to touch his face.

He runs his fingers along my hairline. "It's kind of hard when I can feel your nerves."

I blush, my face warming. "I—"

He brushes his lips across mine. "It's fine. Just try to sleep, okay?"

Relenting to his suggestion, I curl up in the sand, resting my head on his lap so he can play with my hair while I hug against his strong tail. I close my eyes, trying my best to push away all the thoughts from the last day from my mind. Carter hums softly into my mind, a familiar song I can't put my finger on, but I realize I'm too tired to care.

I drift in and out of sleep, startling every time a current tries to shift us in the water. Through my closed lids, I can see the light of my necklace growing brighter and brighter, and it becomes so intense I snap my eyes open to suddenly black waters. The light disappears, leaving me blind.

But that's not the worst of it. My legs cramp, a sudden transformation taking hold of me. A strong current knocks into me, pulling me away from Carter, who I can no longer hear in my mind. I thrash in the sea, tangling myself in the long strands of kelp and try to scream, but my lungs are still full of the ocean since I haven't surfaced for a breath of fresh air.

"You might not fear, but you have not accepted who you are," a familiar feminine voice says.

"But I have," I think, sending the voice into the sea.

"If you remain lost, you will be found," the voice responds. "Heed my warning."

The voice disappears, leaving me in cold darkness in a kelp forest threatening to strangle me. I pull against the ropes, snapping them with my hands, and finally manage to break free to swim to the surface.

The glow of the moon reflects on the water, and I see my reflection staring back at me in the mirror-like surface. Instead of breaking through to air, I stare into my blue eyes, shining silver in the light. Tiny bubbles cling to my face like orbs, and my human body reminds me just how weak I am in this state.

But I can't transform. As much as I will for it to take hold, nothing happens. I remain in the form I'm most familiar with, my lungs burning, threatening to drown me.

Kicking once more, I break through the surface, spitting out water to gulp in fresh air. I don't stay up long. Hands lock around me, yanking me back under, and I scream out through the ocean.

"Ava, calm down. It's me," Carter says, his eyes wide and wild.

I blink the confusion away and realize I'm not in my human form after all. I'm still a mermaid. "Carter, something's wrong," I say.

"We're fine. Everything's fine," he says.

I shake my head, my hair veiling between us. "We have to go."

"It was just a dream, Aves. You created a current in your sleep, and I couldn't hold onto you. I'm sorry I wasn't quick to catch you before you surfaced." Everything he says sinks in, but it doesn't lessen the fear gripping me, begging me to swim away as fast as I can.

"Car—"

A flash of light blinks in the water, cutting off my words. I'd recognize the light anywhere. It looks like the one sparkling from my chest—from Carter's, too. I shouldn't be able to see another merperson's spark, but I'm also not supposed to be able to transform without a ring either. Something in my essence is different. I feel different ever since the ocean dragged us away from a terrible fate at the hands of an unfair and unkind king.

Carter tenses next to me, following my line of vision. Through the glowing water, a shadow cuts through the kelp forest in our direction. It doesn't belong to a large fish or shark. It's definitely another merperson.

I don't even have to tell Carter we need to leave. He hooks his arm around my waist and swims in the opposite direction of the approaching merman. My tail smacks along the long ropes of kelp, and I wave my hand through the water, sending a current strong enough to entangle them so it's nearly impossible to follow us without cutting a way through.

"They're a long way from Pearlestria," I say into Carter's mind, because saying nothing at all squeezes my chest as I fight away the rolling panic. If it weren't for the warning in my dream, they would've stumbled upon us. Pearlestria was small enough that we would've been recognized. The whole ocean could probably recognize us with how merpeople can pass on detailed information—clear images—with their minds.

"It's not uncommon to leave," Carter says. "Look how often we did. It's a big world. We might live in colonies, but we do like to explore."

When we're a few miles away from the kelp forest, Carter loosens his hold on me, allowing me to position myself on his back instead of being pulled along like a doll. Our in-sync hearts slow, and our nerves settle, and after another mile of swimming, Carter finally stops and relaxes.

"That was too close, Ava. I should've listened to you," he says.

I cup his face in my hands. "It's not your fault. Neither of us could've known." I never expected the diamond on my neck would protect us with words of warning. I had no idea what to expect from it, but deep down, I knew it would keep us safe, and it did.

"This is why I'm nervous," he says. "We might not be so lucky near Pearlestria. I don't know what the king will do to us if he discovers we're alive."

I lean my forehead against his. "Nothing," I say. "I won't allow it."

"Ava," Carter whispers into my mind.

"Just trust me," I say.

But I can see it's not me he doesn't trust. It's the rest of the ocean.

I don't blame him. I don't trust it, either.

·14·

POWER ATTRACTS POWER

"JUST ANOTHER MILE," CARTER SAYS into my mind.

His voice startles me awake, and I blink my eyes a few times. I didn't even realize how tired I was until Carter started swimming after he slept for a measly hour, one in which I stayed awake from fear. If he wasn't holding my arms in his, I'd have floated away in the sea.

Nerves tie a dozen knots in my stomach. "Can we reach out to her from here?" I ask.

Carter dives deeper, and I spot the sleepy colony behind the shimmering wall that looks like the inside of a shiny seashell. An intense fear burns in my spark just looking at the place that imprisoned me for weeks. The only thing we have going for us is that all the merpeople hide away in their rock houses, sleeping.

Even the castle lacks activity from the center of the colony, looking more foreboding than beautiful like it used to. Because behind its gem-encrusted walls lies a king who would break my bond with Carter to steal the magic flowing through my veins.

Warmth erupts in my chest, and a bright glow flashes from the diamond necklace over my heart. The sudden light startles me, and I let go of Carter to hide it between the palms of my hands afraid the beacon of light will draw the whole colony right to us.

Carter spins, not letting me get far. "Is someone coming?"

"My necklace," I say, slowly unlacing my fingers. "It's glowing."

Carter's brows furrow, his head tilting to the side. "I can't see it."

Carter would have to be blind not to see how brightly it shines, sending colorful light through the sea around us. It's enough that I consider taking it off to shove in the bag slung across Carter's shoulder.

With a reach of his hand, Carter grabs my wrists and stops me from yanking the chain free. "Don't take it off. I think only you can see it."

"But why is it glowing?"

A sudden current wraps around us, yanking us back.

Through the shift in the water, I spot a lone figure swimming straight for the surface from outside the main channel in Pearlestria. I'd recognize the glittering gold tail anywhere. Luna, King Attilonious' daughter, swims toward the surface to break through. It's something we've done together before when we became fast friends. She tried to run away with me and Carter to go ashore, because she always wanted to experience life on the land, not unlike her mother, the queen. But King Attilonious never allowed it. She still goes to the surface now to dream.

"Luna," I whisper, holding the warm diamond between my fingers. The words stay locked between me and Carter. No one else can hear us unless we want them to.

Carter pulls me close. "Careful, Ava. Luna might be your friend, but she's the king's daughter. She doesn't see the world like we do. Her loyalty will be to her dad."

I frown. I wouldn't blame her, but I'd hope she would stand up to him if it came down to it. It's always nice to have someone on your side.

"I know," I whisper. "I just—I wish she didn't think we died."

His lip pouts. "I wish a lot of people didn't think that."

"I'm sorry." My voice is barely a whisper between us. "I know you miss your dad. I miss mine, too." I miss a bunch of people.

"It won't always be this way. Now, come on. We have to hurry. I want to get out of here before dawn."

Carter swims forward, down to where the wall obscures our arrival. We stop outside the barrier, closest to the spot where Carter and I had shared a small rock house together on the outskirts of the community. If Starla and Mateo are back in Pearlestria, then that would be the place they would stay since they don't have their own home here. Well, it'd be their home now without me and Carter around.

Carter's gaze falls on mine as we share a silent conversation to see who will call for his mom first.

"Starla?" I ask, beating him to it. His hesitation might keep us here well past the sunrise. "Starla, are you here?"

"Ava?" a familiar voice questions. "Oh, no. What are you doing here? Is Carter..." Her voice trails off before she can relay her concerns to me.

"I'm fine, Mom," Carter says, taking over. "We're together."

"You shouldn't be here," she says, her voice whispering through our minds like if she projects it too loudly, the whole colony might hear.

"You shouldn't be here either," Carter says. "We went to San Francisco looking for you, but you weren't there."

She doesn't respond right away. It takes a few minutes of silence before I say, "Starla, are you still there? We know about the sea stone rings, but that's not why we're here. We need your help."

"Oh, Ava. I was hoping the island would protect you," she says. "But I don't know what it is I can help you with. Everyone's been called back to the colonies by King Attilonious."

I close my eyes, twisting my lips to the side at her words. I knew the king removed magic from Carter's sea stone ring, but I didn't realize he called everyone back to the sea on the full moon. And I can't help but think this is all my fault. I caused so much trouble for the king that he probably doesn't want to risk another human standing up to him again if they were chosen as a mate.

"He's scared," Carter says, thinking my next thought for me.

"He should be," I mutter to him, allowing Starla to hear through the water.

"Ava, Carter," Starla says, "you shouldn't talk like that, especially this close to the colony. The king has power that extends through the whole ocean. We don't know what his limitations are. What if he senses you? You two need to leave. Go back to the island. Live life the best you can in those waters."

"The king can't touch us, Starla." At least I hope. "And we're not leaving without you. We need you. One of the lost ones is hurt."

"I'm sorry to hear that," she says. "But I can't return to land."

"Then I'll bring him to the sea. Please, come with us."

"But Mateo. It's hard enough holding this secret," she says.

My hope for Starla's help dwindles the longer our telepathic conversation continues. She's not involved with the people of the island. She doesn't have to live with the consequences of accidentally hurting someone with power. She's a healer. It's all she does. She fixes things while I, like an unstoppable storm, leave everything a wreck in my path.

"Please, Starla. Just this once. I can't go back to the island otherwise."

"Oh, Ava."

Without thinking, I pull from Carter and swim up and over the wall. If she can see my face, look into my eyes, she might agree. I can't go back without trying everything short of forcing her to come with me. Carter swims above me, locking his hands on my waist. I expect him to pull me back over the wall and away from the colony, but he only swims me faster until we're through the door of our old rock house.

Things have changed. It's no longer bare like I used to keep it. Starla brought in more stones for seating and has draped woven sea grass over them. A large chest sits in the corner of our old living room with a few decorative vases she either brought from shore or found somewhere along the way. Within them are stands of kelp that float to the ceiling, and even more fish have moved into the reef lining the perimeter of the room.

The sea glass mural climbing the wall is exactly the same as we left it, the scene reminiscent of the sun setting on water. Though that's the same, Starla's spent time covering the cutouts with seaweed curtains, so people can no longer peer inside without her permission, something we never bothered with because no one ever visited.

"Starla," I whisper telepathically. "We're in the living

room."

The current shifts, a stream coming from the bedroom she had claimed while we lived together. It's smaller than mine and Carter's, and I'm surprised they didn't move into that room. Starla pulls the curtain back, and grimaces at the both of us.

She swims closer, pulling Carter into her arms first. "You never could listen," she says, smiling sadly, a mixture of love and worry marring her soft features. Her eyes, the same blue-green as Carter's, shift to my face before they drop to the diamond hanging around my neck over the T-shirt of Carter's I'm still wearing. "Ava, where did you get that?"

I guess no warm hug for me. Reaching up, I lock my fingers around the glittering stone. "It was a gift."

"That belonged to the queen," she says.

I nod. "I know. The island—it's been doing things to me."

I can't decipher the next look that crosses her face. Surprise? Fear? Confusion? Her perfectly arched brows lower on her smooth forehead, and she cups her hand over mine while I hold the stone.

"Ava's been sleep-swimming and seeing things I can't," Carter adds. "Her water affinity is all over the place. She's the reason we need your help, Mom. She hurt someone by accident while practicing. I don't even know how much longer we can stay on the island. Ava already wants to leave. The others will find out about her, and it's bad enough as it is. Her own sister looks at her with distrust."

Starla pouts her bottom lip and pulls me into a hug. "I'm

so sorry for how everything is turning out for you both. I never imagined Carter would have such a life. You both were supposed to be free to live wherever you chose, make the kind of life you're happy to live. You were supposed to have so much joy, just being together. It's all I ever wanted. What your dad wanted, too. Even after your accidental bonding, I still had hope for that life. If I could face the king myself, I would. I'd do anything to make your lives the best they can be."

"But you can't face the king," Carter says.

"But I can help you." She touches my necklace once more. "I always expected my son would choose a special mate, Ava, but I had never imagined this."

I frown. We've always had tension between us—right up to the moment I realized Starla spared Giselle's life. But hearing her admit all this makes me feel like an utter disappointment. I'm nothing like the daughter she had ever imagined gaining. I've done nothing but ruin everything for her, including her life on land.

"I'm sorry, Starla," I whisper.

She pushes my floating blond hair from my face. "I didn't mean that in a bad way. I just never imagined the queen would pass her essence to you. Power attracts power, and you must've showed her something."

"You knew the queen?" I ask.

"We were childhood friends and grew up together. We had both dreamed of moving from the sea to the land. Your grandmer, Carter, she raised me between here and the land.

Celestiana used to visit, and she met someone—a human. But when her affinity started showing, the king took great interest in her. He swept her on the waves, promised her the ocean, everything she could ever imagine in a mate. And she felt herself pull away from the human she loved. She enjoyed the king's company, and he taught her how to harness her magic, but soon after the coupling ceremony, he wanted her to stop returning to the land. And she had agreed for many years." She stops speaking, her blue eyes blinking a few times as she pushes whatever memory away.

"But she wanted to return?"

Starla nods. "Can you blame her? Once you love the human world, you never stop loving it. She took interest in every new human transformed into merperson and would travel the world to offer her support through the transition."

"Is that why she created the Lost Cove?" I ask. I know the rumors. I know it is said that the queen created the sanctuary for a woman who refused to transform after discovering the mer-secret.

"It is. And she kept it from the king, but it turned too difficult to protect the island and remain in Pearlestria, especially with the bond she shared with the king."

"So, she left." It's not a question. I know it's true. "I can't believe she left Luna behind like that."

"It wasn't her intention. She had planned to give up her magic and renounce her reign over the sea, but in doing so, it'd have gone to King Attilonious. They shared a bond and their magic."

My heart hangs heavy in my chest. "She died to protect that island and to keep the king from getting her magic."

Starla nods. "She gave her essence back to the sea. The sea gave her a human life in exchange and it stopped her from returning to Luna. It broke the bond she had for the king. But without her mermaid essence and the weight of the broken bond—it was too much."

I blink surprise from my face. "You mean...I can give up this life completely? I can renounce my essence." I turn to Carter. "Why didn't you tell me?"

Starla touches my arm. "Carter knows nothing of this. It's an impossible situation. If any merperson could do it, we wouldn't need rings to go to land. The moon would never call to us. The queen had the ocean's magic in her heart like you, but it doesn't go without consequence. You've bonded with Carter through the essence. Renouncing it will break it like it did between the king and queen. The king survives because they both share magic. Carter doesn't. It could very well kill him."

My lips form an O-shape. As much as the idea of returning to the human world as completely human stirs something within me, I could never do it. I could never break Carter's heart like that. I could never risk his life.

"I'd never," I whisper. "I promised you forever."

Carter's mouth pulls up into a half-smile, and then he leans over and kisses my cheek. "I know, Aves."

"Starla?" a masculine voice sounds through all our minds.

"Where are you?"

Carter hooks his arm around my waist and pulls us through the door before Mateo swims into the living room to find us. My heartbeat pounds in my ears, and I panic at the idea that I've spent too much time learning about the queen, and now I might've missed my opportunity to take Starla back to the Lost Cove.

"My love, you caught me," Starla says, letting us hear her conversation with Mateo. "I was about to sneak out. I wanted to surprise you with a few things."

"How about I close my eyes and pretend I didn't see you?" Mateo asks.

I raise my eyebrows, glancing at Carter who shakes his head.

"Perfect," Starla says. "Now, enjoy your day. I'll be back by sunset."

Carter swims me up and over the wall before Mateo can watch Starla leave. My necklace suddenly sparks brightly on my neck, sending a flash of panic to my heart, but it's only Starla who swims over the wall above us.

"We must be quick," she says, looking down at us.

I blow a bubble through my mouth, letting it trickle to the surface. My necklace still glows brightly, sending rainbow sparkles through the water. No one but me sees it, and I tuck it under my shirt. It might be going off because the sun has already risen overhead and the colony will awaken soon.

Carter responds to his mom with a nod. I climb on his

back, and he takes off. I take one last look behind us, fear sneaking into my heart. Making her way down from the surface is Luna, and her eyes meet mine from over my shoulder.

But she doesn't move from her spot.

All she does is watch us leave.

15

REMAIN LOST

"AVA, YOU CAN STILL TRANSFORM?" Starla asks, floating in the middle of the bay next to me and Carter. Her brown hair is tied in a tight bun on the nape of her neck, and she wears a decorative sea grass wrap around her chest, a popular look in the colony, though some mermaids do go topless. It's something I never got used to, even though merpeople don't judge bodies the same as humans.

I pull myself from my thoughts and nod. Tugging my hand from Carter, I hold out my fingers so Starla can see I'm not wearing a sea stone ring. She didn't stay long the last time I saw her, and I was so caught up with Giselle and Bailey I didn't even mention my lack of one before she left.

"I don't even need a ring," I say.

Closing my eyes, I let the transformation take hold of me. After a quick rush of cramps, I change back into my human self, and Carter propels us to the surface to break through. Starla remains underwater, and Carter helps me get my bottoms on and then hands me the bag with the supplies I picked up in San Francisco.

Starla swims behind us, never breaking the surface, and waits with Carter just past the waves where they won't have to hunch to stay underwater. It's my job to get Wes to them so Starla can see what she can do.

My legs give out the moment I reach the shore of the bay, and I stay on my hands and knees for a good few minutes just inhaling and exhaling the briny air. My sopping hair sticks to my face and sand covers me from head to toe, peppering the shirt of Carter's I still wear even though swimming without it would be a million times easier.

"Ava?" Giselle's familiar voice rings through the air. "Bailey! Ava's back!"

Everyone from our little community rushes onto the beach to gape at me getting back to my feet. I wring the seawater from my shirt and force myself to smile. Giselle rushes to me, throwing her arms around me, holding me as tight as she possibly can.

I laugh, pushing her back just enough so I can breathe.

"How's Wes?" I ask, turning my gaze to Bailey.

Her lip quivers and she doesn't even have to say anything for me to know he's either gotten worse or nothing has changed. "He's dehydrated." Her brows pinch together. "Where's Carter? Is everything okay?"

I swallow the lump in my throat. "He's with his mom in the bay. We need to get Wes to her."

Giselle turns to the water. "Why don't they come on land?"

Tears prickle in my eyes, and I blink them away. "It's a long story, but we don't have much time. If you all can help me carry Wes to the water, I can swim him myself."

"I'm coming with you," Bailey says.

I nod. There's no way I'm going to tell her it's better if she remains on land where it's safe, because who knows what'll happen with me around. Instead, Darren, Sandra, and Reyna lead the way to Bailey's bungalow. We all take a section of the blanket Wes rests on and carry him all the way into the waves.

Carter surfaces the moment the others leave me and Bailey, and he takes Wes from us. In Carter's arms, Wes looks years younger and smaller. Water splashes his face, gaining no reaction, and I wonder if the damage done to him can be fixed. He hit his head and stopped breathing before I pulled the water from his lungs—there's a lot that can be wrong. Even if I could get him to a hospital, there might not be anything we can do.

I push the thought away. I refuse to think it. If there was one thing I learned from being a mermaid, it's that magic is real and the ocean doesn't only steal life away. It creates it, too.

We reach the center of the bay, and Starla breaks the surface for the first time. Carter flicks his tail, keeping Wes above the water. I tread water next to Bailey, remaining in my human form though transforming would be so much easier. I remain human not only for Bailey's sake, but because I'm slightly afraid.

What if Starla can't heal Wes, and I lose control of my emotions? I'm much stronger as a mermaid. I can't let anything happen. Not anymore.

"I need to submerge him," Starla says, running her fingers along Wes' forehead.

"He's not like you," Bailey argues. "You'll drown him."

Starla swims back, putting space between her and Bailey. "Then I can't help you. I'm sorry. I need the water to heal him."

Bailey's eyes glass over, her lip quivering. She's torn between her hatred of our kind and her love of Wes. Merpeople are responsible for both of them being on this island. I don't blame her for not trusting us.

Blowing strands of damp hair from my face, I reach out and grab Bailey's hand in the water. "This is Wes' only chance," I say. "Getting him to a hospital might be nearly impossible. And if I do take him to one, I won't be going back for him. You won't ever see him again. But if you'd rather put your faith in a human, I understand. Just do what you think Wes would want."

Bailey rubs water from her face with her free hand. "He'd

let you try," she whispers.

I nod. "I promise we'll do everything we can."

Dipping under, I transform into a mermaid, kicking a current around us that jostles Bailey. She swims closer, locking her hands on my shoulders. I don't argue that she should stay above the water, because she's having a hard enough time trusting us as it is.

"You have to have him back up for air when I need it," Bailey says.

Starla nods. "I'll be as quick as I can."

Carter covers Wes' mouth and nose with his hand, and when Starla's ready, we all sink under together, swimming deeper into the bay. Bailey grips my neck, resting her chin on my shoulder, and I watch Starla prod her fingers around Wes' head.

She brushes her fingers along the fresh stitches and uses her sharp nail to cut right through them. Blood trickles into the water in a small pink-tinted cloud, and Bailey squeezes my shoulders so hard I flinch and grab her hands.

The seconds tick by as Starla massages her fingers in Wes' wound, making my stomach roll. Carter remains silent, still preventing Wes from automatically sucking in water. Bailey pinches me, pointing to the surface, but Starla shakes her head at her. She needs more time.

"I need at least a minute more. If I stop now, there won't be anything else I can do," Starla says.

"But he'll suffocate," I say.

"He's already dying, Ava," Starla says softly. "It's a chance we must risk."

Wes' body jerks in Carter's arms, startling me, and Bailey locks her fingers into my hair, ripping at the strands. She attempts to swim forward, but I yank her back so she can't get in between Starla and Wes.

Bubbles erupt from my sister's mouth, ridding her lungs of the oxygen she needs to survive. She struggles to hold onto me, but if she does any longer, she'll open her mouth and let water into her lungs.

I don't give her the chance.

With the flick of my tail, I shoot us both up to the surface, but I don't break through. I wave my hand through the water, sending her in a current that takes her right to the air. Tilting my head down, I peer down at the others. Carter grips Wes in his arms as he continues to thrash, and Starla holds his forehead between her hands, her eyes closed.

For the first time ever, I see the glow of her spark in her chest. It's like her healing ability calls to me. It lights up the water surrounding them, the glow catching off the facets of my necklace, sending rainbow light through the water.

Bubbles erupt around me as Bailey dives back under, but she won't be able to reach Wes quick enough at her pace. Holding my hand out, I imagine calming the water. I want so badly to stop time to give Starla what she needs to heal Wes.

Carter's head jerks up to look at me, and it's not until our eyes meet that I realize all the bubbles surrounding us lie frozen in the water, suspended in the still bay. I run my hand through the water, gathering up the biggest pools of oxygen created by Bailey's thrashing. It's like I've somehow created a veil between her at the surface and us amid the sea. She continues to fight while the rest of us remain calm.

Diving down, I close the distance between me and Carter, still carrying the balloon sized pocket of air with me. Light shimmers around it, casting it in an iridescent glow, and I maneuver it in front of Wes' face until his mouth and nose break through the barrier.

Carter and Starla freeze, the intensity of their eyes hot enough to ignite something deep in my soul. Carter shifts his hands, Wes gasps a huge breath, and then the water erupts back to life, the bubbles scattering and catching on invisible streams that take them to the surface.

Wes falls limp in Carter's arms, tiny bubbles still clinging to his face and Carter's strong hands.

Starla's spark in her chest increases in intensity nearly blinding me, and a second later, she says, "I've done all I can. His injuries are healed, but now it's up to Wes to decide."

I don't follow Carter up to the surface where he takes Wes and instead remain at Starla's side. When our gazes meet, I fling my arms out and embrace her like I've never hugged her before. She rubs her fingers over my back, pushing my hair away from my skin.

"Ava, what you did..." Her voice trails off. The last time anyone beside Carter and Giselle witnessed my water affinity was when I used it against the king at my failed coronation. Starla wasn't there.

"Do I scare you?" I ask, feeling self-conscious as she studies me.

She shakes her head. "No, but I am afraid for you. If the king were to ever realize you were alive, he'd do everything he could to find you. He'd assure your bond to Carter was broken, and he would force you to bow before him. He won't be kind like he was with Celestiana. He won't try to win you. He'll take what he thinks is rightfully his."

"But I'm not his," I say.

She purses her lips. "He won't see things as you do."

"I won't let him take Carter from me," I say. "I won't bow down to him, either."

She nods, hugging me again. "I hope it never comes to that. I don't want to lose my son—I don't want to lose you."

"You won't," I say. "We'll be safe."

"Please, just take my advice and never come to Pearlestria again. Don't leave these protected waters. I'd much rather never see you again and know you're safe than lose you completely."

I frown. "But Starla."

She shakes her head. "Please, just promise me."

But I can't. I refuse to trap Carter here like he's in some tank, especially since he can't transform back into a human.

I open my mouth to respond, but my necklace flashes brightly, sending fear straight to my very core. "Starla, my necklace. It's telling me danger lurks by. Do you think someone followed us?"

She draws her eyes to the reef. "Even if they did, they can't come in."

That doesn't make me feel better. "You have to go. You have to get back to the colony before Mateo gets anxious."

She hugs me. "Please, remember what I asked."

"I—okay," I say without arguing. A terrible feeling sinks into me, and my first thought travels to Luna. I'm almost a hundred percent certain she saw us, but I don't want to believe she told her dad. And if she did? *Stop. Luna was your friend.*

"Ava?" Luna's soft voice hums through the current and into my mind. "Where are you?"

I freeze, half expecting her to come through the reef at any moment. "Starla, you have to go to her. You have to make sure she returns to Pearlestria with you."

The water shifts around us as Carter swims below us and toward the reef. His hot emotions rush through me, causing me to wave my hand out. I shift the water, creating a current that stops him from exiting the reef into the open sea.

He still tries to fight the current.

"Carter, stop! What do you think you're doing?" I ask.

He spins to face me from fifty feet away. "I heard the princess, Ava. She can't be here. She'll lead the king right to us."

"So, what do you think you're going to do? She was my friend."

"She's the king's daughter."

"That doesn't make her our enemy. If you even think

about doing something crazy, even if you think it's because you want to protect us, I'll transform right now and go back to the beach and stay. Is she worth that to you? Because I don't like what's gotten into you, and I won't stand for it."

The shock that crosses his face strikes me right in the heart, but I don't know what else to say to bring him back to his senses. This feels like it did in San Francisco. It's like he's changed with his merman transformation, and I'm seeing a side of him I didn't know—one I don't like. Being protective is one thing, but wanting to face Luna head on like a threat is different.

I close the distance between us and wrap my arms around him. His hard face softens under my touch. "Let me handle this. I don't want you doing something you'll later regret."

"I'll never regret keeping you safe."

I want to put space between me and Carter for the first time ever. I want to swim away from him and be alone. And it's in this moment I know why. He reminds me of the king in his reasoning. It's unsettling.

Still holding onto Carter, I shift and gaze at Starla from over my shoulder. "Please, you have to go. You have to make sure she goes back with you. Tell her enough to satisfy her, but don't tell her about the humans here, okay?"

"You want my mom to tell her about us? But, Ava—"

I give Carter a stern look, cutting off his thoughts. "The human's secret is more important. This island is theirs, not ours. I won't jeopardize them."

Starla nods, concern lining her brows, but she doesn't argue with him. She swims by, touching Carter's arm once, and then jets through the water without a goodbye and breaches over the reef to the open sea.

"Ava, I don't like this. Our secret is out," Carter says.

I hold his face between my hands. "That's the least of my worries. I can't think about the rest of the world until every-thing is fixed here. I need to check on Wes."

"Let the others worry about him. You've done enough."

"But I haven't."

"Ava..."

"Please, I need to go to land." I don't say it, but I need the fresh air to clear the water from my lungs. I need to think about everything that's happening. I need to figure out what happens next.

If only the ocean would just give me the answers.

16

ONCOMING STORM

I THOUGHT FACING MY SISTER before was scary, but now, after what I did in the bay while Wes was underwater, how I forced her to surface so I could keep him under long enough for Starla to finish healing him, has me beyond panicking to face her. But I have to. Carter can't access the land like I can. He can't even intervene if things get heated.

Carter sits in the sand, slapping his fin against a wave, because he didn't want to remain in the water alone. I'd give anything to have him stand with me right now, but his attitude isn't helping the stress I'm feeling. His anger keeps trickling into me, confusing me in a moment where I'm trying to stay composed.

I kneel in the sand next to him and grab his hands. "Please, you have to chill out. You're making things worse."

He releases a breath. "I'm sorry, Aves. It's just—"

"I know this isn't ideal, but I have other things I need to worry about now. I can't be stressing about you while I need to face Bailey," I say, cutting him off. "And we'll talk about the rest of it later. But I have to check on Wes. Maybe you should go for a swim. It might be good for you."

"I'm not leaving you," he says.

I sigh. "Then please, just keep yourself in control for five minutes."

Standing up, I catch sight of Giselle hovering on the outskirts of the shelters. I wave her over, and she jogs my way, kicking up sand. We meet in the middle of the beach between the community and shore.

"Is he?" I ask, talking about Wes.

"I don't know. Sandra and Bailey are with him. Bailey looked like she wanted to murder someone, so we're staying out of the way," she says.

Great. I knew I had upset her, and now I'm going to have to face her wrath. If Wes dies, she'll surely try to kill me herself. But how could I blame her?

I wring my hands together. "Think you can hang out with Carter? He could use a friendly face."

Giselle grimaces. "I don't know. I can feel his tension from here, and it's ridiculously uncomfortable."

"Please," I beg.

She droops her shoulders. "Fine, but you owe me."

"You can have the jar of jam I brought," I offer.

She purses her lips, narrowing her eyes in a fake glare. "What? No peanut butter?"

I laugh. "Sorry, I got hungry."

With a dramatic sigh, Giselle strolls away from me and heads toward Carter. She plants herself in the space next to him and stretches her legs out in front of her, allowing the waves to wash the sand off her feet.

I wait a minute longer, watching the two of them to make sure everything's okay before I head toward my sister's shelter. Quiet murmurs sound from the other side of the palm fronds, and I stand and eavesdrop for a moment.

I don't catch much of the conversation before Sandra shifts the leaves to let herself out. She offers me a sad smile, pats my shoulder, and then heads toward the tree line that'll take her inland toward the orchard of fruit trees and beyond them, a fresh water creek.

I straighten my shoulders, tempted to turn around and run back to the sea, but before I can, Bailey clears her throat. She watches me stand outside her bungalow, her intense gaze hot enough to ignite me from the inside. I suck in a small breath, steeling myself, and then I hunch down to enter her shelter.

Wes sleeps on a blanket, his clothes damp from the sea water. His head is no longer cut, but he's still not awake. It's enough to send my heart sliding to my feet to splatter onto the floor. I had wished with everything in me that I'd enter her bungalow to see him sitting up and smiling, chatting like nothing had happened, but he's exactly as he was before.

"Bailey." My sister's name nearly sticks in my throat. "I'm sorry."

Her hands curl into fists. "What you did out there, Ava. You could've—"

"Ava..."

I crinkle my nose, hearing the soft whisper of my name.

Bailey hops to her feet, rushing to Wes' side, and I gape at him with my mouth hanging open. He doesn't sit up or move but just blinks his eyes, staring at the palm leaf roof of the bungalow he and Bailey have shared for who knows how long. Neither of them has ever told me.

"Wes, God. You're awake. I've been so scared," Bailey says, tears dripping down her cheeks to roll off her chin to pelt Wes in the face.

He reaches up and wipes his fingers across her tears, smearing them away. "What happened?"

"Our boat was dragged beyond the reef, and we jumped, but you hit your head pretty hard. You've been unconscious for days." The words spill out of Bailey's mouth faster than her tears do from her eyes. "But all that doesn't matter now. You're okay. Ava saved you."

I back away from the two of them, wanting nothing more than to leave them to their private moment, but the second Bailey says my name, they both glance in my direction.

I freeze and force myself to smile. "No, Starla saved him. I was just the errand girl."

Wes' eyes study me for an uncomfortable moment before he asks, "You left the cove for me?"

"I couldn't let you die," I say.

He nods his head but doesn't look surprised. "Thank you," he says. "I owe you my life."

My hair smacks my cheeks as I shake my head. "It's fine, really."

"Ava," he says.

"It's fine," I repeat.

I can't stand the look of gratitude and awe crossing his face, so I do the only thing I can think of. I back out of the bungalow, telling him it's fine once more, and then leave Wes and Bailey alone.

His voice echoes through the air, drawing everyone's attention to Bailey's shelter, and I run. Something feels so strange about everything. I can't get far away fast enough. I even ignore Carter and Giselle as they call my name.

I run along the shore and don't stop running until the hum of voices disappears, the bay can no longer be seen over my shoulder, and I'm greeted by comforting waves that invite me to swim among them.

I strut into the water, pushing through the waves until I have to swim. I don't transform and keep swimming in the surf, heading out to the rocks not far from the reef. I pull myself onto them, facing the ocean, and for the first time in a long time, I sob.

My chest heaves, my eyes burning from tears, my whole body shaking with each shuddering breath. I muffle my wail with the palm of my hand, just letting things sink in. I've been bottling up everything, trying to keep myself strong, but the events of the last few days sneak up on me.

From the moment I realized Carter couldn't return to his human form to the drunk guy who frightened me on the beach—almost being spotted by mermen, our trip to Pearlestria, Starla healing Wes, Luna showing up, and Wes telling me he owes me his life even though I was responsible for his injuries. Each moment plays over and over in my mind, and the longer I think about everything, the harder I cry. I cry so many tears I'm sure the sea has risen. The salty water washes over my bare legs like it's attempting to hug me, but I flick my hand, sending the wave in the opposite direction.

A dark head of hair pops from the water, and Carter swims closer through the current I created. Without a word, he pulls himself onto the rock next to me and wraps his muscular arms around me.

"Ava, I'm sorry," Carter whispers. "I wish I could pull every bad thing you feel out of you and take it into me."

I sniffle, wiping my face with my palms. "I feel so lost," I whisper. "What is the point to all this?"

He holds me tighter. "I wish I had the answers. All I know is you're strong and brave and the most powerful person I've ever met. We're going to get through this. We're going to figure out how to make this all work so we can have the happiness I've been trying so hard to give you."

"It's not all about me," I say.

He kisses my temple. "I know, Ava. And we'll figure it out. Let's just take a moment to breathe, okay? You've been through a lot."

I hold his hand in mine. "So have you."

"Then we'll process this all together. If there's one thing I know about us, it's that we can get through anything."

His words bring a smile to my face.

Gently pinching my chin, he turns my head so I have to look at him. His beautiful smile, the one he saves just for me, lights his face brighter than the spark in either of our chests. It shines brighter than the low-hanging sun. Probably the rest of the universe, too.

"You always know what to say to make me feel better," I say, leaning my forehead against his. "Did you know I happen to have the best mate in the entire ocean? The entire world even."

He chuckles. "I don't know...I think *I* might."

I grin wider and shift my legs over Carter's tail. We sit in silence, just holding each other. For the first time in a while, it feels like as long as Carter's holding me we'll be okay. That the world will be okay.

I can only hope.

A flash of lightning sparkles on the horizon, drawing my gaze away from Carter. It's the first storm I've ever seen out here, and it looks massive, coming this way. I don't know why I thought this island was protected from more than merpeople, but I guess magic has its limitations and a storm is one of them.

Wind whips through my salty blond hair, blowing it off my damp neck, causing me to shiver. Carter holds me close to him in the sand, because I wasn't ready to return to the water. Something has me on edge, and I feel like the shore is safer than the water. Most merpeople usually wouldn't leave the ocean, but now they can't. No one can follow me.

"If you want to sleep on land..." Carter says, his voice trailing off.

I raise my eyebrows. "The only way I'm sleeping on land is if you do it too and with the way that storm looks, sleeping in this spot doesn't seem like an option."

Leaning over, he plants his lips to my cheek. "The surface will be rough, but if we go to the deepest part of the bay, it won't be so bad. I wish I had time to build you a house like back in Pearlestria. I know how much sleeping in the open bothers you."

"We'll work on it in the morning, okay?" I say.

"Hey, Aves," Giselle calls from behind me. She strolls through the sand, flicking her gaze from me to the ocean. "Sandra wants us to pack up to head inland. You sure you two will be okay out here?"

I grimace. "We have to be. Carter can't spend the whole

night out of the water."

"I guess we'll have to invest in a saltwater swimming pool when we get off this island," she muses, smiling brightly at her idea.

I don't have the heart to tell her if we ever make it off this island that Carter and I won't be making a permanent residence anywhere, and he definitely won't be living in some pool all so I can have a human life.

"You have some big dreams, Gi," Carter says with a smirk.

"Hey, I know people. I can make it happen."

"I'm sure Sapphire will be dying to know why you're suddenly interested in enormous aquariums. You really want to let her in on our secret, too?" I ask.

Giselle frowns for a split second before rolling her eyes. "Matty would complain that Carter has definitely set the bar too high considering how obsessed we were with mermaids...before, you know."

Talking about Giselle's cousin and our friends back in Azure Waters both pains me and lifts my spirits. I miss everyone immensely and can't stop wondering what they're up to. Sapphire and Matty are surely living it up in LA. Their penthouse apartment probably does have a saltwater swimming pool...of course it's probably on the roof of the high rise they live in.

More lightning strikes in the clouds, startling me. Giselle hugs herself, and I'm sure she wishes I'd come to shore to stay with her. The storm rolling in looks nothing like anything we had in Azure Waters. Thunder and lightning were as rare as a downpour.

"You two stay safe, okay?" Giselle says, stepping farther from a wave that sneaks up on me, smashing into Carter's tail and up and over it to splash me in the face.

"You, too." I climb to my feet so I can hug my best friend for a moment.

The others gather near the shelters, packing things up to take inland to wherever it is they're going.

Carter pulls himself into the surf first, watching me from the swells, and I wave once before waltzing into the whitecaps.

"Ava!" a masculine voice calls out. I turn to glance at Wes over my shoulder. "Ava, wait! Where are you going?"

"Underwater," I say.

"No, you're not. You're coming with us."

Wes' eyes shine with a wildness I've never seen before, and he rushes toward me. He reaches out to me, trying to lock his fingers on my arm, and I stumble away, doing the only thing I can think of. I push him back and run into the water.

"Ava!" he screams again.

"Get back, Wes," I warn.

He doesn't.

In a blink of my eyes, Carter's between us. Fear washes over me at his anger, and I hold my breath as he wraps his arms around Wes in the surf.

I turn my gaze away. I can't look.

This time, Bailey's the one to scream.

17

BAD FEELING

"WES!" MY SISTER'S VOICE CUTS through the wind whistling around us.

Carter doesn't let Wes go, but he doesn't hurt him either. All he does is restrain him so he can't get any closer to me.

I hate that I automatically assumed the worse, but after San Francisco and the way he reacted hearing Luna's voice, I wasn't sure what to expect. Without being able to transform, something's changed in him. He's more protective of me than ever.

"I just need to talk to her!" Wes hollers, thrashing in Carter's arms, trying to fight my mate amid the waves. "Why won't you let me go?"

I wish I had transformed back into a mermaid so Carter and I could leave, but I'm afraid Wes would now try to follow.

"Ava!" Wes yells again. "Ava, please, you have to tell him to let me go."

My heart rams against my ribcage at the desperation in Wes' voice. But my own desperation prevents me from wanting Carter to give Wes a moment to talk to me. Something in him has snapped, freaking me out, and I have no idea what's wrong. Ever since he woke up with my name on his lips, I felt something was off.

"Wes, come on. We have to go," Bailey says from her place on the sand.

He ignores her.

The others stand back on the beach, almost like they're afraid of the ocean...or maybe they're afraid of me. I have no idea. All I know is it takes everything in me to close the distance between me and Wes as he continues to fight against Carter's strong hold.

"Wes?" My soft voice barely whispers over the wind. I need to get his attention before he ends up hurt by accident. "What's the matter?"

The moment he hears my voice, he stops struggling against Carter. His wide green eyes look almost brown in the night, and he's wearing only a pair of shorts. His long hair falls from his knotted bun, and the way he gapes at me frightens me even more.

He doesn't respond to me for an uncomfortable minute.

"Wes? Are you okay?" I ask, hoping he'll say something.

"I—" Wes opens and shuts his mouth, confusion crossing his thick brows. "I'm not sure. Something feels wrong. You can't go."

Lightning strikes, startling me, and I fall into a wave and sink under. Hands grab onto me, pulling me up, and then another pair of hands yank me away. Carter holds me against him instead of onto Wes. He slaps the waves with his strong tail, forcing Wes to stay back while keeping us afloat. I cough and spit out the water I inhaled, gasping as another wave attempts to rip me from Carter.

Wes raises his arms up in surrender and doesn't move forward. Another wave rolls into us, pushing him toward shore, but he fights to stay in the surf. His intense stare bores into me, crawling under my skin. I wish he'd say what he was thinking so I could understand the weirdness he's forcing upon me.

"You should come to shore with me, Ava," Wes says, offering his hand out.

Carter swims us farther away. "I think you need to go back. You're still recovering." The tenseness bunching Carter's muscles has me on edge.

"He's right, Wes," I say. "You need to rest, and I can't leave the water. Things have changed since the full moon, and I won't abandon my mate."

"Please, Ava," he says, his voice getting lost on the intense wind. "Ever since I woke up, I've had a horrible feeling that something was coming. I didn't realize what it was about until I saw you enter the waves. The feeling was about you. I don't know how to explain it. You saved my life, and I can't live with myself knowing that something will happen to you."

He says it with such certainty that it leaves me on the brink of panicking. I have no idea what's gotten into him and why he has this sudden need to protect me. I'm not even the one who saved him. All I did was get Starla to come here. But it's like the water got to his head—maybe it did.

Or maybe it was my magic. I did use it to pull the sea from his lungs. I also used it to give him the air he needed to remain under long enough for Starla to heal him. Did it somehow get to him? Maybe it's lingering in the shadows of his mind and that's why he's acting so strange.

I shake my head. "Wes, you're probably nervous because of the storm, but I'm a mermaid. I'll be okay." Shifting in Carter's arms, I give my mate a look. Carter releases me, letting me stand in the chest high water on my own. "Come on, let me walk you to shore."

As the words escape my mouth, another wave knocks into Wes, dragging him under. A yell echoes from the shore, and my attention draws to Bailey as she rushes toward us, not even caring that huge waves collide against the sand, threatening to rise all the way to the shelters to wash them away.

Before Bailey can enter the surf, Wes pops out of the wave. I close the distance between us and stop him from getting sucked back under. His green eyes meet mine, and he locks me in his stare.

"Okay," he says. "I guess you're right."

"I promise I'll be fine." I help Wes closer to the shore with Carter right behind us.

Another flash of lightning lights up the night, and I nearly jump from my skin. When we're close enough to the shore, I let go of Wes' arm as Bailey closes the distance. She reaches out for him, but a strange look crosses his face, all wild eyes. He shuffles around Bailey and charges me. I don't even have time to react. His sinewy arms wrap around me, and he drags me from the water, throwing me onto his shoulder.

Carter yells out, swimming onto the shore and out of the waves, but without being able to transform, he can't get to me. Wes holds his hand out to the others who try to close in on us. I scratch my nails into his back and then thrash, doing everything I can to get him to let me go. His strength overpowers me, and he walks backward away from everyone.

"Wes, don't do this," I say. "Please, you're scaring me."

"I have to, Ava," he says. "You need to stay on land."

"Please, I'll be fine," I say.

"You can't know that."

Tears prickle in my eyes. I can't believe this is happening. If I wasn't worried about hurting him, I'd bring the whole sea upon us to wash me away, but he's not acting like himself, and I'm afraid I'm responsible.

"But I do. Now, please. Just put me down."

"I'm sorry. I can't. You're coming with me."

Wes didn't stop running until we were far from shore and deep within the island. I couldn't see where we were heading in the dark, but I could hear the trickling creek until the skies opened up to release a waterfall of rain on us.

And now, I press my back into the hard rock of a cave, wishing with everything in me that I wasn't here. I'd rather brave the open ocean than be here.

A flash of lightning streaks through sky, lighting up the cave. I jump, hugging myself tighter. Carter's out there in the storm, facing waves comparable to the ones I create, and I can't stop the fear from slicing through me. Luckily, no crazy emotions come from him—just a whole lot of annoyance. It makes even me annoyed.

"You going to stare at me all night?" My voice echoes over the pelting rain. "It's creepy."

Wes' forehead crinkles at my words. "I'm sorry. I didn't realize I was."

I raise my eyebrows. "What has gotten into you? You know you're jeopardizing my relationship with my mate, right? And my sister." Because I know I'm going to have to stand between Carter and Wes even though a part of me wants to toss Wes to the waves. And Bailey? I'm sure she's thinking I'm getting in the middle of her and Wes. God, why did this have to happen?

Wes' mouth hangs open like he had no idea his actions were going to impact things. "You never have a bad feeling before?"

"My whole life is one big bad feeling. But that doesn't mean I should run and hide all the time. I shouldn't be in this cave, Wes. I don't want you getting hurt again because of me."

"Because of you?" he questions, his voice only a murmur.

I nod. "The accident. I had no idea I'd create such rough water."

He's silent for a moment, letting my confession sink in. I expect him to start yelling, to throw all his hatred at me. I expect him to tell me to leave. But he doesn't do any of that. All he does is rub his cheeks while gazing at me.

After an almost painful minute, he says, "Accidents happen."

"This one shouldn't have. I shouldn't be here," I repeat.

"So, you think I'm feeling this way because of you? Bailey said you saved me when I hit my head."

I purse my lips, remembering back. Remembering the choice I thought I had to make between saving my sister or saving Wes and then pulling the water from his lungs while attempting to bring Bailey back over the reef. I didn't think about it until this very moment, but one thought fills up my mind. It's so intense I can't think of anything else until I say it out loud.

"You drowned," I whisper.

"What do you mean I drowned? I thought I just hit my head."

"My water affinity saved you. I pulled the ocean from your lungs and gave you your breath again." Confusion and fear prickle through me. Obviously, I didn't give Wes my essence. Carter was my one unexpected transformation after the king ended Carter's life—something I shouldn't have been able to do as a human-born mermaid—and I would have known. It's why I can feel Carter more than ever. Why my love for him feels ten times more powerful. But what if saving Wes the way I did messed with him? He might not be in love with me, but his sudden need to protect me is totally unwarranted.

"Don't humans who get brought back to life turn into merpeople? Isn't that what happened to you? Giselle said—"

"You're not a merman, Wes. The full moon passed and you didn't transform. But I think I did something else to you. I don't know." I push off the ground and get to my feet. "But I need to find out, and the answers don't lie in this cave."

"You can't be serious. This can wait until morning," he argues.

I shake my head. "No, I need to go. I don't belong here."

"Ava, I'm not letting you leave."

I raise my hand out, keeping it aimed at him as he gets to his own feet. "I'm not letting you stop me."

"Then I'm coming with you," he says.

"No, you can't. Stay here."

He rushes me, but I'm prepared this time. I dodge around him, clocking him in the shoulder hard enough with my fist that he falls back into the cave wall with a thud. I run from the cave and into the dense forest. It's nearly pitch-black apart from the lightning storm above.

I glance once over my shoulder, half expecting Wes to be on my heels, chasing me, but he's nowhere to be found. I just hope he realized how crazy he was acting, especially knowing about what I did to him, that he won't risk his life in this seemingly unrelenting storm.

Through the dark trees, I carefully hike through the forest, following the pull in my heart. It's the only way I know which direction to go, because without the sun or the moon, I'm basically traveling blindly. And even in the day, I'm not sure I'd have any idea of where I'm going because I've never traveled far up the creek. Wes has been on this island for years. He probably knows the terrain by heart.

My bare feet sink into the muddy water, pooling all around from the heavy rains. The wind whistles in my ears, cutting off the noise of everything else. If I didn't shield my eyes from the rain falling on my head, I'd have a hard time seeing.

"Ava," a voice whispers. It takes me a moment to realize it's in my mind. "You must return to the sea. The answers you seek lie beyond the barrier. Your fear will keep you lost forever. Now, come to me."

Thrashing my head, I shake the voice away. I take another step forward through the dark trees. The sparkle from my necklace lights up like rainbow beams. It glows brighter and brighter, so brightly that the world around me can be seen clear as day even though morning won't come for hours. It's then I realize I'm walking on the edge of a ravine, halfway filled with running rainwater. I automatically step back, but the soggy ground beneath my bare feet gives way, and I slide into the few feet of rushing water.

The world slips past me as I'm caught in the rainwater river. I flail, looking for anything to grab onto, but none of the roots hold. My screams echo through the air, catching on the wind, and my stomach flies into my throat when I hit a sudden drop that propels me toward the edge of a cliff—the same cliffs with rocks that can only be accessed by the ocean.

Huge swells crash into the cliff, sending white waves through the air, lit up by the lightning sporadically striking within the clouds. Horror and fear rush through my mind. All I can think about is how I'm going to die at any second. There are too many rocks below. I'm bound to splatter against one of them.

Squeezing my eyes shut, I wave my hands out, calling on a miracle from the ocean, praying that I haven't used all my miracles up. My feet break through a swell rising over the rocks. It cushions my fall, and I sink under and let the current drag me away. The ocean glows around me, my body thrashing in the rough waves too enormous to swim in. There's no way I can even make my way to the surface for a breath, one I desperately need.

"You must trust yourself," a voice says into my mind. "Let it all go."

I do exactly that. I inhale a long, burning breath of the ocean, filling up my very essence with the sea I've become so connected to.

A dozen images flash through my mind, none of which are my own. My body screams in pain, my head feeling like it'll suddenly explode. And then I feel nothing at all.

I black out.

18

CELESTIANA

"MY DAUGHTER, YOU'VE MADE IT to me," a feminine voice says, the melodious sound so soothing and heartwarming that I want to wrap it around me like a blanket after facing a frozen sea.

"Like I had a choice. This storm—"

"Is the consequence of remaining hidden, my daughter. You can't stay lost forever."

Celestiana hovers before me in crystalline waters undisturbed by ocean life, currents, or even the gentle wave of her silver tail. A tail so sparkling, it almost looks as if rainbows project from it. Her black hair floats in a thick braid, and a silver and diamond crown glitters on her head. She looks exactly like her memories, but this isn't a memory.

"I'm not your daughter," I say, projecting my thoughts into her mind. "I'm not even a daughter of the ocean. I was human-born."

She smirks, like what I've said was funny. "But you were chosen."

"By Carter," I say before she can tell me the ocean picked me.

"A suitable warrior for a suitable queen," she says, closing the distance. Raising her hand, she brushes her fingers over my cheek and pushes the veil of blond hair from my face. "I always knew Starla and Mateo would raise a fine man with a love of the land who would choose a mate worthy of the sea."

Confusion knits my brows. "I don't understand. I was afraid of the ocean. I didn't want to be a mermaid. All I wanted—want—is to go home to my family."

"Which is why you've been chosen. Your desires can never be under Attilonious' rule. By his need to protect the colonies, he's grown too distant from the land. He's isolated the kingdom. His distrust of humans will hurt us all in the end."

"Why are you telling me this? You can't expect me to face the king and demand him to renounce his crown. He'll kill me," I say. "And if he doesn't, then what? I'm not some queen to look after the sea. This is all crazy." With a flick of my hand, I yank off the necklace and hold it out to her. "I don't think I want this after all."

She doesn't respond, just looks at me with the same smirk she had when I told her I wasn't her daughter or a daughter of the ocean.

I hold up the necklace again, dangling it in the water between us, but she doesn't grab it. "Take it, please. I already hate how everything is. I don't want any more madness in my life. I've already almost killed one human, and now he's acting strange toward me. Keeping this necklace puts everyone around me at risk."

She still doesn't take it. Instead, she strokes my cheek with her knuckles. "You're pure of heart and that makes you exceptional."

"Do you not care about the humans you gave up your magic for on that island?" I ask.

"I care immensely. There's a man there who kept a part of my heart before I was enchanted by Attilonious' magic."

"Darren?"

Her smile is enough to tell me it is him. He's one of the few who never told me how he ended up there, but he wasn't the first to arrive.

"He tied me to the land. He gave up everything for me willingly, but we were never bonded. I couldn't ask that of him. It was more than him that I loved. It was his humanity. The king thought I was fleeing for him, but I was fleeing for me. I was selfish."

That makes two of us. "If you care about Darren, you

wouldn't ask me to keep this. You'd tell me how to fix Wes and tell me where I can go with Carter that's away from here. You'd tell me what to do about Luna knowing we're alive, too. You remember your real daughter, right?"

For the first time since I opened my eyes, the queen frowns. "Luna will make a good ally. She knows the seas better than anyone. And as for Wes, you've given him a gift he'll repay with his loyalty. It never hurts to have ties to the land and the sea."

"His behavior will get him killed," I say. "He kidnapped me over a bad feeling."

"He knows the time is coming. He knows the dangers that lie within the deep."

I blow a bubble through my lips. "Dangers you want *me* to face."

"My daughter, please. You can't see past your fear. The king does not care for those who are not under his rule. Your empathy and connection to the world outside the sea will help the colonies flourish."

"How? No one can leave the sea."

"It's not only the king's magic that can unite the sea with the land." She moves her hand to the spark in my chest. "The answer lies here."

"You mean *I* can create sea stone rings?" If I wasn't floating underwater, I'd be crying. Relief and joy washes through me at just the thought. If I can infuse Carter's ring with magic, I can give him the life on land he deserves. We can still have a life outside the ocean.

She nods without a word. I expect her to give me the answer, to give me something more to work with, but the light in the crystal clear water dims, leaving us in darkness. The sea shifts, a current swirling around us, stirring up sand from the sea floor, and the queen drops her hand from me and lets me go.

A huge swell sweeps me away from the queen, and I tumble through the current of the unforgiving ocean. The only light comes from the spark in my chest, but it's not enough to see where I'm going.

My lungs erupt in pain, a burning sensation so intense it makes my eyes widen. I swallow water, and panic rushes through me when I realize I'm no longer a mermaid. A flash of light draws my attention above me, and I kick my way toward the surface lit by the massive storm.

Before I break through, fingers lock on my hips and spin me around. I meet Carter's jewel-like eyes only inches away. With a flick of his tail, he ascends to the surface, taking me with him. I expel the water from my lungs, coughing and spitting, gasping breath after breath.

"Ava, you have to transform," Carter says.

I squeeze my eyes shut, willing the transformation to happen, but my mind wanders elsewhere and nothing I do triggers the cramps to come. Carter struggles to hold me above water in the raging waves, and I fall under a swell. It rips me from Carter, thrashing me about.

My head spins, and I can't focus on anything but the lack of oxygen, how my lungs scream, and how no matter how hard I fight, I get nowhere.

I just want it all to stop.

I project my thoughts into the sea, and the ocean complies. The waves die down around me, the water turning utterly still. The ripple of the now unmoving current shines around me in thousands of tiny bubbles, and I slowly gather them the same way I did for Wes, collecting them into a huge sphere that I can breathe.

I inhale the bubble of air, filling my lungs to the brim, and kick my way to the surface. Lightning flickers above, and rain cascades down like a waterfall, but the ocean remains as calm as it is on the most tranquil days.

"Ava," Carter's voice sounds out through the air. "We have to go back."

It's in this moment I realize we're in the open water and away from the island. I can't even see it from our spot. Fear grips at my heart, threatening to send it bursting from my chest.

"I can't transform. Can you swim me?" I ask.

Carter nods and pulls me closer so I can hold onto his neck. He swims us forward, staying above the surface instead of going under. He probably would if I wasn't gasping, but I can't help it. Everything is too much. Now that I'm not drowning, I can't stop thinking about the queen and the dream—if it was even a dream.

I hug tightly to Carter, just feeling the smooth muscles of

his back. His fingers lock with mine, their strength cutting off my circulation. I'm sure he's afraid if he's not gripping me I'll somehow wash away even if the ocean is placid despite the storm pelting us.

A sudden blink of light erupts in my vision, my diamond glowing brighter and brighter. It's a warning, something I can't ignore knowing we're quite a distance from the protection only the Lost Cove brings. If I'd just listened to Wes and stayed put, I wouldn't be out here. I wouldn't be putting Carter at risk, because he followed the pull of my spark. And now, someone is close by.

"You have to dive. Someone's nearby," I say.

Carter stiffens. "I hear them."

"What are they saying?"

"They're talking about Luna." Carter nearly spits the words. "There's hostility between her and the king."

"It was fate for Luna to see us. She is our best ally, Carter. She knows the ocean probably as good as her father," I say. "She can help us."

"Help us to do what?"

"Get away from here. We can find somewhere to go on land," I say.

"Ava, I can't."

"You can. I just need to figure out how to help you. The queen, she—"

"This is why you were out here?"

"I think her magic forced me away from the island. She

doesn't want us to remain lost."

"I don't under—" Carter suddenly dives, dragging me down with him. His voice is lost to me since I can't hear him.

His fear washes over me, and I peer through my blurry vision. It's hard to make them out, but up ahead I spot two dark figures in the water. One of them hovers upright, combing their fingers through the unmoving bubbles, creating swirls that glitter every time lightning strikes.

I do the only thing I can think of, I thrust my hand forward, anger and fear rushing from me, and jumpstart the ocean, turning the calm waters violent. I'm not fast enough, though, because I meet the glowing amber eyes of a mermaid seconds before she's caught on a current and swept away along with her mate.

Carter remains swimming in the rough waters though he'd be faster if he'd dive with me. At least here, we're less likely to be followed. Because I'm sure our secret is out. It won't be long until the whole ocean hears of our sudden appearance.

Cramps rush through me, my transformation suddenly taking hold, and I inhale a long breath of water, letting it sink deep into me to push away all my thoughts. I can't help feeling betrayed by the ocean that gave me this life. It's like it was the queen's plan all along.

I don't care who she thinks I am or what she thinks I should do, I'm so over having my life messed with. I'm over fearing all the time.

I'm so over this supposed fate.

"Ava," Carter whispers in my mind. "Do you hear them?"

I close my eyes and concentrate. Faint voices echo through my mind, and a chill runs up my spine. They're calling for their queen. But it's not Celestiana's name they're saying. It's mine.

Shivering, I force the voices away and swim faster.

"This is bad, Aves," Carter thinks to me.

I hold him tighter. This is the queen's fault. It's the ocean's fault. They're forcing me away from the island, and once again I'm losing control over my life. But this is different. I'm not supposed to sit back and hope for the best. I need to fight.

"We'll be okay," I whisper. I'm afraid to tell him what's on my mind. I'm afraid to tell him I have a feeling that everything is about to get worse.

19

SOMETHING WORTH FIGHTING FOR

"OH, NO," I WHISPER, PUSHING to my feet in the sand. "Everything is gone." The ocean did this. It's trying to force me to leave, first by revealing me to the merpeople and now this. The storm passed an hour ago, but I've been too nervous to re-surface. I ran away from Wes during the worst of it. If he followed, he could very well be dead, and once again, I'd be to blame for another bad thing happening.

"They'll rebuild," Carter says from his spot in the sand. "I'm sure it's not the first hurricane to roll through."

I kick my bare foot against some debris. "This is my fault.

The ocean doesn't want me here anymore. It's a warning just like Celestiana said."

There's nothing left of the shelters on the beach. The storm wiped them all away, leaving behind remnants in the form of broken wood, palm fronds, and what's left of the pieces of furniture that either washed ashore, was made, or brought by one of the few merpeople that would do deliveries before the king stole their ability to come on land.

"Hurricanes happen all the time, Aves. Celestiana—she was just a dream."

"It was very much real, Carter," I say. I bend down and collect a few ratty blankets that were left behind and then push an old trunk out of the water, dragging it up to the tree line. "Why else would all this be happening? You saw what I saw. How can you deny it?"

"Because what she wants is a death sentence." I shared my vision of Celestiana through a kiss, revealing everything she told me about King Attilonious, about him dooming the colonies by cutting them off from the human world, about my supposed purpose. I can't blame him for being skeptical. I think the queen's crazy, but I know only more trouble will befall on the island if we stay.

"There's still no denying the truth, no matter how much you want to."

"Then what do you expect us to do?"

Voices murmur from somewhere beyond the trees, cutting off our conversation. It's the others making their way back.

"Wes, you have to calm down. I'm sure Ava is fine. What you did was insane, you know." It's Bailey.

I puff a breath of relief through my lips, realizing that Wes is fine, and he managed to find the others again.

"You don't know that," Wes says. "I looked everywhere for her. She doesn't know the island like we do. What if she's lost?" I cringe at the abnormal shrillness in his usually deep voice.

"What has gotten into you? Why do you even care?" Bailey asks.

I grimace. I can't help it. The coldness in my sister's voice freezes my heart. I'd hoped maybe she'd be a little bit concerned about me, but I guess I should get used to the idea that she will never be.

"Ava and I think it's because she brought me back to life after she lost control," Wes says, repeating our conversation from last night. He's so casual about it, that it sounds like what I've done is totally normal.

"What?" Bailey's voice erupts through the air.

I scramble backward, putting space between me and the tree line as I spot the group making their way to where they'll discover the mess the storm left behind. I turn to run back to Carter, but then a familiar voice calls my name, cutting Bailey and Wes off.

"You're safe!" Giselle says, rushing past them to me. She slings her arms around me and pushes me back toward the water. "Oh, my God, Aves. Last night was nuts. Wes showed up like a lunatic in a panic because you ran away from him. He hasn't shut up since. Bailey is freaking out. It's drama-land. Like, if the ocean didn't try to drown us, I'm pretty sure the rest of us would make an escape just so we don't have to hear Wes and Bailey argue over you anymore."

"I shouldn't be here then," I say.

"Of course you should be here." Wes' voice draws my attention away from Giselle.

I ignore him and stroll toward Carter.

"No, actually, she shouldn't," Bailey says. "She's messing with your head, Wes."

I cringe, refusing to look at Bailey.

"Hey! Ava's not doing anything," Giselle says.

"Are you kidding?" Bailey throws her hands up. "All she's done is mess things up around here. This place wasn't meant for her kind."

"It was created by her *kind*." The heat in Giselle's voice makes my eyes widen. I've always known she was protective of me, but she's never been one to blatantly put herself out there.

"She's right," Wes says.

Bailey points her finger at Wes. "Stay out of it, Wes. You can't see it because she got into your head."

"It was an accident," Giselle says. "It was my fault, not Ava's. I was pressuring her."

"To do what?" Bailey asks.

"Gi, stop," I say.

"No, Ava. Bailey has some stupid problem that no one else has. I think she's just jealous."

"The last person I'd be jealous of is her," Bailey snaps.

"Come on, Aves," Carter says.

Wes steps away from Bailey. "Stay, Ava."

There's too much going on. My mind whirls with everyone's voices as they try to speak all at once. All I want to do is run back to the water and dive.

A huge wave swells up next to me, crashing into the shore. It surprises everyone, knocking us onto the beach. I shake sand from my hair and get to my feet while the others slowly get back to theirs.

"I'm sorry." I can't help apologizing. This whole conversation has me on edge. Celestiana did say that Wes would continue to show loyalty no matter how much I don't want it. "I didn't mean to do that."

"What do you mean by that?" Bailey asks, glaring. All the others fall silent.

I sigh. What's the point in hiding it? "I can control the sea," I finally say.

Giselle strolls closer to me, putting herself in the path between Bailey and me. "And she's awesome. She's going to help us get off this island, now cool it."

Bailey ignores Giselle. "So, it was you that day? You're the reason we had to jump from the boat." She doesn't wait for my response, because I'm sure it's clearly written on my face. "I should've known."

I wring my hands together. "Bailey, I'm sorry."

She swings her arm out to point at Wes. "Look what you

did to him."

"It was an accident," Wes says, standing up for me.

Bailey huffs. "One she's responsible for."

Wes scowls. "Bailey."

"No, I don't think so. You will *not* stand up for her. She did this. She probably caused the storm, too!" She turns her attention to me, pointing her finger. "I want you out of here."

"Hey, you can't do that," Giselle says.

"Go!" Bailey screams.

She charges me, fury lining her blue eyes. Carter grabs me by the ankle, yanking me off my feet to pull me into the water before Bailey can get close enough to touch me. I'm pretty sure she'd have attacked me if she could have. But now, Wes grips her shoulders.

She struggles against him. "Let me go."

"No, you need to calm down," he says. "Ava isn't our enemy. You can't blame her for this."

"He's right." For the first time since seeing the others come through the trees do I notice Darren. He stands back, lingering next to Sandra and Reyna, who look like they want nothing to do with any of this. "This is the doing of King Attilonious. None of us would be here if it weren't for him."

Bailey turns her gaze to Darren. "That doesn't make a difference. He's not here. She is."

"You should be happy about that," Giselle says, speaking up. "That guy is a monster."

"Ava," Carter says, drawing my attention to him. "Someone's calling for us."

All the others fall silent at the sound of Carter's words.

"We have to go," he says.

Fear stirs in my heart. I knew we were spotted last night, but I was hoping we'd still have time. The last thing I need is to have the whole ocean calling for us. A thousand thoughts spin through my head, making me dizzy. I can think of a million terrible things the king could do to lure us out, but neither Carter nor I even want to think about them. His family would be the first to face the king's wrath.

I release a small breath and turn my gaze to Bailey. "You'll be happy to know I was spotted last night, and the king knows I'm alive." I half hug myself. "You'll get your wish, because I can't put you all in any more danger."

"What?" Giselle and Wes ask in unison.

I squeeze my eyes shut. "I'm not abandoning you, Gi, but Bailey is right. I can't stay on this island. But I'll figure out how to get you off. I promise."

"Aves, please. We can figure this out," Giselle says.

"Come on, Ava," Carter says.

Tears line Giselle's eyes. "You can't go."

"I have to. I have to figure out what happens next."

"But—"

"But nothing. I can't hide forever. The ocean has made it quite clear."

"Aves, please."

"Trust that I'll fix this."

"How?"

"It's time to face what I've been running from."

"Ava, no!"

I sink under the waves before Giselle can talk me out of leaving. Carter pulls me deeper into the bay and away from my last connection to the land, one I'll have to fight for if I'm ever going to keep it. The queen was right. I'll never get everything I want under the king's rule, and now that he knows I'm alive, it won't be long until our magic collides. I just hope I can survive in the end. For everyone's sakes.

Sucking in water to fill my lungs, I push away all my fear as my transformation takes hold. Fear will leave me lost forever.

I'm done being afraid. I'm done hiding.

For the first time in a long time, I feel brave. I feel like I have a fighting chance. Because even if I can't do anything about the king, even if I can't get my old life back, I can at least say that I tried. Not only for myself, but for everyone else. With others at risk, I finally have something worth fighting for.

20

NEVER BE FREE

"AVA, CARTER." THE FAMILIAR, FEMININE voice sounds through my mind. "I know you're around here somewhere. Please, you have to talk to me. My dad knows you're alive." When Carter said someone was calling us, I had expected his mom. I wasn't expecting Luna.

Carter holds me beneath him, his chest pressing into my back and his strong arms locked just below my ribcage. I'd usually hold onto his back, but I think he's afraid I'll let go and leave him behind, so he's not taking any chances. It's almost ridiculous, because I'd never out swim him.

"Luna, you shouldn't have come," I say, projecting my thoughts back to her. "What if your dad followed you?"

"He didn't," she says.

"And how do you know?" Carter asks, speaking up.

Up ahead, a figure comes into view. It takes us swimming a good few dozen feet past the reef to see the open ocean clearly. Luna's hair floats around her like a black veil, and the sun from above glints off her golden tail.

"Because my dad left Pearlestria before I did," she says.

"So, why did you come here? Didn't Starla tell you we were protected?" I ask.

Carter closes the distance between us and Luna. Her dark sapphire eyes glow in the water, and she surprises the both of us by flinging her arms around us the moment Carter swims us upright to meet her face-to-face.

"My family," Carter says, fear lining his thoughts, projecting into me. "Are they—?" I hate to admit the thought crossed my mind, too.

"It was your mother who sent me. The colonies are under lockdown. No one that isn't a king's guard can leave. They're now searching all the seas for you. I could only leave because I stole this." Luna holds up a small bracelet with an onyx stone on it. "It's a guard's key."

Carter holds his hand out, and Luna drops the bracelet into his palm. He studies it for a long moment. "Can you steal more?"

She shakes her head. "If I could, I would. But it wouldn't

make a difference. Your mom and grandmer have been locked away in the castle."

"And my dad?" Carter asks.

"With the king," she says.

Carter grimaces.

"Why would he be with the king?" I ask.

"Leverage," Carter says. "I can't think of any other reason."

I could see that. King Attilonious isn't stupid. He knows the importance of family and bonds. If he were to find us, one way to get us to comply would be to threaten someone Carter cares about.

"Oh, God," I say.

"Carter," Luna says. "Mateo offered his services to the king. He wants nothing more than to have you back. I saw his face when the king made the announcement. He didn't know you were alive, did he?"

I shake my head. "Only Starla."

"We have to go to Pearlestria then," Carter says. "We have to get my mom and grandmer."

Before Carter can swim forward, Luna raises her hand. "That's not why I'm here."

Fear squeezes my heart at her words. Realization settles into my bones with the sad look Luna gives me. She doesn't even have to utter the words for me to know what the king is planning to do. He threatened my entire human life once to get me to comply.

"My family." My thought is barely a whisper in my mind.

Luna nods. "I'm so sorry, Ava. I came here as fast as I could."

"We have to go to Azure Waters, Carter," I say.

"What if it's too late?" he asks. "We'll risk our lives for nothing."

"I don't care," I say. "I'm going whether or not you follow me."

He squeezes my hand. "Ava, I'll follow you anywhere. You know that."

I turn to Luna. "Go back to Pearlestria. Help Starla."

Before she can nod, Carter releases me and bolts forward, locking his hand around Luna's wrist. "No, Ava. We need her."

"What do you mean?" I ask into his mind. "You're crazy if you think I'm going to let you hurt—"

"The king doesn't know that," he says only to me. "But you can't tell her. It has to look real."

I swallow the lump forming in my throat and glance at Luna. "I'm sorry, Luna. I guess you're coming with us."

"Please, Ava. You don't have to do this. You know I'll help you," Luna says.

Carter grips her in his arms while I hold onto his shoulders. She doesn't fight or resist, but she's been begging me for miles to just let her help. The desperation in her voice almost causes me to tell her the truth—that there's no way we'd ever hurt her, but Carter's right. Luna is the one mermaid in the ocean that would make the king stop in his tracks if her life were in danger.

She'll be the key to surviving this.

"He's your father, Luna," I say. "If it comes down to his life or mine, you'll choose his. I'm not stupid."

"You don't know him like I do. This won't work," she says.

"Well, I have to try."

A sudden swell jerks Carter off course, and I tumble through the water away from him. The ocean sways back and forth the closer we get to Azure Waters, and I suppress my fear as much as I can. Fish get trapped in strong currents, making it nearly impossible for them to swim. They cruise with the waves, just going with the flow.

I fight my way back to Carter, creating our own current to fight against the unnatural one that tries to stop us in our path. A shadow falls over us, and I glance up at the rocking boat on the surface above. The vessel rises and falls in the water, stirring up waves that glimmer in the sunlight. The humans aboard are probably freaking out over the strange waters that shouldn't be this rough on a beautiful day.

"Carter, swim faster," I say. We're both exhausted from our night without sleep, and I'm surviving on adrenaline to get us through this.

"You have to do something, Ava," he says into my mind. "The water is too rough. It doesn't even change the deeper I go."

Closing my eyes, I concentrate on the relentless current. Bubbles fizzle around us, stinging against my skin in a blast of heat. This isn't like controlling the bay back at the Lost Cove.

This is different. The ocean here buzzes with magic that isn't mine. It's foreign and intrusive and threatens to suppress every attempt I make to bend the sea to my will.

The diamond around my neck sparks, sending rainbow light around us, shimmering off all the tiny bubbles, and then suddenly the waves stop around us. Carter jolts forward, cutting through the placid waves faster than ever. It's like he's flying through the water. I manage to keep the water still in our own calm current that slices through the rolling ocean still hell-bent on destroying everything.

A familiar kelp forest comes into view up ahead, the kelp vines thrashing in the waves that threaten to uproot them. Another vessel, one much smaller than the one before, rocks on the surface. My heart nearly seizes in my chest at the sight of a body tangled amid the kelp. It's not only the shores of Azure Waters I need to worry about; it's the fishermen and boaters, too.

I release Carter and swim right for the body. Carter yells out my name, but I don't stop. I summon a current strong enough to sweep me from Carter so quickly he doesn't have a chance to grab onto my tail.

The spark in my heart flashes in quick successions, racing with my heart thudding against my ribs. Without even stopping to check out the body, I latch my fingers to the back of the fisherman's shirt and hoist him to the surface where his boat rocks on the rolling waves.

A scream rips through the air, startling me, and I nearly sink back under. A girl with golden hair, a shade darker than mine, holds onto her seat in the boat, trying to stop herself from falling overboard.

Everything in me yells to dive. Instead, I ignore my inner voice and hold the guy in my arms with one hand while hooking my other arm over the side of the boat.

"Grab him," I say, trying my best to push the fisherman back into the boat.

The girl hesitates for only a second before sliding over to help me. With a flick of my wrist, I pull the ocean from his lungs, and he gasps and spits. A mix between a moan and a yell erupts from his mouth, and he snaps his eyes open. Saltwater sprinkles over his face. The man's brown eyes meet mine for a second, and he reaches up and runs his rough fingers over my cheeks.

"Ava!" Carter yells, surfacing from behind me. "What are you doing?"

I graze my fingers across the sloshing waves, coaxing them to settle down under my touch. It's enough to get the boat to stop rocking. "What do you think? I'm saving them."

"They know our secret," Carter says.

"Well, I'm not letting them die, and I'm not taking them back to the Lost Cove. No one will believe them," I say.

The man sits up higher, and they gape at me for a long moment. Carter propels closer, Luna still locked in one of his arms. She doesn't say a word as he grabs my hand and pulls me away, taking us underwater.

"That was incredibly stupid, Ava," Carter says, dragging

me with him.

"Then maybe that's what I am," I snap. "I'm sorry I'm not like you. I'm sorry if I care about—"

He stops swimming and surprisingly releases Luna to draw me into his arms. I want to yell at him, to push him away with a current. Because hovering here is slowing us down. We don't have time for this.

"I'm sorry, Ava," Carter says.

"We have to go," I say.

He shakes his head. "Not until you know I didn't mean what I said. I love you, and I love that you care so much about others. We're about to face the king and there's no way I'm going to have us go in there with you thinking I don't care about anything apart from you. Because I do. If I didn't, I wouldn't be here. I wouldn't want to stand against a tyrant who wants nothing more than to destroy us for not complying. If that means we give away the secret of our people, then so be it."

I slowly nod my head and lean in for a kiss. "That's one way of taking power from the king," I say with a smirk. But that's the last thing I want. Not everyone is like Giselle, or Wes and Darren even. I can't fault the king for keeping the secret from humans. I just don't agree with how he goes about it. I don't agree with murdering people or forcing anyone into the merpeople life. "But we need to find another way."

I turn to glance at Luna. I had expected her to swim away as fast as she could, but she remains exactly where Carter released her. Looking into her sapphire eyes, I study her face for a long moment.

"Luna, you can leave. I can't go through with using you as leverage to get the king to comply. It's not who I am. You're my friend, and I don't want you to accidentally get hurt," I say.

Carter frowns but doesn't argue. He knows I'd like nothing more than to see the two of them leave me altogether so I don't have to worry.

"Ava," Luna says, her voice nearly a whisper. "Listen."

I calm my roaring thoughts and do as she says. A murmur of voices drifts into my mind, cooling my blood. Carter stiffens next to me. He pulls me closer to him like he can stop me from falling apart and disappearing into the waves.

"Please, they could be anywhere in the world, my king. This isn't necessary," Mateo says, his voice projecting through the water.

"It must be done." The king's voice strikes me right in the heart, edging my vision in shadows. "There are consequences for rising against me."

"I'm asking you as a father to show some mercy. Had I known Starla was hiding them, I'd have told you sooner. My mate, she cares immensely about our children. You know she's always had a love of the land not unlike the quee—"

The water shudders, cutting off Mateo's words.

"She should've been the one to tell me."

"They're just children," Mateo says. "They don't under-stand."

Another shudder cuts through the water, startling me.

"This must be done. It's too much of a risk. Ava is too connected to the land," the king says.

"But she's a daughter of the sea."

"Her mindset is dangerous. I can't risk all the colonies."

"Please, my king. Give me a day. I'll find them myself. I'll bring them to you."

"No. It still must be done. All her ties to the land must be severed. She must have nothing left."

The next shudder in the water is enough to break me and Carter apart. Luna gets washed away from us on a current. The whole ocean bends to the will of the king. The sea around us presses into me, slowly growing higher and higher, lifting me toward the surface.

"No!" I scream, my voice projecting through the water.

"Ava, it's too late. We have to get out of here," Carter says, locking his fingers to my wrist.

"I'm not leaving!" I yell.

Squeezing my eyes shut, I force the ocean to freeze. A sudden calm falls over the sea, and the only thing I can hear is the sound of my heart thudding in my ears.

"King Attilonious!" I yell. "If you want me, you have to stop."

"Ava, no," Carter says only to me.

Our gazes lock for a long moment. "Don't let him catch you, okay?"

"What are you doing?" he asks.

"I'm saving Azure Waters."

"But, Ava," he argues.

I shake my head. "Trust me." I kiss him gently on the lips.

The water bubbles around us, quivering again under the king's power. Without another word, I pull away from Carter. Luna grabs his arm, stopping him from following me. I just hope this works. Because if it doesn't, I'll never be free.

21

A WARRIOR FOR A QUEEN

THE DIAMOND AROUND MY NECK glows so brightly I have to squint to see through the turbulent water. My whole body shakes with nerves, but I don't let it stop me from swimming along the familiar shore. A weird sensation crawls over me, and it's like I'm suddenly being pulled toward a force that leaves everything in me screaming in the most horrible way. My stomach knots, my fingers clench into fists, my body reacting to the dread stealing all the freedom and strength I usually feel with every flick of my tail.

I suck in a gulp of water through my mouth and push it

out through my gills. The usually cold water off the coast of Azure Waters turns warmer and warmer the closer I head toward the harbor. The heat slows me down, making it hard to stay focused.

I jerk in the current as another jolt cuts through me, and a swell yanks me toward the surface. King Attilonious wills the ocean to rise, and it takes me fighting free of the current to stop myself from being pulled into the harbor where dozens of boats dock. I can't see them from here, but I'm sure they're helpless against the power of the king.

"Stop!" I project my voice toward the figures in front of me, lurking below the surface. It takes everything in me to keep swimming even though I'd rather turn around and flee back to the safest spot in all the ocean—not the Lost Cove—but Carter's arms. Because with him, I don't feel like a weak, insignificant mermaid with a death wish. His strength reflects into me and steels me against everything I'm afraid of. With Carter, the world doesn't feel out of control. Because he's my world and has been my world for weeks. But Azure Waters? The rest of the ocean? That's our universe.

King Attilonious, in all his terrifying, god-like glory, points his golden staff directly at me. The diamond at the end, the other half to the one blazing on my neck, lights up like a beacon, but not a beacon of hope. It's like a sign that destruction isn't far away. That even if I can control the waters, even if I have magic in my essence, that maybe I'm still not powerful enough to face the king who has been reigning over the seas for more than a century.

I imagine Carter locking his hands around me to pull me forward with his strength, channeling my warrior mate into myself. Even though I made him stay behind, his presence lingers in my essence. He's always with me regardless. It's enough to push me forward.

The water quakes around me. Instead of knocking me back, it drags me forward in a nearly boiling current hot enough to redden my skin. I cry out, my voice erupting in the water with a dozen bubbles. I wave my hand, drawing water from the outside of this hot current leading to the king and wrap myself in a stream of icy water cool enough to fight against the king's rage. But it's not enough to slow me down or protect me.

A small army of merpeople surrounds the king, blocking him like he somehow needs their protection. Mateo is among them, his dark hair longer than the last time I saw him, and when our gazes lock, a strange look crosses his face—one I don't want to find myself caught it. It's not the usual love and adoration he's previously had for me. This one is dark and crawls under my skin, leaving me wanting to curl up in a ball and cry.

Beside him is a muscular mermaid with white hair despite the youthfulness of her gorgeous face. She narrows her saucer-wide, honey eyes, tightening her lips into a glower. She hates me without even knowing me, all because of the king. On her other side is another merman, one as brawny as Mateo but a good foot shorter. He wears no emotions on his face. I can't read him at all.

The hot current dissipates when I'm ten feet away from the king, and I flick my tail, propelling myself another five feet back. The king looms over his small army, his salt and pepper hair flowing behind him in a current he creates on his own. His sapphire eyes, as dark as the night without a moon, bore into mine for a second before his gaze flicks down and stops at the diamond around my neck.

I cover it with my hand, gripping it in my fingers like it'd somehow stop him from focusing on it. He tries to intimidate me with his sheer size, a good few feet longer than I am. His thick brows lower, nearly covering his eyes, and he bares his teeth in a smile that awakens the fear I've been suppressing.

"Where is your mate?" King Attilonious asks, peering around the ocean like Carter will try to sneak up on him.

"You need to stop this," I say instead of answering his question. "These people are innocent. They don't deserve your wrath." Waving my hand, I motion to the shore. My remodeled Victorian house is nestled right on the beach two miles away. Maybe the distance will keep them out of this mess.

"You can only blame yourself. I had offered you a great life and a powerful kingdom, and how did you repay me?" the king asks. King Attilonious is as delusional as I remember. A great life? No. A powerful kingdom? It wouldn't have been mine.

My nose crinkles. A million responses fly through my mind even though I know he's not expecting me to answer his question. I consider yelling that a life being imprisoned to the sea is not a great life at all. Having Carter ripped from me is not a life

I'd ever want to live. Being by the king's side as his queen is equivalent to hell in my mind. But all my thoughts remain locked away. Anything I say will set him off. I'm not here to start a war. I'm here to save the place I grew up. I'm here to save my family and friends. Everything I've ever known.

"Please," I say, desperation squeezing my chest. If there was one thing I learned from the few moments of being around King Attilonious is that standing up to him only leaves him needing to prove how mighty he is. "I'm begging you. I'll do whatever you want. Just leave Azure Waters alone."

He holds his staff out to me, a smug smile on his face. My heart races, causing my hands to shake. If I were breathing air, I'd be panting. His drawn out pause threatens to send me into full blown panic.

King Attilonious straightens his shoulders. "No. You'll do what I say regardless."

With a wave of his hand, he shifts the ocean above us, sending an enormous tidal wave toward the shore, one big enough to pulverize anything in its path. For the first time since seeing Mateo again do I see something flash in his eyes— sadness? Pity? I can't tell.

It's enough to set me off. With a flick of my tail, I propel forward and straight for the king. The current around me thrusts me at the king, moving me faster than I could ever possibly swim. I beg the ocean to bend to my will.

The diamond around my neck flashes, and I thrust my hand out, sending the small army of merpeople out of the way.

Something flickers in King Attilonious' eyes, but I don't even get within a few feet of him when he raises his staff, sending a pulse through the water directly at me.

It hits me in the chest, knocking me back, making it hard to gasp water. The edges of my vision darken, the sky shimmering through the surface turning dark. The ocean continues to rise, but there's nothing I can do. The last thing I see is the glow of the queen's diamond as it lights up my vision.

But even with the magic of the queen's heart, I know I've failed.

Bright sunlight shines overhead, bouncing off my cerulean scales. I dig my hands into the powdery sand, only to sink deeper into the unfamiliar shore around me. The last thing I remember was the king at the harbor of Azure Waters ready to wipe my beloved town off the map.

But now, I'm somewhere I've never been.

Fear pulls at my heart when I concentrate on Carter but can't feel him at all. If King Attilonious hurt him, I don't know what I'd do. I can't stand the thought of losing him again. He was supposed to stay away. He was supposed to trust me to take care of things. *But you failed.*

"It's not the end of the world, my daughter," a familiar voice says.

I exhale a long breath, loosening the nerves tightening my chest, making it hard to breathe. "What happened? Where am I? Am I dead?" A million questions try to escape my lips all at once. There is no other explanation as to why I'm here and why I can't feel Carter anymore other than the king ended my life before destroying the rest of my human world forever.

A cool hand rests on my tail, and I draw my gaze to the glittering sharp nails of the queen. "You mustn't be afraid," she says without answering any of my questions. "You'll figure this all out."

"I don't think I can," I say. "What's even the point anymore? I should've never left the Lost Cove."

Celestiana frowns. "And I thought you were a suitable queen."

I should be offended. But I'm tired. Exhausted. A hopelessness comparable to the moment Starla took my sea stone ring away from me burrows deep into my soul, my essence, threatening to shred me into tiny pieces to scatter along the shore like the glittering sea glass that sparkles in the warm sunlight above.

I bend forward, pulling my tail up to my chest and then wrap my arms around it to hold me in place. "I told you I don't want to be a queen. I don't want magic. All I want is my life back. I want to go home, but I don't even think I have a home anymore."

"So, you want to renounce your mermaid essence?"

"I—" I pause. Could I just go back to being a human? I could move somewhere land-locked and forget that the ocean exists. Carter and I, we could...we couldn't do any of that. If I gave up my mermaid essence, I'd have to give up Carter. The permanent change would sever our bond like it did between the king and queen.

"Something holds you back," she says.

A tear drips onto my cheek. "Carter."

"The perfect warrior for the perfect queen," she says.

It's not the first time she has said this, but it doesn't make me feel better. Carter's lived most of his life on land. It wasn't until me that he lived in the water. He might have been gifted the ability to be a warrior, but he doesn't have the training the king's guards do. Mateo was right. In this moment, I feel like a child. I feel like I know nothing.

"I don't want him fighting for me," I say.

"He will fight with you. He'll protect you. Your magic reflects your emotions. Together, you will set things right," she says. "The colonies weren't always about living a simple life. Life isn't about just existing. The ocean didn't instill its magic into us only to have a king lock us away and cut us off from the human world many used to freely go into."

"And what about our secret?"

"Do you know why you triggered your transformation in front of your human companion and revealed the secret to her?" the queen asks.

I shift to meet her soft smile. "Because I lacked control."

She shakes her head. "Because you could trust her. The ocean has spent forever, for as long as anyone can remember, protecting us. Only the ones worthy of our secret discover it."

"That's why you created the Lost Cove. It wasn't only to

save those humans because they discovered our secret," I say.

She beams me a smile. "I created the island to protect those the ocean saw as worthy allies. A way to keep us connected."

My sister flashes through my mind. She's not exactly my ally. "But Bailey, she—"

"She will see."

"I don't know," I say.

"Then you will show her."

An ominous storm materializes in the distance, turning the crystalline sky dark with thunderous clouds. Lightning strikes, startling me, and before I have a chance to say another word to Celestiana, a huge swell crashes over us, sweeping me away.

Dark waters encompass me, dragging me deeper into the sea until I can no longer see the surface above. I flail in the current, trying my best to swim. But it's too strong, and I'm too exhausted.

"Ava," a voice whispers into my mind. "Ava, my daughter. It's okay. You're okay."

I snap my eyes open and jerk my arms out, sending a forceful current in front of me. It crashes into a pearlescent wall before bouncing back to send me flying into someone else's warm arms.

"Let me go!" I scream, struggling to break free.

"Shhh. You must calm down before you hurt one of us," Starla says.

I freeze at the sound of her voice and spin to face her. The moment I meet her blue-green eyes, ones the same color as

Carter's, I sink against her, letting her hold me in a hug tight enough to force away the nervous shakes that grip me.

"Starla," I whisper, projecting my thoughts only to her. "My home. My parents. The king." Panic, grief, anguish, despair—so many heart-wrenching emotions wash over me, threatening to send me to the sea floor where I want to curl in on myself and disappear.

Everything feels so heavy—my thoughts, the sea, the shimmering room around us—closes in on me, trying to smother me. I can't breathe. I can't get my gills to work. To pull oxygen from the water.

I need to escape. I can't be here.

I need to find Carter.

Despite Starla hugging me and whispering to me that everything will be okay, I feel like I'm dying, like the ocean is rejecting me. My skin tingles, my heart thrashing in quick, painful beats, and I start to panic, thinking I'm about to transform into a human at any second.

"Just breathe." The two little words drift into my mind, settling deep in my essence. Carter's voice flows into me along with his emotions, pushing all of the horrible thoughts away. His calmness blankets my panic and the intensity of his love burns away all the doubt and despair from my very being. *The perfect warrior for the perfect queen...*

For the first time, Celestiana's words ring true. And it's in this moment I realize I've been wrong. I thought in Celestiana's mind that Carter was supposed to protect me, fight for me, die for me—do everything in his power to see to it that I'm safe and alive and free.

But that's not what being my warrior or mate means. He's not here to serve me. I'm no queen. I'm his other half, and we're in this together. Together, we're whole. Carter isn't my warrior in the sense that he must do everything for me, but he can help me do everything myself. He can make it possible for me to be strong, to be powerful, to stay in control. Through our bond, we share a connection unlike anything in the world. He's my mate, my love, my everything. He brings out the good in me. He'll get me through it all. Together. Always together.

I suck in a deep breath of the ocean, letting it fill me to the brim. The water soothes the fissures in my soul that threaten to break me apart and leave me useless. With every breath, every beat of my heart, the weight of my situation lifts, freeing me.

"Carter," I whisper to only him. "You shouldn't be here. If the king discovers you..." I can't bear to put my thoughts into words.

"Don't worry, I'm safe. Luna says the king doesn't know she took a guard's key so he'll never expect me to be here," he says. "You're getting out tonight."

"But your family," I say.

"Ava." Starla touches my shoulder, drawing my attention away from the wall. I turn and meet her gaze and then realize we're not alone. Grandmer, Starla's mom, hovers just behind her daughter with a sad smile on her face. "You need to listen to Carter."

I frown. "You know?"

"I'm the one who called to him when Mateo brought you here. The king wanted you in his chambers, but Mateo convinced Attilonious to let you be with us for now."

I grind my teeth, just the thought of waking up in King Attilonious' chambers freaking me out. Does he expect that since he ruined my life I'll submit to him and be the perfect little queen? Ew. I'll never resort to that.

"How are you so calm about Mateo, Starla?" I ask.

She pouts her bottom lip. "He's doing what he thinks is right for our family."

"He wants me by the king's side," I say.

"He wants you alive, Ava. He wants Carter alive. He's not aiding the king because he's against you. Someone must be there for you if things don't go as planned," Grandmer says, speaking up.

"They already haven't," I say.

"Calm down, Ava," Carter says into my mind. "You won't have to worry for much longer." But he can't make any guarantees. I'm locked in a room in the castle with no escape.

A sudden rumble causes the water to quiver, and the boulder blocking the only entrance and exit moves out of the way. Light streams in through the cutout, brightening the darkness of the room lit only by my spark.

"My queen," a masculine voice says.

"Carter," I say only to him. "I'm being moved."

"Your king requests your presence," the merman says, poking his head in. I don't recognize him.

I hug myself. "No. I don't want to see him."

"Please, my queen. I don't want to restrain you," the merman says. He swims into the small room, forcing Starla and Grandmer to move to the outskirts of the room.

I hold up my hand, willing a current to push him away. But it's not strong enough. He locks his fingers around my arm and tugs me with him.

"Stop!" I yell. "Let me go!"

But he doesn't, and no one tries to help me. Another mermaid grabs my other arm, allowing the merman to block the exit to the room again, cutting me off from Starla, who tells me to be strong.

"Don't resist, Ava," Carter whispers into my mind. "Don't give the king a reason to hurt you."

"I'm scared," I whisper.

"I'm here," Carter says. "I know you can do this."

But I'm not so sure I can.

Because I really don't want to.

22

REBEL

I WAVE MY HAND THROUGH the water, sending a current into the closest mermaid, who holds up a sea grass woven top. Her dark auburn hair veils her face as she flies across the open room, hitting her back on the pearlescent wall.

"Queen Ava," another mermaid says. "Please, we're trying to help you." The mermaid swims closer, cringing when I hold my hand up, but I don't use any of my magic. Her steel gray eyes line with sadness when I sink to the floor and curl in on myself.

A small hand touches my shoulder and then shifts to push

my hair from my face. I roll over and stare up at the young mermaid. She motions for the other two to leave the room, and they listen without arguing.

"I know this is hard," the girl says, shifting in the sand so her forest green tail doesn't brush mine. "But the king asked that we make you presentable."

"I don't want to see him," I mutter.

She cups my hand. "I know. It pains me to see you like this."

I sit up, surprise widening my eyes. "Why? You don't even know me."

"I was here during your coronation. What the king did..." Her voice trails off in my head. She tightens her hand around mine. "Thinking about it makes my heart hurt. You promised yourself to someone else. It doesn't make sense for the king to have done this."

I consider telling her the reason he has. I consider spilling my heart to her, so she can see what pain I'm in. So she can make sense of all this. But I can't. The words stay locked deep in my mind.

"Thank you for sharing your thoughts," I say instead of what's on my mind. "And I'm sorry for not complying. I'm glad you understand."

She nods, moving away so I can compose myself. "I'm not going to make you change for the king. I'll keep the others away as well."

I tilt my head. "No, it's fine. I don't want you to face his fury. Not on my behalf. Let's just get this over with." As much as I want to be stubborn, to send everyone away and let no one near me, I wouldn't put it past King Attilonious to punish those who comply with my will instead of his. Carter was right. I need to do what I'm told so the king doesn't hurt me.

I swallow the rising lump in my throat.

"Relax, Aves," Carter says. "I'm still here with you."

"I love you," I whisper.

"Don't say it like that."

"Would you like me to help you with your top, Queen Ava," the mermaid says, pulling my thoughts away from Carter.

I shake my head and unhook my bikini top myself, using my arm to hide my bare chest even though the mermaid doesn't gape at me. She tucks my bikini top into a small bag and hands me the grass woven top with tiny pieces of blue sea glass strung through it.

I struggle for a moment, trying to tie the top around back. Without asking, the mermaid swims behind me and does it herself before quickly running her fingers through my hair, untangling the knots as she goes. She twists my blond locks into a braid that stops just past the strap of my new top.

The mermaid moves around to sit in front of me and holds out a dainty silver crown, one studded with sparkling diamonds and pearls, and sets it on top of my head despite my protests. She holds up a mirror so I can see myself. I frown.

I hate it. I hate everything about it. I don't want to look the part of a queen, which the king expects me to play. I don't want to find myself beautiful as I stare at my reflection—my sad cerulean eyes the same shade as my tail, how my skin shimmers in a pearlescent sheen, giving me a glow I could never manage as a human. How perfect my hair looks even underwater, and how the queen's heart around my neck projects enchanting rainbow beams, even though I'm sure only I can see them.

But what I hate most is Carter isn't here to see me. I'm not dressed up for him to appreciate. I've been dolled up like a pretty little mermaid queen to please the one merman I want nothing to do with. One who will probably kill me if I fight too hard. The thought makes me sick to my stomach. I don't want to be pretty for him. I don't want the king to look at me like some jewel he can hide away in his treasure chest. I want to be repulsive.

"What's the matter?" the mermaid asks.

I cover my face with my hands, sobbing silently. My tears blend with the salty sea, my chest heaving. If I could get sick, I would, but I can't even remember the last time I've eaten. San Francisco? That feels like an eternity ago.

"Please, don't cry," Carter whispers into my mind. "I can't bear it."

"You should be here. You should get to see me right now. Not him." The words escape so sharply the sand stirs from the floor without me even moving. Fear pokes me in the mind, but the mermaid doesn't react. I didn't accidentally send the words out for the entire ocean to hear. "I don't want him to see me like this."

"Queen Ava?" the mermaid asks.

"It's going to be okay, Aves," Carter assures, talking over the mermaid.

"Everything is so screwed up," I say, projecting my voice for everyone to hear. "I hate this."

"Would you like to try another top?" the mermaid asks.

I thrash my head back and forth. "It's not that. It's all of it."

The mermaid floats in front of me, a grimace marring her delicate features. "You look lovely, Queen Ava."

"That's the point. I don't want to," I say.

I cover my face with my hands again, but this time, I don't cry. Instead, I drag the sharp nail of my index finger down my cheek. A small pool of blood tints the sea pink in front of me, causing the mermaid to gasp. The thin cut only hurts a little, and it'll heal by nightfall, but in this moment, it's a glaring mark on my once flawless skin. It's my way of protesting. Rebelling. The king can try to have power over me all he wants, but he can never truly control me.

"I need a healer!" the mermaid calls.

I reach out and grab her arm. "No. I'm through here. Take me to the king."

"But you've injured yourself," the mermaid says, trying to reach up to touch the cut.

I turn away. "I'm fine. I'm perfect. Take me to the king."

"But—"

"I *said* take me to the king."

The mermaid nods, her lips tilted downward, and swims across the room to the cutout where the muscular guard with short dark gray hair waits for me. The moment his eyes fall on the cut on my cheek, I know King Attilonious will be displeased. It gives me the courage to straighten my shoulders and let him take me by the arm.

"Now's a good time to give me all your strength, my warrior mate," I whisper to Carter in my mind. My heart tugs as I try to pinpoint where he is, and I know if I just follow the pull, it'll take me into his arms.

"You're the bravest being in the universe," he whispers into my mind. "You're strong and smart and everything I could've ever dreamed of. The king doesn't stand a chance against you, my mate—my queen."

A smile crosses my lips, hearing him whisper through my mind. It's the first time he's ever called me his queen, and while it sounds cheesy, it feels honest and so full of love that I already feel a thousand times stronger. I feel like I can face whatever the king has to throw at me. Because he can't break me. He can't make me bow.

"Against us," I whisper back, sending my thoughts only to him.

The guard guides me through a tunnel and into the grand room of the castle filled with remnants of sunken ships. Before, I thought everything here was collected from accidental shipwrecks. But now? I know the pieces are trophies collected by the king from ships he probably destroyed without reason, just because he could.

Voices murmur through my mind, drawing my attention from the glittering room to those who hover around me. Dozens of smiling faces greet me, some reaching out to touch my arm or my tail, totally invading my space. As much as I want to jerk away and lash out, I don't. The merpeople are merely excited about my arrival, lost in their own naivety which I can't blame them for.

Forcing myself to smile, I gently touch the cheeks of those close enough for me to reach. I hum to myself, trying my best to push out the harmonious voices overtaking my thoughts, making it hard to think. The melody stirs sadness in my heart for a split second when I realize I'm humming a song my mom used to sing to me long ago. I can almost hear her voice now.

The guard motions for the others to back away and swims me up to the balcony that overlooks the grand room. It'll lead to the throne room and then the king's chambers, the last place I want to be. I'd rather stay where everyone can see.

Suddenly, the room falls silent and merpeople start bowing around me. A shadow falls over me, and I steel myself to face King Attilonious as he hovers on the balcony. The guard tries to force me to bow next to him, but I hold my head high and bring my eyes to meet the king's.

Something indecipherable flickers on his face, so quickly I nearly miss it, before he offers me a brilliant smile, one that would've once dazzled me. But he can't charm me now. I will not allow him to have any sort of power over me.

"Welcome home, Ava," King Attilonious says, bending low to bow before me. "You're as beautiful as ever."

I grin. I can't help it. Not because I'm flattered by his compliment, but because I now know what the look I saw was. Dissatisfaction. But he can't react. Something like a cut or blemish would never get in the way of the bond between mates. But I'm not bonded with the king. I'll never be.

I don't respond to his compliment or bow. All I do is cross my arms and continue to grin. I catch sight of the guard next to me, and he gives me a funny look, mouth hanging open with squinty eyes—one that almost looks fearful, probably because I don't do anything.

Even the king looks uncomfortable.

The king closes the distance between us, grabbing both my hands in his, and then he brings them up to kiss my knuckles. I clench my jaw to keep from grimacing. But I can't stop the falter of my smile when he leans over and tries to kiss me on the lips.

I turn my head, and his lips brush against my cheek. "Try that again, and I'll make a scene." I direct the thought only to the king.

With narrowed eyes, King Attilonious leans away from me but doesn't let me go. He nearly drags me from the crowd and through the throne room to his chambers, leaving the crowd cheering like what they witnessed was the most magical thing ever.

"You will not disrespect me!" King Attilonious bellows,

swinging his staff toward me.

A current knocks me across the room, and I skid over his black sand pool. Heat rushes around me, threatening to boil me. I twist on the floor, my once neat hair now loose from the braid. I grip the diamond on my neck and inhale a breath of the hot water. It courses through me, igniting my spark even brighter, and I thrust my arm out, sending the hot current right back to the king.

He sways in the current, but the strength from his tail combats the shift in the water. "I am your king, and you will accept your place by my side. The ocean picked you for me and gifted you with an affinity found only in those meant to be royalty."

"The ocean did not pick me, Carter did. For him. Not you." Celestiana was right about him being so closed off from the world. He's not some king trying to protect his kingdom. He's protecting what he thinks is rightfully his. Me included. He sees no reason and his power has gotten to his head. "I will never accept a place by your side."

In a bout of rage, he hits his staff on the ground again, except this time, I'm prepared. I deflect his current and remain in my spot on the sand. I'm only ten feet away from the balcony that leads to the open water of the colony, and if I can make it there, it'll be harder to stop me.

King Attilonious holds his staff up but doesn't hit me with his magic. "Oh, but you will. It won't be long before I find your mate. He won't be able to stay away from you. And when he comes, I won't attempt to sever your bond."

I hold my face expressionless. I refuse to give him a reaction.

"He'll feel whatever you feel. You might be able to withstand my power, but can he? Can you watch your mate suffer?"

My lip quivers, giving him the reaction he was looking for. "I won't allow it."

"Allow it? Do you honestly think you're a match against me?"

"I don't get it. Why not just kill me? Why go through this trouble?" I don't know why I feel the need to ask, but if my existence is so horrible to him, why bother?

His mouth twitches, and I'm sure he's thought about it. "My kingdom is important, and the colonies have already accepted your place."

I remember now that there's never been an uprising because the merpeople adored him. Hurting me wouldn't risk the colonies. It'd risk him.

"It doesn't have to be this way, though. I want my queen to be happy. I want you to want to be by my side. You've been gifted, and I can help you," he says, closing the distance. Lowering himself to the floor, he reaches out and brushes strands of my hair away from my face. "If you swear your loyalty to me, I'll stop the hunt for Carter. I'll release his family. I might even grant you freedom to leave Pearlestria with a guard. I need our kingdom united, and you've put a rift among our people. That's something I can't allow to continue."

"Me? You did that yourself. You couldn't just leave me alone," I say.

"To give away our secret? To put everyone at risk because you're a stubborn, spoiled mermaid?" Nothing he says will faze me. "I cannot allow it. I'm giving you an opportunity most yearn for. Sometimes we have to do things we don't like because it's the right thing to do. It's time you learn that. It's time to learn your place in the ocean."

"And if I resist? If I don't comply?" I ask.

"That's not an option. I'll make you see."

The water warms around us, and I realize it's not by the king's doing. It's me. Rage rushes over me, and I swim up from my spot, putting space between us. The king is quick to propel toward me, but he doesn't have a chance to touch me before a figure darts between us.

"Dad, stop!" Luna yells, projecting her voice out.

King Attilonious freezes, staff aimed and ready to strike me, but Luna blocks his way. She holds her hands up, trying to fill the space in front of me so that King Attilonious can't get a shot.

"Move, Luna," he says, trying to knock her away with a wave, but I grab her hand and swim with her.

"You will not stand against me, my daughter." The viciousness in the king's voice makes me pull Luna back.

"You can't hurt her," she says. "I won't let you."

"You don't understand, Luna. She'll destroy us all. She doesn't understand our traditions and ways. Without me, her power runs wild. It must be given to me. Do you even know what she wears around her neck?"

Luna peers over her shoulder at me, glancing at the necklace. She doesn't respond to her father.

"That was your mother's. It was a wedding gift from me. It was lost with her," he says. "Ava should not have it."

Luna turns from the king to meet my gaze. "Is that true? You mean?"

This is not the conversation I want to have right now only feet from my escape. But how can I deny Luna the answers she seeks? If my mother disappeared when I was a merbabe, I'd want to know the truth.

"She renounced her mermaid essence," I say quietly. "The queen's heart was a gift to me."

"But why would she do that? I knew she loved the land, but I don't understand," she says.

"Please, Luna. I'll explain everything. But not here. We have to go," I say, sending my thought to her alone.

Luna gives me a tiny nod and turns to face her father. Neither of us has time to react when he swings his staff out and knocks Luna away. She flies through the water and clatters to the floor. Her black hair veils her face, and she lies there unmoving.

"Swear your loyalty, Ava," the king says, closing the distance.

"No," I say.

"Do it now!" he roars, grabbing me by the hair and shaking

me once. I swing my arm out and smack his shoulder, using the force of the current to knock him away from me. With a flick of my tail, I propel toward my only exit, praying I can somehow get through the protective barrier of Pearlestria the king set to imprison us all.

I don't make it far.

Strong hands latch around the base of my tale and yank me back. Bubbles erupt from my mouth as I scream out in the water. The king pins me down, one hand digging into my shoulder and the other one locked around the chain on my neck.

The diamond burns brightly, setting the entire room aglow. The king brushes his fingers on the diamond, and the stone floor quakes beneath us. It shocks the king, stopping him from stealing the stone from my neck. He swims up, putting space between us and then aligns his staff with my heart.

I squeeze my eyes shut, bracing for the impact, for what could possibly be the end of my life but nothing happens. Peeking through my eyelashes, I stare at King Attilonious through the fastest current I've ever seen. It blocks me from the king, moving so quickly his staff can't touch me.

He snarls, swimming back. My chest heaves as I inhale and exhale cool water, trying to calm down my racing heart.

"This isn't over," he says, the new calmness in his voice making me shiver. "You will swear your loyalty to me and our kingdom."

I don't respond. I can't.

Without another word, King Attilonious leaves both me

and Luna in his chambers. Two guards enter the room, one blocking each exit.

My chance of escaping seems impossible now. I don't even know how we'll get through the barrier imprisoning all merpeople here.

"Ava, say something to me," Carter says in my mind. "Your emotions are all over the place."

"Carter, you have to get as far away as possible. The king is depending on you showing up," I say. "I can't let him get to you."

"I'm not leaving without you," he says.

"Please," I beg.

"Ava, don't ask me again."

So, I don't. Instead, I look around the king's chambers. The king was right. This isn't over. It's just begun.

23

BETRAYAL

"I COMMAND YOU TO LET me go," Luna says, jabbing her finger into the guard's rock-hard chest.

Moments after the king left, three healers came into the chambers to fix the damage caused to the both of us, including my self-inflicted cut on my face. It took two of them and the guard to hold me down, and also Carter talking me out of blasting them all into a wall, to allow them to mend the scrapes on my still tender tail.

"I'm sorry, princess. We're under strict orders," the guard

says, keeping his eyes trained above Luna's head.

"Then I want to talk to my dad," she argues.

A bubble of panic rises in my chest at the thought of King Attilonious returning. "It's not worth it, Luna."

She turns to glance at me, her lips barely a visible line as she presses them together. My thoughts must be written all over my face because she immediately backs away from the guard but not before kicking up an arc of black sand from the pool into his face with a flick of her tail.

He closes his eyes, the tiny grains pelting him, but he remains firm in his position in front of the exit.

With a wave of my hand, I send a cool current at him, making him waver in the water. He brings his attention to me for the first time since his arrival. His firm mouth hides under facial hair, but it doesn't conceal how he clenches his jaw under my scrutiny. He's obviously uncomfortable, and I use that to my advantage. Too bad the king's messenger, Tide, isn't here. I could probably scare him away easily enough.

I wiggle my index finger at the guard and wink, and he flushes. One thing I remember from my weeks within the walls of this colony is that it's unheard of for a coupled mermaid to show attention to anyone apart from their mate.

Giselle would laugh hysterically if she were here. She'd attempt to make the guard even more uncomfortable for the sheer fun of it. All I want is for him to turn around and stand guard outside the door.

"Carter?" I whisper through the water with my mind. "I'm

trying to get the guard to take post outside of the chambers. What can I say that'll make him leave?"

"Compliment his tail," Carter says. A small chuckle sounds through my mind, making my heart soar.

Heat crawls up my neck for no other reason than this feels super awkward. I force myself from my spot on the floor and swim closer to the guard. Luna tilts her head to the side, studying me. I smirk at her before hiding my smile with my hand.

"What's this guy's name?" I ask only to her.

"Why?"

"I'm going to compliment his tail."

Her mouth falls open. "That's something you say to a potential mate," she whispers only to me.

I suck in my bottom lip to stop myself from laughing into the water. "Just tell me his name."

"He goes by Blue," she says.

Inhaling a deep breath of the ocean, I rise in the water so I can meet Blue's eyes, though he trains them on the ceiling above my head. I float in place for an excruciating moment, taking in his hard features, from the sharpness of his nose to his dark brown eyes. Nothing about him is blue.

"Where's a good place to rest my hand, Carter?" I ask only to him. My heart constantly aches because I can't follow the pull that wants to lead me to him.

"Should I be worried?" he asks.

"You should bask in my brilliance," I say.

"You know I bask in your everything."

His words bring a huge smile to my lips, and Blue visibly stiffens. I might not even have to say anything at all to him before he swims out of here to escape the awkwardness I'm about to thrust upon him.

"And to answer your question, grasp him on the crook of his neck and shoulder, and tap right below his gills."

"So, Blue," I say, projecting my thoughts through the water.

Luna watches me in fascination while the guard refuses to look at me at all. I wonder if any of my fake advances will even work. He could be immune to my charm, and then I'll just embarrass myself.

"Have you ever been to shore before?" I ask.

He doesn't respond.

I tighten my jaw and flick my gaze to Luna. "I'm starting to feel unwelcome in my own kingdom."

Blue fidgets in place and says, "I'm sorry, my queen. The king didn't mention if I'm allowed to speak to you."

"Why wouldn't you be?" I ask. "He's not my mate, you know."

"Yes, your highness. But you are my queen."

It's starting to get awkward on my part as I lose my bravado. "Which means you should at least be courteous enough to respond when I'm speaking to you."

"My apologies, your highness. I've never been to the shore before. I'm not familiar with human customs," he says.

"But I'm not human." I float a few inches closer, and his

caudal fin brushes against mine. He doesn't move away but tenses.

"I'm sorry, my queen. I just know—"

I reach up and grasp his shoulder, sliding my hand up his tight muscles to the spot Carter mentioned. "You don't have to apologize to me, Blue. I'm happy to have you in my presence." I gently tap my finger to his neck. "Your tail is the—" Prettiest? Strongest? Oh, God, this is so uncomfortable.

"Pardon me, my queen. I'm being summoned," Blue says, nearly barreling through the cutout that leads to the grand room.

I meet Luna's wide eyes and offer her my most dazzling smile. I swim the few feet between us and nestle myself next to her, flopping my tail down in front of me, stirring up the black sand of the pool.

"What? I was tired of him watching our every move," I say.

"We're still not going to be able to leave," she says.

"I have a plan for that, too."

"What is it?"

I can only smile. Being stuck in a room with nothing to do but think and talk to Carter has given me the chance to plan my escape. It's going to be a long shot, but I'm going to risk it. I just need to create a distraction. One that sends not only the king from Pearlestria but his guards, too.

"Carter's going to rescue me," I say. "Because there's no way he's going to allow the king to try to steal my power. The ocean gave me a warrior for this reason. The king might be mighty, but he doesn't stand a chance against my mate."

"Ava, tone it down," Carter says in my mind.

Luna reaches out and touches my hand. "This is a terrible idea. You don't know what my dad is capable of."

"Oh, I know," I say, gripping the necklace. "Celestiana, your mom, she told me he'll be the cause of our destruction." I let my thoughts project through the water for all to hear. "She wants nothing more than to make sure things return as they should be."

Luna frowns. "You talked to my mom? I don't understand."

I nearly regret telling her. Her brows hang low on her head, and she pouts her bottom lip. It's in this moment I realize how unfair all of this really is for both me and Luna. I shouldn't be in this position, and Luna, she should be the one to hold her mother's essence, the essence that blinks in the diamond around my neck. But Luna only knows the sea while I know the land.

"It's hard to explain. Can I show you?" I ask.

"Ava, we're running out of time," Carter says in my mind.

"I have to do something first," I tell him.

Luna nods, drawing my attention back to her. Leaning forward, I do the only thing I know how to do to allow her to glimpse my memories. I press my lips against hers, sending the thousands of images the queen bestowed on me into Luna's mind. One after another flickers through, showing Luna her mother's life from her time on land, visiting her human grandfather to her falling in love with Darren to how the king swept her into the world of royalty, even to the moment she gazed upon a young Luna knowing she might never see her daughter again.

Luna jerks back and covers her mouth with her hand. "Oh, Ava," she says. "It was really her."

I nod. "I wish it was you who could talk to her."

"But you've given me something I never thought I'd ever get. I don't know how to thank you," she says.

"I might have something in mind."

"Anything."

"I need you to betray me," I say.

24

SINK OR SWIM

"ARE YOU INSANE?" LUNA ASKS, her voice projecting through the water. She stands near the cutout where Blue waits outside. He's eased closer since I tried telling anyone nearby what the queen had told me. "I'm not going to let you risk your life like that. I know you don't want to be here, but my dad is so powerful. You know what he's capable of."

"Luna, keep your voice down," I say. "This is supposed to be between you and me."

Luna swims in a quick circle. Her black hair veils her face, and she sinks to the stone floor and brings her tail up to her chest to rest her chin on it. "Someone could get hurt. You might not care about everyone here, but I do. You should just tell him to leave. If he were my mate, I'd want to protect him. You're selfish, you know."

My nose crinkles at her words. I tell myself I'm selfish all the time, but it sounds weird coming from someone else, even if she doesn't truly believe it.

"Please, Luna. You have no idea what it's like. I'd rather fight and die together than remain here for the rest of my life." Dramatic? Definitely. True? Absolutely. But I don't plan on dying any time soon.

A pout crosses her face, and she brings her eyes to mine. "I thought we were friends. I might not be your mate, but I thought you cared about me. I stood up for you to my dad."

"I know. And I appreciate it. But this—" I motion around the room. "This isn't what I want."

"I'm sorry, Ava," Luna says, her voice nearly a whisper.

A moment of panic blossoms in my chest, pulling at my spark so hard my hands fly up to hug myself. Blue enters the room, and then another guard flies in from outside. They both close in on me like I'll suddenly do something to escape. And I'm about to.

"What have you done, Luna?" I ask, throwing my hand out.

"I'm sorry," she whispers again.

"Carter, you have to run! They know you're here!" I scream, letting my voice project through the water.

"Be brave, Ava," he says only to me.

I spin around in a circle, thrusting a current at the guards as they try to close in on me. They fly back a few feet, barely fazed by my attempt to keep them away.

"Queen Ava, you must calm down. We have strict orders from the king. He says if you try to fight us that he won't bring back your mate alive," Blue says. "He's already been spotted on the outskirts of the kingdom."

It takes everything in me not to blast the two guards away. "I swear if any of you hurt him, I'll—"

"My queen, that's the last thing any of us want. I grew up with your mate's father," the other guard, who I have no idea what his name is, says. "I don't want anything to happen to his son."

"Then why are you helping Attilonious?" I ask. His admission throws me off. Most of the merpeople have been kind and compassionate, but it's like all they can do is feel bad. Only Luna's been brave enough to stand up with me.

"He is our king," the guard says.

"He's not my king," I say.

"But he is," Blue says.

Luna swims closer and takes my hand. "Ava, it's going to be okay."

Closing my eyes, I summon the courage I can feel coursing from Carter as he evades the king and his guards. I hold on tightly to his love, his loyalty, all his strength. Because I'm going to need it to do what I'm about to do next.

I can't escape Pearlestria as a mermaid, but the king's imprisoning magic can't hold me here if I change forms. He didn't account for the fact that I can still transform into a human. He doesn't have a clue.

"I know it will be," I say. "Because I'm counting on you to not let me die."

She nods once, still gripping my hand, and I will my human transformation to take hold. Cramps seize my muscles, sending me bowing, but they disappear a second later before my lungs scream in pain. Silence veils over me. The only sound I can hear is my racing heart beating in sync with Carter's as he lures the king away.

And he's not just luring him anywhere. He's taking him to the one place he's never supposed to go. Because the Lost Cove is where we have the advantage. It's where Celestiana's magic resonates in every molecule of the water, water I'm familiar with.

Opening my eyes, I stare through the dark room, nearly blinded. Without my mermaid vision and with the sun already set, I have to rely on my other senses to get me out of here. But in my human form, I can't make it alone.

Luna pulls me to her and away from the two guards. My necklace erupts in magical light silhouetting them long enough that I wave my arm in their direction and send a current their way.

The water quivers from the force in which they strike the wall, and Luna yanks me toward the cutout leading to the open sea of Pearlestria. Shadows edge my vision from the lack of oxygen, and I fight to stay awake.

Something hits me hard in the side, and a muffled scream sounds through the water. I'm ripped away from Luna, a pair of strong arms locking around me. I thrash, fighting as hard as I can, but with every passing second, I become weaker and weaker. And as a human, no one can hear my thoughts. But I refuse to transform back. I'm not even sure I can in this moment.

A flash of gold erupts in my vision, the sparkle of Luna's tail cutting through the water in my direction. Bubbles fizzle around me, and I manage to elbow my captor right in the gills, forcing him to release me. I thrust out both hands and send a cold current right at the guard, knocking him away. His spark blinks as he lands in the channel between the houses where all the unsuspecting merpeople hide away. I don't know why I can see it, but I can.

Kicking my legs, I swim a few feet in the direction I think is the surface. It's hard to tell in this state. I sink lower despite my kicking, and my hope dwindles to the ocean floor. Luna was supposed to swim me to the surface, but she's nowhere to be found. She was supposed to help me cross the barrier. The guards were supposed to let her because they shouldn't have wanted to see me drown. How can they let their queen die?

But maybe I'm not really their queen. The king can call me that all he wants. Everyone can pretend I'm royalty. But when it all comes down to it, I'm a human-born mermaid, who's coupled with a boy who loves the land more than the sea. In the end, I'm not the queen of the ocean. I'm not as powerful as the king.

I'm no one.

Celestiana was wrong. The ocean was wrong. Carter isn't the perfect warrior for the perfect queen. I'm an accidental mermaid, and he's my hero.

"Ava," a voice says. It's not in my mind, but I can hear it through the hum of the ocean around me. "Ava-girl, stay with me."

Strong hands encircle my waist and drag me from the spot I float above all the rock houses of Pearlestria. The ocean zooms around me, and I close my eyes, taking comfort in the heat of the sturdy body that sends the icy chill away from my bones.

My ears ring with every heartbeat, and the water grows warmer and warmer. Moonlight trickles into the now crystal clear ocean, and Mateo concentrates on swimming me to the air I need to breathe.

In one thrust, Mateo sends me to the surface. I spit, expelling the ocean from my lungs. Pale moonlight sets me aglow in the middle of the endless sea, and relief rushes over me with every gasp of breath.

A swell rises next to me, and Mateo breaks the surface. "Ava, what are you thinking? You could've died."

I bob under, struggling to stay afloat. "I don't belong here, Mateo."

"You have to transform back. If King Attilonious discovers you've figured out a way to leave, he'll kill my son the moment he catches him."

"He won't catch him," I say.

"How are you so sure?"

"Trust me."

"The only thing I can trust is that you've gotten in over your head. I know you didn't choose this life and my son made a grave mistake, but please, you have to reconsider what you're doing. You might have bonded with Carter, but you obviously don't share the same feelings mates usually feel. If you care about Carter even a little, you'll transform and return to the castle," he says.

Anger sneaks up on me. "No wonder Starla didn't tell you we survived. You have so little faith in me and Carter. And if *you* love Carter like you claim to, you'd help me swim across the barrier. You'll take me where I need to go since I'm obviously not transforming so you can drag me back to the castle. Carter's counting on me to be there for him. And so you know, I love Carter more than the sea, more than land, and more than even myself. So don't you dare doubt my love for your son."

He doesn't move from his spot, so I start swimming away the best I can, following the pull of my heart that'll lead me directly to Carter. Every few feet I sink under from utter exhaustion that I know I'll have to transform. But I'm no match for Mateo's speed. He's as fast as his son.

I stifle a frustrated sob, stroking my arms out while kicking my legs. The motion awakens a small current to help move me forward, but it's still not fast enough. My hope dwindles, sinking every time I do.

"Ava," Mateo says, swimming up next to me. "I'm sorry. I can't take you to where you need to go, but I will help you cross the barrier, and I won't stop you. I just—I can't risk my mate's life for disobeying the king. I hope you understand."

Relief floods over me in a warm wave, and I nod my head. Locking my fingers to Mateo's broad shoulders, I hold on while he swims me forward, remaining above water so I don't have to hold my breath. The water shimmers with tiny bubbles the farther away we get from the castle, and then Mateo stops where there's a visible line of bubbles—magic—before us.

I release him and tread in place. "Thank you, Mateo. You have no idea how much this means to me."

"Just take care of Carter, Ava," he says.

"Take care of yourself, too."

I hug him in the water, and he embraces me, pressing his warm lips to my cool forehead in the same way my dad used to kiss me. The gesture stirs sadness within me that I push away, because in this moment, I can't think about all the things I miss. All the ways I've been wronged. I must remember and hold onto all the good in my life. All the love. All the strength. All the people I still have that rely on me and who I rely on.

Because I'm going to need it.

I'm never going back to Pearlestria as the king's queen if I ever go back again.

Mateo releases me and throws me up and into the air. I land feet first in the water and transform the moment my head dips under. When I spin in place, Mateo's already swimming back to the colony, leaving me alone.

In this spot, I'm too far to hear the voices of the merpeople of Pearlestria and too far from the Lost Cove to hear Carter. The ocean feels lonely despite its vastness.

With a flick of my tail, I propel myself forward, cutting through the water as quickly as the magical current I've created can take me. I just hope I'm not too late. Because once the king discovers the Lost Cove, he'll do everything he can to break the magic, leaving the inhabitants defenseless.

If the king gets through the protective barrier, he'll send the island to the ocean floor.

But I won't let that happen.

I might not be the queen everyone wants me to be, but I'll fight for the land.

I'll fight to protect the humans.

One way or another, King Attilonious' reign will end.

I just hope I don't end with it.

25

LAST CHANCE

I COAST THE SURFACE SO I can get a clear view of anyone who tries to sneak up on me from below. I doubt they'll be able to, not without me knowing since the diamond on my neck will warn me.

I've never swam this far alone, and it's less pleasant than I thought it would be. I don't know if it's because I'm bored—on land, I've always traveled with music or something—or if it's because I'm freaking out a bit. Who knows? But I can't wait to hit familiar waters. I want nothing more than to return to shore.

Up ahead, a frenzy of blue sharks crowd the sea for what

looks like forever. I push away my human fears, because the biggest predator in the ocean to me is King Attilonious, and swim right into the fray of things. A few sharks bump into me, making it hard to swim. I'll get pretty bruised up if I continue, but it's safer to stay in the frenzy since merpeople would usually dive down to swim around it.

Most of the sharks are shorter in length than I am, considering I'm longer as a mermaid than in my human form, but the sheer amount of them swimming around me, feeding on a school of mackerel, makes me keep my arms clenched against my chest.

A smaller shark brushes against me, its skin feeling almost like sandpaper compared to my slippery scales. I nudge it away and finally give up after another shark bumps into my tail. Diving down, I swim out of the frenzy and into the open sea.

The silhouettes of the sharks above me send goosebumps over my skin. But they don't leave me as on edge as the bottomless ocean below me. I can only see so far and every blurry figure of an ocean animal makes my heart pound and my stomach clench in knots.

Pushing myself harder, I swim as fast as I can. The ocean floor rises below me, the pull in my chest stronger than ever. I haven't swam much outside the reef barrier of the Lost Cove, but I'd recognize these familiar waters. Part of it feels like home—like as long as I'm here, things will turn out okay.

Heat crawls from my chest to my neck, and bright light erupts, sending a stream of dazzling, colorful beams through the water. Without seeing the king or his guards, I can sense them near. I dart down, staying along the bottom of the shallows, navigating around the tropical fish surrounding me in such a way it feels like they're protecting me.

"Follow the barrier. See if there is any weakness in the magic. All I need is a small crack, and I can blast it wide open." King Attilonious' voice sneaks into my mind as he projects it out for his small army of merpeople to hear.

"Carter?" I whisper, afraid that if I push my voice too hard the others will hear it. "I'm here."

"Thank God, Ava. I was getting worried." I blow a bubble through my lips, hearing the sound of Carter's voice in my head.

"It's all okay. I'm okay. But I don't know how to get to you. The king has his guards circling the reef. I'm afraid of coming any closer," I say.

"Don't worry, Aves. I'll come for you. Just stay there," he says.

My heart clenches at the thought of Carter leaving the protection of the cove. He shouldn't have to risk his life to get me. The king doesn't even know I'm here.

"No, Carter. I don't want you to come out here. It isn't safe for you," I say.

He doesn't respond for a moment, and I wring my hands together, afraid he's already on his way, that he'll ignore my pleas and get us both caught.

"I have an idea," he finally says. "But you might not like

it."

I crinkle my nose. "What is it?"

"I'm going to need you to transform."

I hide among the kelp growing right before the shallows dip into the open sea. Flicking my gaze from the surface to the area around me, I anxiously await for the shadow of the boat to cross over the reef.

King Attilonious disappeared minutes ago to swim around the reef himself, and a lonely guard hovers in the sea, peering at the reef like it'll somehow open up and let him in. The magic only allows the merpeople loyal to the inhabitants of the Lost Cove in, and since none of the guards or the king knows of their existence, they won't be able to get through unless King Attilonious can break the protective barrier.

My heart soars in my throat the second the shadow of the small boat crosses the reef. I bob back and forth in the suddenly choppy water, and I realize what's happening the second I see a paddle break the surface.

"Carter?" I ask. "Who's in the boat? I thought you were going to push it over."

"The guard would be curious if he knew it was empty. This was the only way to get him to back off," Carter says.

And he's right. The moment the guard spots the boat, the merman swims away from his spot looking at the reef. The ocean essence protects us from being seen from boats, but it still doesn't stop the unease that comes with seeing humans on the surface. I should know.

A huge swell rises, lifting and dropping the boat in attempt to keep its passenger from floating to the open sea. No human can leave the island just like no ordinary merperson can cross the reef. Swimming forward, I close the distance between me and the boat.

"My king, there are humans on the other side of the reef," a voice says, cutting through my mind.

"Humans?" King Attilonious asks.

"A boat just crossed over."

Panic slips through me, and I close my eyes, concentrating on transforming into my human self. I kick to the surface, spitting out water, and strong hands lift me from the choppy water and drag me into the boat.

It won't be long until King Attilonious comes to investigate, and I wouldn't put it past him to flip the boat over. If he does, he'll realize I've escaped Pearlestria.

"Here, Ava. Put this on," Wes says, drawing my attention from the rocking waves. He hands me a dress without looking at me.

I slide it on over my head and take one of the paddles. "You're crazy for coming out here. The king will get to us at any second. We need to paddle."

Wes nods, dipping his paddle into the rough water, and we both struggle to bring the boat back over the reef. The ocean wants to send Wes under, but there's no way I'm going to let him fall overboard, especially not with the king around.

"Come on," I say more to myself, slicing my paddle through the water.

Something knocks into the boat, sending my heart to my feet. It definitely wasn't just another swell trying to knock the boat over. The force was intentional, hard enough to knock the paddle right from Wes' hand. It drifts away, leaving us with one.

With a wave of my hand, I create a current strong enough to propel us toward the reef. I didn't want to use my magic, but I was left with no choice. And it's still not strong enough. A huge wave cascades over us, filling the boat with a foot of water. Hands reach from the sea and lock onto the edge of the boat. My voice rings through the air as surprise grabs hold of me.

I meet King Attilonious' dark, heated gaze.

Without hesitating, I grab onto Wes' hand and pull him with me. We dive over the edge of the boat and away from the king. Blindly, I flick out my hand, shooting a wave of water behind us. Strong hands grab me by the waist, and I scream through the water, thrashing and kicking, refusing to let go of Wes.

"Ava, it's me," Carter says, pulling me from the king who raises his staff in our direction.

Thrusting out my freehand, I blast King Attilonious with an icy current, knocking his staff sideways. The motion is enough to propel us back, and Carter breaches from the water, taking both me and Wes over the barrier and back into the bay of the Lost Cove.

A huge wave swells from the other side of the reef, rising high into the air. The king sends the ocean directly at us from his spot, even though he can't cross over. It's in this moment I realize that even though King Attilonious can't reach us, the ocean—the water he controls—can, and it won't be long until he tries to sweep us all away.

"Ava!" King Attilonious' voice stabs me in my mind. The force of his words nearly leaves me breathless as another wave steals my oxygen away. "I'm giving you one opportunity to return to my side. If you do, I'll leave this place alone. I'll let that little human who is helping you live. But if you don't, you can consider yourself an enemy, and I will not rest until I take back what is mine."

I don't respond to him. The shock of being able to hear the king, even in my human form, frightens me. We shouldn't be so connected. I can't even hear Carter in this state.

"Come on, Ava. You need to transform," Carter says. He's holding onto both me and Wes in the unrelenting waves created by King Attilonious.

"Take him to shore," I say, motioning to Wes.

"What are you going to do?" Carter asks.

"I'm going to try to stop the king from wiping us out," I say.

Carter presses his lips to mine for a quick second, just long enough that I can feel his strength and courage wash through me. "I'll be right back."

I nod instead of arguing. Sinking under, I transform into a

mermaid. A thousand bubbles prickle against my skin. The water shudders around me, scaring the ocean life away. Fish scatter, swimming in all different directions, and the water grows hazy as sand swirls through the current with every new wave.

Holding my hands out, I push back at the water, imagining it bending to my will. My cold current hits King Attilonious' hot one, forcing it back toward the reef. I swim forward with it, doing my best to calm the water around me.

"This is your last chance, Ava," the king says again. "I will punish Carter's family on your behalf. Their lives will be on you. Are you really going to let that happen? All because you're too stubborn to see how the world works."

I still refuse to respond to the king.

Carter swims up next to me, taking my hand in his, and we both stare at the dangerous sea before us.

"Carter, he's threatening your family," I say.

He holds me tighter. "He's bluffing."

"And if he isn't?" I ask.

"I'm not letting you go out there. I won't let him win," he says.

Closing my eyes, I focus on the love radiating from Carter—the love that pushes away the panic threatening to be my undoing. "I think he might've already won."

"If he had won, he wouldn't be trying so hard, Aves. You've got him scared. He thinks you're a threat to him. It's why he's doing this."

"He's not afraid of me," I say.

"He's shaking."

Carter's words ease the fear clenching my chest, and I suck in water to push it out through my gills. We hold tightly to each other as another wave cascades over the reef, high enough to reach the shore. I push it back with a flick of my hand, and the sudden movement drags us forward. This push and pull of magic leaves me dizzy, and it takes everything in me to constantly fight the king's attempts to make me comply.

"Carter, I don't know how much of this I can take," I say. "There has to be something more we can do."

We meet each other's gazes in the water. Carter's bright bluish-green eyes look like two jewels, sparkling at me. I know he'd attempt to fight the king if I asked him. He'd be by my side, keeping me safe, while I try to get the king to back off. But even now, even in the Lost Cove, I still don't feel as powerful as I need to be to get King Attilonious to leave us alone, to revert things back to how they were. It'll all come down to who wants it more, and I'm not sure that's me.

"He'll give up, Ava," Carter says. "When he does, we'll think things through. We'll beat him on our terms. We'll use our strengths against him."

I blink a few times as his words sink into my bones. Carter's right about one thing. I need to turn this power struggle around to where it's on my terms. The king holds strong because he knows how to control his power. He knows the ocean doesn't have a choice. He's all powerful in the water. But there is one place he isn't.

"The land, Carter. I thought I could defend us because I knew the water here, because Celestiana's essence is the strongest here, but I was wrong. The only place I'll be able to stop King Attilonious is on land. We have to get him to shore," I say.

"But I can't go there," Carter says. "And the others. What about them?"

I reach out and cup his face in my hands. It might be a long shot, but it's the only way any of us will have a fighting chance. I can't stay here, fighting the waves forever. I can't hope and pray the king will give up so we can rest. Because that'll give the king a chance to get stronger.

All this has to end now.

It has to end on my terms.

I'm fighting for the land and the sea, and that's why I have to use them together.

"The others will be fine, but I need you in the water, okay? I need you to keep the guards away," I say. "Do you think you can do that?"

He hesitates, not because he doesn't think he's capable of keeping the guards away, but because he's unsure if he's capable of leaving me. But he has to be.

"We can do this, Carter," I say. "We *have* to do this. We haven't been through so much just to stop now. I'm not going to risk being apart from you anymore. I'm not going to let the king threaten your family or our lives just because he can't get what he wants. The ocean needs us. The land needs us. Do you remember why you chose me, Carter?" I ask.

"Because all I could see was our future. How much I felt connected to you because you loved the land as much as me," he says.

"And I can see that future now," I say. "I can finally see what you saw in me."

He smiles, pushing away the fear in his eyes. It's the same smile I saw on him the first time our eyes met on the dock. It's the smile that is only for me. "You're the perfect mate for me, you know."

"Forever," I say.

I lean over and kiss him. Not like it's the last kiss we'll ever share, but like the first real one we shared on the night of my transformation when my life was changed forever. This is the kiss that'll linger with me to remind me what I'm fighting for. The kiss that'll make sure I do everything I can to see that I win. Because I'm tired of not getting to make the choices in my life. I'm tired of feeling like fate controls me.

"Ready?" Carter asks, pulling me forward in the rolling bay.

I straighten my shoulders, channeling Carter's bravery into my heart where his essence entangles with mine. "Yeah. Let's get our lives back."

26

DON'T DESERVE OCEAN MAGIC

REACHING MY HANDS OUT AND pulling them to me, I summon a wave from the other side of the reef. At the same time it crashes over me, Carter jumps from the water and over the protective barrier leading to the open ocean where the king's guards wait.

A heavy body collides with mine, sending me tumbling through the bay. A cloud of sand engulfs me, turning the clear water hazy. I don't have a chance to move before the king jabs his staff into my chest, sending a shuddering pulse over me.

Shadows edge the corners of my vision. Locking my fingers

around the staff, I use it to pull myself from the ground when the king jerks his arm back. I cling on to his staff, refusing to let it go. King Attilonious grabs me by the hair and forces me away from him. I land on my back in the sand at the bottom of the bay.

I'm up in seconds, swimming backward in the current while sending a stream of cool water in his direction. It slows him down just enough that I can flip to swim toward the shore and to the spot I need him to be.

Heat courses over me as the temperature shifts from warm to hot to match the king's rage. I flick my tail hard, propelling forward. I don't glance behind me. I don't have to. I can feel the tingling sensation of King Attilonious' magic sliding over me, threatening to send me back to the bay floor.

A shockwave erupts from the queen's diamond on my neck, and King Attilonious yells through my mind in surprise. It's like the stone does everything it can to protect me, to make sure I end up where I need to be.

"You can't escape me, Ava. I will have your power, even if you don't willingly give it to me. I'll take it," the king says.

"You won't," I say. "It's not yours to take."

"You could've made this so easy on yourself. All you had to do was pledge your loyalty to me. It didn't have to come down to this." Nails dig into the base of my tail, and King Attilonious jerks me toward him, forcing me to stop. "You could've had the whole ocean at your fingertips."

Swinging out my hand, I hit him with a current that snaps

his head to the side. "I don't want the ocean!"

"And that's why you don't deserve what it bestowed upon you, you ungrateful girl." King Attilonious' eyes burn bright through the water. Power radiates from him, shimmering around us in a million tiny bubbles zinging over my skin, engulfing me in a tingling sensation that creeps into my very essence with every breath of water I suck into my lungs.

It stings me from the inside out, threatening to consume me and rip my own mermaid essence from my heart. I struggle in the king's grip as he holds me before him in the water. His eyes bore into mine. My heart races, lighting up the water around us in quick successions. It feels like it'll leap from my chest and land against the king where he can snuff out my spark of life.

"It's over, Ava," he says.

But I refuse to believe it.

The surface lightens overhead, the morning pushing away the darkness of night. The ripples shine purple, and I wish with everything in me that I could kick to the surface to watch the sunrise one last time.

"Don't give up, Ava," Carter whispers into my mind. "I'm coming for you."

"But the guards," I whisper.

"They're gone," he says. "Just hold on."

But I don't think I can.

The shadow of a boat crosses overhead, and I pout my bottom lip out. The humans of the Lost Cove don't stand a chance the moment I'm gone. It breaks my heart.

Tears drip from my eyes and disappear into the sea. King Attilonious draws me closer, and I can't find the will to resist when he presses his lips against mine. A thousand images crash into my mind, and my whole body burns as he slowly steals my life essence and magic away.

"Ava!" Carter's voice erupts in my mind.

The king stiffens and pulls away. He raises his staff at my mate, ready to blast him with the ocean's magic. A splash shifts the water from overhead, drawing the king's attention away for a split second. My mouth drops open the moment I see both Wes and Giselle enter the water, each holding a spear in their hands like they stand a chance against the most powerful being in all the seas.

King Attilonious jerks his staff toward my friends, aiming it away from Carter, and a pulse cuts through the water, sending a hot current their way.

My heart stalls, the blink of light in my chest freezing. It glows so brightly I'm sure the king sees it. A look of shock crosses his face, and we fly through the water on a wave that blasts from me, sending us both toward the shore.

The ocean moves with my instincts instead of bending to my will, and it catches me in a now placid surf while the king still flies through the current until he hits the sand, sending a cloud into the water. But he's not down for long, and I'm too slow. He slaps his mighty tail, shooting him forward. The weight of his body knocks me back, pulling me deeper into the water.

The world spins as another figure smashes into the king, ripping me from him. Carter grabs King Attilonious from behind, hooking his muscular arm around the king's neck. The king tries to elbow him in the face, but Carter is quick to move, scratching his sharp nails over King Attilonious' throat. The ocean rises, turning the shallows of the shore a few feet deeper, and it pushes Carter and the king forward fast enough that Carter loses his grip.

In one swift motion, the king grabs my mate and launches him through the water in front of him. He raises his staff, splitting the waves so Carter drops to the sandy floor. Water expels from Carter's lungs, forcing him to breathe in the dome of air. It surprises him, slowing him down. He only has time to roll into the wave to get out of the way, but King Attilonious smashes down his staff into Carter's tail, spearing him.

Carter yells out through the water and through my mind, sending me flying toward the king. Pain washes through my tail, the raw emotion coming from Carter. I don't let it slow me down. It merely pushes me faster.

I ram my shoulder into King Attilonious' back. He turns his attention away from Carter and back to me. With a thrust of my hands, I slam into the king's chest while kicking my tail, and I push us so close to the shore that when he tries to flick his tail, it smacks on the sand and forces both our heads above water.

Surprise widens the king's eyes before rage narrows them.

He locks his fingers around my arms and flips me over his shoulder. I hit my back on the sand, and a wave washes over my face, causing me to choke.

King Attilonious rises above me, lifted higher on a wave, and he holds his staff up to me. The surf slides over me, heavier than I've ever felt it. It locks me in place, and all I can do is watch as King Attilonious prepares to try to steal my magic.

"Ava," Carter whispers into my mind. "You have to transform. Do it now."

As King Attilonious swings his staff at me through the water, aiming for the spark in my chest, I close my eyes and let the transformation take hold of me. Cramps seize me for a second, causing me to jerk up, and the staff whips my shoulder. A scream rips from my mouth, and my whole body shudders with a pain so intense that I fall back to the sand. A wave rips me away from the king, dragging me toward land, and he zooms after me. His long fingers wrap around my ankle, but I don't let him grab hold of me. I transform back into a mermaid and slap him in the face with my cerulean tail.

Pulling my hands toward my chest, I summon the water around the king, and it propels him closer to me. The massive wave sends us to the shore so far that I plow into a young palm tree. It cracks, falling forward, and lands on the king's tail. He hollers and picks it up to throw it off of him. It lands in the receding waves and rolls into the surf.

King Attilonious narrows his gaze on me and rides a small wave in my direction. Closing my eyes, I will myself to transform into a human. I expel the water from my lungs and scramble to my feet.

A hot whitecap crashes into me, knocking me sideways, and I flail as I'm dragged closer to King Attilonious. He locks his hand around my neck, squeezing my airway. Shadows edge my vision, trying to steal my consciousness.

Lying under his power, I've never felt so utterly wrong. Because even out of the sea he controls, he's still powerful. He's twice as strong and heavy without the water cushioning us. His weight presses me into the sand, and I know at any second, I'll break.

I open and close my mouth, trying to force air out so I can talk. "Ple—" I can't do it. He's not even going to let me say final words.

This is it.

A shadow falls over me, blocking the halo of sun around the king's salt and pepper hair. He huffs, bending closer, and loses his balance. His hand slides from my throat and into the sand, but the weight of his tail still crushes my legs.

King Attilonious growls, grinding his teeth, and a palm-sized rock lands in the sand next to us. Then another and another. The inhabitants of the Lost Cove throw everything they can find at the king, giving me the precious moment I need. With a flick of my hand, I call the ocean to me, pulling a wave from the bay. It crashes onto us, lifting the king from me, and I scramble away.

Hands lock onto my waist, pulling me deeper, and I meet

Carter's blue-green eyes. We share a look, one that speaks volumes without even being able to communicate with me in my human form, and he propels us forward where the six people we've been sharing this island with attack the king with whatever they can get their hands on. They won't last long though, because the ocean swells around us, and as soon as King Attilonious gives his command, it'll wipe everyone away.

Holding my hands out while Carter swims us forward, I steal the ocean back, forcing it out to sea instead of land. Carter pushes me onto the beach, and I get to my feet, still holding off the waves King Attilonious struggles to control. My torn dress clings to my wet skin, and I clutch the stone around my neck.

"Attilonious!" I yell, my voice echoing through the air. "You've lost! The ocean here belongs to us."

He shifts in the sand, the sun glittering off his golden tail. He raises his staff, trying to break the hold I have on the water, but I refuse to give it up. He can try all he wants, but these sands are mine. The land, the shores—they're mine.

All the king does is laugh, mocking me as I try to stand tall before him. "Is that what you think, Ava? That just because you wear the queen's heart—part of *my* heart—that you can steal from me? You will give back to me what is rightfully mine. Don't think I won't sink this entire island. Celestiana was just as foolish as you for even thinking she could ever save these humans."

I glance from the ocean behind me, seeing Carter's spark through the sand-clouded wave to the tree line where I spot

Giselle holding onto one of the palm trees, preparing herself along with the others if I can't stop Attilonious.

"I won't let you," I say.

"You don't have a choice." King Attilonious brings his staff down hard on the unmoving water, breaking my hold on it, and the wave cascades over us, blocking the morning sun from my vision.

I will my mermaid transformation to take hold and suck in water the moment it slams into me, leaving me trapped on the sea floor.

"Carter!" I scream in my mind. "Save the others!"

"But the king," he says.

"Save them," I say again.

King Attilonious wraps me in a hot whirlpool, cutting us off from the rest of the world. Even if Carter wanted to save me, he could never get to me. I'd rather him save the ones I care about. The ones who were never supposed to be in this mess to begin with.

"Tell me, Ava. Was this worth it?" The king's voice echoes through my mind.

I cringe, feeling his thoughts overpower mine. He hovers over me in the water, his staff gripped in his hand. The diamond on the end glows as brightly as the one on my neck, and I blink a few times to try to see through the shimmering haze of bubbles.

I don't answer his question and instead say, "You'll doom everyone. You know the land and the sea should be united. You know it wasn't always this way. Even your own daughter has the land in her blood, just like Celestiana. Like me."

"And that's why you'll never be as powerful as I am. You don't deserve the magic of the ocean." King Attilonious aims his staff at my spark. This time, there's no one here to stop him.

"And neither do you," I spit out.

He slams his staff against my chest, hitting me in my heart. I arch my back, the force of his power shuddering through me. It leaves me immobilized as he leans over me, pressing his lips against mine to take my mermaid essence away.

Cramps roll over me, seizing my tail and tingling up my back to where my dorsal fin presses against my ripped dress. Fire courses through my veins, and I thrash and claw at the king as I feel my very essence slip away.

I transform into a human, the spark in my chest slowing down and fading. The king isn't just killing me, he's taking away everything Carter had given me. He's severing our bond and forcing me to renounce the ocean against my will.

My lungs scream, aching to breathe in air that'll never come. Because the king isn't letting me survive this. He's not going to just let me live with the dark hole that ices my chest as the remaining fire of my spark smolders out.

The king pulls away, his dark eyes glowing through the blurry water. The spark in his chest shines brighter than ever— or maybe it's because my vision grows dark the longer he keeps me from breathing the air.

My lungs can't hold off any longer, and I take an automatic breath of the ocean. It burns down my throat, filling my lungs in pain and bitterness. When I close my eyes, all I envision is Carter. I'd give anything to see him one more time. To kiss him one more time. But none of that is possible. The last face I'll ever see is that of the king. He truly wanted me to die knowing that I could've never beaten him, that all the fighting I did was for nothing in the end.

"Ava," a voice whispers to me. "Don't let go." It's Carter.

But I can't hold on anymore.

With the remaining strength in my body, I lock my fingers around the queen's heart. King Attilonious aims his staff at me once more. He slams down his staff, striking the diamond I clutch to my chest, sending a jolt of power around us.

It cuts through his hot whirlpool, breaking the king's hold. Rainbow light shimmers around me, and in this moment I realize that both of our diamonds have shattered. The magic within them leaks into the sea.

But none of that matters now.

Because no matter how hard I tried, the king still stole everything from me.

"Ava, my daughter," a familiar voice whispers. "Do not fear. If you fear, you'll be lost forever."

I close my eyes and let the voice take me away. The ocean wraps me in its comforting embrace, pulling me from the king.

Two bright, blue-green eyes glow in the waves in front of me and a love unlike any other washes through me.

It's the last thing I feel before the world disappears.

27

TIME FOR CHANGE

"I'VE FAILED." I SIT IN the sand in my human form, stretching out my legs in front of me.

"You didn't fail, my daughter. You broke the king's hold on the ocean," Celestiana says from next to me. Her silver tail slaps against the waves on our tropical paradise island with glittering sands and crystalline water that goes on forever in front of us.

"But he stole the ocean away from me. I felt it. I felt it leave me. And now..." It's hard to spit the words out. "And now I'm here with you. Wherever this is."

Her dainty hand reaches out and touches mine. "Oh, Ava. Just because you're here doesn't mean you're dead. We're linked and always will be. Attilonious underestimated you and your connection to the sea. Even he doesn't have the kind of power to take away what has been given to you by the ocean."

"You mean I'm alive?"

"Very much so. All you have to do is open your eyes," she says.

I tense. I'm not so sure I'm ready to face the destruction caused by the king. "But the king."

"Isn't the king anymore. He can't harm you ever again. The ocean made sure of it," she says.

I close my eyes, just letting it all sink in. The warm sun pushes away the coldness clinging to my bones, and I suck in a few deep breaths of balmy air. "What happens now?" I ask, holding onto the serenity of the moment and the paradise created for me and Celestiana.

"The ocean has given you everything you need, including your warrior who can follow you anywhere. You'll make a beautiful queen."

"I don't want to be queen. I want to go home with Carter and figure my life out," I say.

"You'll make it work. This is nothing you can't handle. You don't have to choose between the land or the sea anymore."

I snap open my eyes to look at her, but she's gone. Warm arms cradle me, and I shift and meet Carter's gaze. Sparkling tears glitter on his cheeks, and he showers me with a dozen kisses, making me laugh.

"I wasn't sure you'd ever wake up," he whispers.

"It's only been a few minutes," I say, brushing sand from his face.

"No, it's been hours."

I frown, but Carter kisses the expression from my lips. He kisses me so passionately, so deeply, it's like his very essence travels from his heart to his lips to fill me up and leave me gasping for more of his love.

We break apart, and he just cradles me some more like he'll never let me go again. He holds me against him, resting his chin on the crook of my neck without saying a word. And he doesn't have to. We could spend the rest of our lives without speaking and be okay, because all that matters is that we're alive and free from the king's reign.

"Ava," a soft voice says from behind me.

As much as I don't want to move, don't want to pull myself away from Carter, I force myself to my feet. It's only then that I realize Carter sits in the sand just as human as I am. He has a small gash on his shin from where Attilonious speared him with his staff, but it's already healing.

Whatever I did, whatever happened after I allowed the ocean into me, has done something to break the king's hold on Carter's merman essence. *The queen said the ocean gave you everything you need to figure it out...including a warrior to follow you anywhere, meaning between the land and the sea.*

Carter stands with me, holding a tattered blanket to cover

himself. Giselle closes the distance between us, and I wrap my arms around my best friend. We cry together, all snotty and heaving chests, full on sobs that even Carter can't rub away.

"I knew my BFF was awesome, but damn," Giselle says, laughing through her tears. "Does this mean it's finally over?"

I pull away and turn to look at Carter before turning back to Giselle. "Yeah, it's over. We can go ho—" I snap my mouth shut at the thought. I'm not even sure Azure Waters is still there after what the ki—what Attilonious did.

Giselle stifles a gasp. "What aren't you telling me?"

Carter puts his arms around the both of us. "We'll figure it all out."

Someone clears their throat from behind us, and we all turn to meet the gazes of Bailey, Wes, Reyna, Darren, and Sandra. My heart slams against my ribcage seeing the unmoving body of Attilonious at their feet, in all his naked, human glory. His salt and pepper hair hangs limply over his face as he lies on his stomach with his cheek pressed into the sand. Seeing him like this fills me with pity, and a tiny bit of sadness—not for him but for Luna. He was her dad after all.

"He's still breathing," Wes says, nudging Attilonious with his bare foot.

Carter tenses next to me. "Not for long."

I lock my fingers through his, stopping him in his tracks. His brows hang low over his oceanic eyes, and he studies me for a minute as I gather my thoughts.

I should be the first person to want Attilonious dead. I

should send him into the waves and drown him myself for everything he's done. But something holds me back. I'm not a murderer, especially of someone who can't even get to his feet—feet that are brand new, in a body that is brand new, even in a life that is all new to him. What the ocean gave to him was taken back, and now he'll live out the rest of his life as the species he refused to unite with.

"He's no longer a threat to us," I say, turning away from Carter to the others. "Killing him goes against everything in me. He will not be harmed. Do you all understand?"

"How are you so sure? He's the reason we're all here." Bailey crosses her arms over her chest. "And there's no way I'm living on this island with him."

I rub my lips together, tasting the ever-present saltwater that clings to me. "You don't have to. You can all come with me. We'll work things out. We can have our lives back. I figured I could use this island to help the colonies adjust, so they can enter the human world if they want to. What better way to protect the ocean than from on the surface and below?"

Darren and Sandra look at each other for a moment, then Darren says, "My life is here. There's no place for me in the human world anymore."

"I'm afraid that goes for me, too. This is my home. It might not be much, but I don't think I want to leave," Sandra says.

Sadness rises in my heart. I can't imagine going through what they're going through. The world isn't the same place it was when they left. A lot has changed in twenty plus years.

Brushing my hand through my tangled hair, I stare at them. I try to think of a million reasons to convince them to leave the island, but nothing sounds as good as their reason to want to stay.

"What about the rest of you?" I ask.

Wes slings his arm around Bailey's shoulder. "Whatever she decides. We're both here for you, Ava. Whatever we can do to help you, we will." I'm not sure if it's really him talking or the fact that I saved his life—either way, I guess it doesn't matter now. We're all in this together.

"I have a husband to get back to," Reyna says, cutting in when Bailey doesn't speak right away. "I haven't been here as long as any of the others."

Bailey looks at Reyna and then to the sand like she'll find the answer written on the beach before her. "I don't know what I want. It's been so long. Mom and Dad, they—"

"We'll work it out. I'm your sister, Bailey. If you want to leave, I won't abandon you. Even if you choose to stay, I still won't abandon you. But Attilonious. He can't leave. The ocean won't allow him to." I don't have to test my theory to know. Attilonious is truly one of the lost now.

Bailey nods. "I want to leave then, even if going home isn't an option for me."

It might not be an option for any of us, but I'm afraid to say it. Carter hugs me from behind, leaning down to rest his chin on my shoulder. He's thinking what I'm thinking, but the only way we'll know for sure is if we see things for ourselves.

Before I can make a plan, Attilonious moans from the ground. He spits sand from his mouth and pushes himself up to steady his upper body on his hands without getting to his feet. Everyone takes a few steps back, putting distance between them and the fallen king, but I stand my ground with Carter by my side.

"Attilonious, your reign of the sea has ended. If you attempt to fight or hurt any of us, the ocean will end your life," I say.

He falls back to the ground and just lays there without a word. I'm not in the mood to coddle him or tell him it'll be okay, because I don't care. He got what he deserved. As long as he knows his new place in this bright new world, I'm satisfied with never looking in his eyes, never hearing his voice in my mind again.

"Carter? Ava?" a familiar voice asks from the water. "Oh, thank God!"

Carter tugs me from my spot in front of Attilonious and into the lapping surf. We meet Starla and Mateo in chest high water, and they nearly tackle the both of us. Mateo spins me around, creating a current with his tail. Starla hugs Carter for so long that he laughs and pulls himself away.

"The guards returned to Pearlestria. They said something had gotten into the king. Something you did changed things for them, Ava. They refused to stand by the king against you," Mateo says.

It wasn't me who got to them. It was the very ocean surrounding us. It was the queen's essence lingering in these waves and in my heart, even without the diamond that bound us.

"And then the magical barrier disappeared, and we came as soon as we could. Is Attilonious?" Starla asks.

A small wave splashes me, and another head pops up to the surface. Black hair veils Luna's face, and she meets my gaze with serious eyes.

"Where is he?" Luna asks.

"Luna," I say. "It's okay. Everything's going to be okay. Attilonious, he—"

She pouts, grief crinkling her eyes in the corners. "He's gone, right?" she asks, interrupting like she can't bear to hear me say the words out loud. "I knew he'd push you, and I knew this would be a possibility. I was just hoping you could work it out. But I felt something shift in the water. I know I shouldn't have followed Starla, but I couldn't stay in Pearlestria and wait. Can you take me to him? Or did the sea... Oh, my Ocean—" Tears spring from her eyes, and she thrusts her arms around me.

I shake her for a moment as she breaks down without even letting me get in a word. "Luna, listen to me. Attilonious is alive."

"But—"

"I broke his hold on the ocean by shattering the diamond that held his magic, and then I stole it from him completely. The ocean took his merman essence after. He's human now," I say.

"Oh, Ocean," Luna says, her eyes widening. "I must go to him."

"He's on the shore," I say.

Luna dives underwater without another word, leaving me and Carter with his parents.

"You know what this makes you, Ava-girl, right?" Mateo asks. "The ocean has chosen her true queen. The colonies, they'll be—"

I crinkle my nose, raising my hand to stop him. "About that—"

"My beautiful, brave, powerful queen," Carter says, smiling so wide I softly punch him in the shoulder. "She's about to make some big changes."

Starla nods. "Good. I think change is exactly what everyone needs."

"We won't be long. A day or two tops," I say, wrapping my arms around Giselle. "Luna and Mateo are going to stay here the entire time."

My best friend squeezes me tighter. "The first thing we're going to do when we get home is going to eat at the Taco Palace. I'm dying for tacos."

I laugh. "I'll bring some back with me."

"Enough for everyone," Wes says, grinning from his spot in the sand next to Bailey in front of the fire.

A few feet away, sitting in the lapping waves, remains Attilonious with both Luna and Mateo. It'll be a hard adjustment for Attilonious, but he'll get through it for his daughter's sake. It helps how much she loves the land. It shines so brightly in her eyes that it'll shine a new light on her father.

"Of course," I say to Wes, drawing my eyes from Attilonious. "We'll see you all soon."

Carter slides his hands around my waist and pulls me with him into the water where Starla waits for us in the waves. Our first stop will be to Azure Waters, and then we'll head to San Francisco where we can get what we need since Starla had hoped to return to land one day.

We swim to the middle of the bay in our human forms, and Carter locks his fingers through mine, staring deeply into my eyes. The sky shines purple with twilight, and I lean forward to kiss him once more.

"Don't be afraid to transform," I say, knowing Carter's hesitating. "As my mate, you don't need the sea stone anymore. Celestiana told me so."

"What about the others?" he asks.

"I can't restore the magic of the sea stone rings until the full moon," I say. "We can use the time until then to get things ready. I want to use this island to help anyone who wants to visit the land adjust. With the way Attilonious ruled, it was nearly impossible to go to land. Your parents were lucky they had your grandparents."

Carter once told me everyone had a choice. They could live on the land or in the sea. But knowing what I do now, his lifestyle was an exception. Merpeople can't just emerge from the water to join the human world. They need help. And I'll be able to give it to them. All of those on this island now can help me.

"And the colonies are lucky they have you," he says, running his fingers along my cheek to push my hair behind my ear.

"Us, you mean."

With a deep breath, Carter pulls me under the water with him. His hands never leave me as we transform together. Starla swims up next to us, hovering amid the placid bay. I swirl my finger through the water, creating a small whirlpool. The magic of the ocean resides in me more powerful than ever. I no longer have to struggle with the water. I no longer have to fight Attilonious' control. The magic is just there now—in every bubble, in every current, in every creature. It's not a gift bestowed upon me. It is me.

"You okay?" Carter asks, sending his thoughts into my mind.

I bob my head, leaning forward to kiss him. "I'm better than okay. I feel free."

He smiles into my lips. "We are free."

"I want you to show me everything," I say. "I want to go everywhere with you."

"I like the sound of that, Aves. You and me and the ocean."

"And the land."

"Always the land."

28

THE AFTERMATH

THE SHALLOWS OF AZURE WATERS don't look any different from the last time I was here. The faint memory of Attilonious' rage warms the water around me, but it's not real. The water is still cool like usual, and soon to be colder when I transform back into my human self to face the aftermath.

"Want me to look first?" Carter asks, his voice wrapping around me in a comforting familiarity that eases the nerves bunching the muscles on my back.

"Or I can," Starla says, holding one of my hands.

I shake my head as much as I want him to. "No, I have to

do this myself."

"Then whenever you're ready."

I consider popping to the surface without transforming, but I'm afraid if I don't, then I might take one look and dive back into the deep. I need to return to shore and see things for myself. The only way to get my life back is to summon my courage and face what I've left behind, no matter what it is or how hard it is to face.

Closing my eyes, I borrow the strength and courage resonating from Carter and hold it in my heart as I transform. We hover together for only a second and rise to the surface to expel the sea from our lungs, leaving Starla behind.

Bright stars shine overhead, and the beach in front of us is speckled with soft, man-made light. It sends relief through me, and I swim forward, breaking away from Carter. I head directly to the empty beach in front of my house. I never thought I'd ever see it again, but there it is, looming in front of me with a light shining from upstairs.

"Ava," Carter calls from behind me.

I sink to my knees in the sand just outside the surf and cry into my hands. Even though the small fence that surrounds my back patio is broken, even though wooden boards cover all of the downstairs windows and most of the windows of my neighbors for as far as I can see in the dark, everything is still standing. Azure Waters is still here.

And I'm home.

"Ava, you have to stop," Carter says.

He races to me and wraps his arms around me before I can run to my back door. Because I don't care if I'm dripping wet and half naked. I don't care if there will be a million questions. I can't wait any longer.

"I need to see them, Carter," I say.

"Please, you have to think this through. No one knows what people think or how much the police are involved. Your parents thought we were traveling together when you stopped calling them. It's been over a month. What if they assume the worst about me? I know you want them to know you're okay, but we need to know what we'd be returning to. We'll call when we get to San Francisco."

Tears burst from my eyes at his rational thinking, and I hate that he's right. I can't just knock on the door and tell my parents that I've just washed ashore. I can't pretend my phone died or I went somewhere without reception. Giselle was amazing at faking my presence, and since she couldn't do so after she was taken to the Lost Cove, who knows what's going on. All I know is it could be anything. Starla and Mateo were never contacted, but it could've been because they were hard to find. I'll have a lot of explaining to do, and it'll take too much time to do so tonight. The others of the Lost Cove depend on me now. Giselle and Bailey depend on me. The merpeople colonies depend on me.

Carter pulls me back into the surf, petting my hair and holding me as we go. I stare at the light on the second story of my house until he lowers me under where he transforms into a merman before me. I take an extra minute, just listening to the silence of the sea, and then gulp in a breath of water as I transform.

Starla treads in the exact spot we left her, and she hugs me close, glimpsing the sad look crossing my face.

"Things are better than we expected," Carter says for me. "I promised Ava she could call her parents when we get to San Francisco."

"Ava," Starla says. "You sure about that? I know you said you wanted to return to the land, but it might not be safe for you to do that here. I thought maybe you and the others could join me and Mateo in San Francisco. There's still a lot you need to learn, things I can help you with."

I used to fight so hard against Starla and her mermaid traditions, but she might be right. It doesn't change the fact that I'm going to call my parents. Celestiana said only those worthy of the mermaid secret find out. If the ocean lets me tell them, then I know I can trust them. There's not even a doubt in my mind about it.

"I know," I say. "But I can't just let them think something happened to me. And my sister, I want to at least try for her."

Starla nods. "It seems you've made up your mind then."

"I have."

"And I stand by her decision," Carter says, speaking up.

Starla reaches out her hand to me and takes mine in hers. "Then so do I. I just want you to prepare yourself if things can't work out."

"Thank you, Starla. I mean for everything. I don't think I could do this without you."

"I'd do anything for you. You're my daughter," she says.

I smile. "And I'm so glad for that."

Sunshine glitters off the murky water of the marina not far from Starla's apartment. It's not until this moment that I realize how little I know about Carter's parents. Sure, I basically grew up with them through Carter's memories, but some things never really stayed with me.

Like the fact that the store Starla and Mateo own not only has everything ocean-related any beach-goer could ever need, but they also have a number of boats that they do day and evening cruises with, including one for personal use. It's how Carter got his job on the Ocean Jewel before we met when he wanted to leave home and make a life for himself. While he wasn't raised in the water, he was raised on the water. It's just so strange seeing things through my own eyes instead of through his memory.

"She's all set," a woman with dark hair pulled into a ponytail says, stepping onto the wooden dock where Carter's parents are slip owners, even with a live-aboard permit for their own small yacht, well, small in comparison to the Ocean Jewel, the only other yacht I've been aboard. This one can be manned by Carter alone, and he's done it numerous times.

"Thanks for coming down here on such short notice, Nicole," Carter says. "I'll have her back in a day or two. Just taking a short trip with my m—fiancée."

If my heart could escape my chest and splash into the water, it would. Hearing Carter call me his fiancée to a stranger—stranger to me—is something I didn't expect. The smile he gives me when he glances at me nearly makes me melt into a puddle. I think the manager of his parents' shop is about to do the same.

"Of course. I was thrilled when your mom called and told me you were in town," Nicole says. "It's been too long."

Carter hugs her. "I know. Been busy. But my mom asked me to watch over things while she and my dad are gone."

"I bet they're having a blast in Hawaii. If I didn't know any better, I'd think they weren't coming back," she says.

Carter laughs and his uneasiness washes over me. "They changed their minds when I told them we were considering moving here."

She only laughs and hugs Carter once more. We stay on the dock until Nicole disappears and then Carter helps me aboard the Sultry Mermaid. I couldn't stop laughing at the name. Carter said Mateo named it after Starla, which warmed my heart.

The sleek slate gray and white yacht looks nearly new. I run my finger along the tan vinyl seating of the wraparound lounge area that includes a fridge and wetbar right by the cockpit. All whites and tans, the rest of the craft is more spacious than I realized, and it's basically like an RV on the water with a master stateroom. A cushioned headboard sits behind the queen-sized bed, and gleaming storage cabinets line the perimeter, which could fit everything needed for a long ocean excursion. A privacy curtain blocks off the stateroom from the galley and the saloon with white seating and six portholes that give us a view of the marina around us. It's amazing. I'm slightly sad this isn't some romantic getaway but a rescue mission.

"All set?" Carter asks.

"As soon as I call my parents," I say.

"You still sure about it?"

I nod. "Give me a minute?"

Carter leaves me sitting in the saloon, clutching the prepaid phone we picked up on the way here from Starla's apartment. I figured if I do it the second before we head back to the Lost Cove, it might make things easier on me, and I won't want to dive into the ocean and swim back to Azure Waters alone.

My breathing blows static into the receiver when the phone rings three times. It clicks on the fourth, and I nearly hang up. My mom's voice sounds through the line, causing my voice to stick. I blink away my tears, wipe my nose on the sleeve of my shirt, and then release a long breath.

"Hey, Mom. It's me."

I'm greeted with utter silence for a few seconds, and then my mom says, "Ava? Oh, my God. Where are you? Are you okay?"

"I'm fine," I say, my voice only quivering a little. "I'm in San Francisco. I'm sorry I didn't call you sooner. Things have been crazy."

"It's been over a month!"

I cringe as my mom's worry turns into anger. "I know, and I swear I'll explain everything to you, but I can't right now. I just wanted to let you know I'm okay. I'm still with Carter. And Giselle, she—"

"What trouble have you gotten yourselves into? You've been lying to me. If Sapphire didn't tell us you'd come to town without telling us and had lunch with them, I'd thought you were dead. You know, I thought you could tell us anything. If you needed help, you should've called. Then you had to drag Giselle into whatever the hell you've done."

"I'm sorry. I didn't mean to worry you. I swear I have a good reason. But I need to know if I can come home," I say.

"Of course you can. Why wouldn't you be able to?" she asks.

"Well, if the whole world thinks I went missing...or if you called the police."

She sighs. "What have you done?"

"Mom, please."

"I'm not stupid, Avie. We saw you withdrew all the money from your bank account and lied about traveling. When Giselle didn't call Anaya back after a few days, she went to the condo and saw Giselle cleared out her clothes. Then Anaya found the emails on Giselle's laptop...you were never in Washington. I knew we should've put more thought into your sudden attitude change and your need to travel after meeting Carter. God, I hate to ask, but what has he gotten you into that made you need to leave and stop all contact with us? I'm scared for you. We have great lawyers. Whatever it is, you can trust us. I thought you knew that."

She doesn't mention Giselle's rental boat, and I wonder if Attilonious had sunk it completely. I thought for sure that they'd have called in search parties. I thought they knew us better than thinking we'd run off without word.

I'm sure if it had been any longer, things would've been different. But now, we're just inconsiderate kids avoiding the law.

"We're not in trouble," I say.

"So, what? You just ran off?"

"I swear I'll explain."

"I don't like this, Avie. We raised you better than this. Carter's changed you," she says.

I sigh. "You're right. It's just not in the way you'd expect."

"Then just tell me."

"Tomorrow, okay? And only you and dad. Please, don't tell anyone we're coming home."

"I have to tell Anaya. She's been worried sick about Giselle."

I huff into the phone. "Please, Mom. Wait until after you talk to me."

"Ava."

"I mean it," I say, closing my eyes. "If you tell her, I can't promise we'll even stay."

"What do you mean?"

"I have to go, Mom. I love you. Tell Dad I love him, too. You can tell Anaya Giselle's safe, but I mean it. No one can know I'm coming home."

With my words, I hang up. I can't listen to my mom beg and plead with me any longer. I need to do what we've been planning to do.

Walking back up to the cockpit, I slide into the warm seat next to Carter, who sits waiting for me at the helm of the yacht. I rub my hands over my face, smoothing out the worry wrinkles creasing my forehead.

"Everything okay?" he asks.

I meet his eyes. "I think so. My mom's pissed, but we got pretty lucky. They think we're criminals on the run or something."

Carter laughs. "Why does everyone always assume I'm some bad guy?"

"Oh, I don't know. The life changing secrets, maybe?"

He smothers his laugh by biting his lip. "If all else fails and we have to pretend to be criminals, we still have a shiny new castle in Pearlestria, my queen."

I playfully slap his arm. "Don't even start."

"But it's fun."

I roll my eyes, though it feels so good to have Carter be able to tease me about that now. It's almost like the last few weeks never happened. Almost. "Come on, my warrior. Let's get going. We have people to save."

"And then we can enjoy the yacht," he says with a smile.

I lean back and grin. "I'd enjoy even a rowboat as long as it's with you."

29

HOME

CARTER DROPS THE ANCHOR JUST outside of the reef that surrounds the Lost Cove. If it weren't for Starla guiding our way, we'd have had a hard time finding it. The magic remains quite powerful here, and it'll keep those who remain on the island or who choose to spend time in the bay safe from the outside world. It is very much still a trusted merpeople-access only place, which makes it perfect to help transition those who want to explore the land.

Holding his hand out to me, Carter helps me over the fold-down sun bed to the short swimming platform. We lock our fingers together and jump from the yacht to swim the rest of the way to the shore.

"Gi!" I yell, hopping into my bikini bottoms to meet her on shore. "We can go home! We're in probably a hell of a lot of trouble with our parents, but we can go home."

She jumps up and down in the sand, clapping her hands. "Seriously?"

I nod. "It's happening. It's really happening."

We both squeal and hug each other for a long moment while the others gather around us. Starla hugs Mateo in the surf and I spy Luna and Attilonious keeping to themselves a good distance away.

"And us?" Bailey asks, stepping forward.

I take a deep breath. "You're coming home, too. Both you and Wes."

"You mean you're going to share your secret?" she asks.

"Yeah. How else am I supposed to explain that I found you on a random island that no one knows about? Or you know, how I'm going to be unreachable every full moon or longer. But I trust Mom and Dad. They might have a hard time believing us, but I guess we'll find out."

Bailey rocks on her heels. "I guess so. Hey, if it doesn't work out, there's always this island you can drop them off on."

She makes a good point, even if she's joking, but I hope to never have to bring someone here against their will again. I need to trust that Celestiana was right, that only the worthy discover the truth. And I know deep in my heart that my parents are worthy. They wouldn't want me to have to abandon them for the sea. I might be a mermaid, but I'm still Ava Adair.

"It'll work out," I say.

"If you believe that, then so do I."

Maybe the relationship I've wanted to have with Bailey is still possible after all. Fate might've ripped us apart and put a huge wall between us, but we're strong enough to tear it down. We're strong enough to get back what we've lost.

"I do."

"Then let's get off this godforsaken island already."

We grin at each other before we hug. Carter helps Wes with the small rowboat, and Giselle, Bailey, and Reyna get into it. I transform back into a mermaid and swim alongside Carter as he pushes the boat over the reef. It only shakes for a minute before Carter ties it to the yacht.

Carter transforms back into a human and helps the others load the rowboat with the supplies Darren and Sandra, and even Attilonious, will need since they have to start over again. Carter and I leave the others on the yacht to make one last trip to shore.

Darren helps Carter with the supplies, and I remain in my mermaid form to meet Mateo, Starla, and Luna, who has left her dad sitting, staring at the ocean.

"As soon as I get everyone home and everything settled on land, I guess I'll return to Pearlestria," I say. "At least for a bit." Thinking about returning to Pearlestria leaves a bitter taste in my mouth. I know Attilonious is no longer there, but I don't even know what to expect. The merpeople are expecting some mighty queen to guide them, not some uncertain mermaid who just wants to eat tacos with her best friend.

"Don't be nervous, Ava. The colonies already love you," Starla says.

"Thanks," I say. "I'll try my best."

"And I'll be here for you too, Ava," Luna says.

I hug her. "We can teach each other."

"Definitely."

Hands encircle my waist, and Carter presses against me in the water. "We're all set to go. You ready?"

I spin and kiss him. "More than you know."

We leave the yacht anchored just off the coast of Azure Waters and swim to shore. It's been a long boat ride, taking Reyna back to her home in Orange County and staying only for a moment to make sure she was safe.

Carter swims with Giselle and Bailey in each of his arms while Wes holds onto my shoulders until we make it close enough for them to swim on their own.

The private beach behind my house is quiet due to the time of night, but I didn't feel right about docking in the harbor and finding a ride home. I need to be able to leave if I have to without getting trapped.

Who even knows how my parents will react after my phone call yesterday. I just hope they don't have police waiting to question us.

We all lie in the sand for a moment, chests heaving. Carter helps me to my feet before he helps the others, and we stand near my back patio just looking at the boarded up window on the door. *This is what you've wanted all along. Just knock.*

Taking a breath of salty air, I curl my fingers into a fist and knock on the door. Carter drapes his arms over my shoulders, pressing against my back. My knees tremble, and I consider sitting down right on the concrete since the patio furniture is no longer there.

Just when I think I'll have to go around to the front to let us all in through the guest house above the garage, the door cracks before opening completely. Both of my parents hover in the now empty entertainment room in their pajamas. I expect them to drag me inside to yell at me, but my mom surprises me with a hug, and then my dad wraps his arms around the both of us.

"You have no idea what you've put us through, Ava," Dad says, pulling away. "Where did you all even come from? Looks like you swam here."

I release a nervous laugh. "We did. We have a yacht off shore."

"Ava," Mom says. "I don't understand. You've been living at sea? What have you gotten yourself into?"

My chest tightens as I summon the courage to give my parents the explanation I owe them. "Sort of. It's all going to sound so crazy," I say. "You see, it all started on vacation."

My dad turns his narrowed eyes to Carter. "So, this is all

your fault."

"Dad," I say. "Let me explain."

"Well, let's first get you all some towels and take this into the kitchen," Mom says. "I have a feeling I'm going to need to sit down. And cake. I'm going to need cake."

A few minutes later, we all sit around the kitchen table; our kitchen untouched by the water damage the entertainment room acquired, with cake in front of us. I start with our vacation on the yacht, how I met Carter, and just let the truth spill out. Everyone sits in utter silence, and Carter squeezes my hand on top of the table, his plate of cake just as untouched as mine is.

"It's all true," Giselle says, speaking up. "I've seen it all myself."

"I don't even know what to say," Mom says. She turns her eyes to Wes and Bailey. "How do you two fit into all this? Are you mer—I can't even say it."

Bailey straightens in her seat. I skipped over revealing she's my sister and their daughter. Revealing I'm a mermaid was hard enough. I didn't even tell them about how serious my relationship with Carter is or how I'm kind of mermaid royalty.

"We met Ava and Carter when they washed ashore the island we were stranded on. They helped me and Bailey escape. We're just lost humans, really. It's been ten years since I've seen civilization and eight for Bailey."

My parents have been so concerned with me that they haven't paid anyone else much attention, but now that my mom looks at her lost daughter, her eyes light up with recognition. "Bailey?" Mom repeats my sister's name. A strange look crosses her face, and she gapes at my dad before turning to me.

"Bailey didn't drown, Mom," I finally say. "It's all really complicated, and I want to explain everything, but you have to understand—"

"Oh, God. Bailey," Mom says, cutting me off. She jumps from her seat and hovers in front of my sister. "I was so distracted with—" She takes a breath. She can't even repeat anything I've told her yet. Can't really blame her. "I don't know why I didn't see it before."

My dad follows her lead and hugs Bailey. I remain in my seat next to Carter. Tears blur my eyes, and I just soak in the happiness radiating from my family. My parents don't even care I revealed I'm a mermaid. They don't even care things are going to be different. They're just so happy we're all here in this moment together, exactly how it should've always been.

"So, is it okay if we stay here for a while?" Bailey asks. "I know it's been so long—"

"Of course you can. You can all stay. I want you to all stay," Mom says.

"Mom," I whisper. "I want to stay here. I do. But I have things I have to take care of."

My parents stare at me for a long moment in silence, almost like what I revealed was something they could just ignore because I'm home, in my human form, and I brought our family back together.

"You're leaving already? You just got home."

"I know," I say. "But it's all going to be okay. Things have changed for me in a good way. It's safe for me to come home whenever I want, and I'm still going to start college in the fall. But right now, I have to go for a bit."

"You're going with her?" Dad asks Carter.

He nods. "Yes, sir. I've made a vow to your daughter. I'll always keep her safe."

Both my parents hug me and Carter, and then I turn and wrap my arms around Giselle. Bailey and Wes hug me last, and I've never felt more at home even if I'm not going to stay. Because these people are my home, and knowing they're on the land will always bring me back to Azure Waters.

Carter leads me back out to the beach, and the others follow behind us but remain on the back patio. The moon shines above us, creating a path on the ocean, and I smile over my shoulder and wave once before wading in.

I never thought I'd ever get the chance to live my life how I wanted to since the moment I transformed into a mermaid. I always thought I'd spend my life on the run, constantly hiding my secret, and then I thought I'd never get to see the land again. I've struggled between wanting to love the ocean and blame it for everything wrong in my life, but after everything, the ocean was never my enemy. It brought so much love and happiness into my life, something the girl on the dock, standing in front of the Ocean Jewel, would've never imagined or thought possible.

"You know, we don't have to return to Pearlestria tonight," Carter says the moment we both transform.

I smile in the water, pulling him so close that our lips meet. "I wasn't planning on it."

He presses his tail against mine. "Good. I was serious about enjoying the yacht."

"And I was serious about enjoying you."

With a smile, Carter dives us deeper and into the ocean that once again feels like our own private world.

EPILOGUE

UNITED

THE FULL MOON HANGS LOW on the horizon as the night disappears into day. Hundreds of merpeople from all over the world gather in the bay of the Lost Cove. I've spent the last three weeks traveling to all seven colonies, trying my best to remember the names of every merperson in the kingdom.

Together, there are nearly a thousand merpeople, only four of which were human-born like me. The whole, plenty of fish analogy is totally wrong when it comes to merpeople, and Luna was right about thinking she'd never find a mate, because I'm pretty sure she was destined to find one on land.

Carter swims next to me as I'm basically passed around and hugged and kissed by everyone. I'm actually starting to get used to merpeople affection, and it no longer feels like they're invading my space but welcoming me into their own.

Tonight is the night everyone's been waiting for. Under the full moon, I'll officially accept my place as a liaison between the land and ocean. I'm not accepting my place as a ruler but as a guide. I want the colonies to flourish the way Attilonious wouldn't allow. He was too concerned about protecting us from humans instead of entrusting those who can work together with us to help protect not only the ocean but all that is in it. To make life better for everyone.

Carter swims us to the deepest part of the bay where the moon's rays sparkle on the glittering sea floor. I open the small chest of rings brought by Luna and hold my hands over them, feeling the magic of the ocean and the pull of the moon between my fingers.

A thousand sparks blink through the bay like dazzling stars as I turn my attention to the merpeople of the ocean, sparks I feel connected to now more than ever. Sparks that remind me of the gift bestowed on me, how my life is connected to everything good about the sea.

"As the moon sets and the sun brings a new day, it'll also bring a new life to our colonies. It's time to bring our knowledge of the sea to the land and bring a piece of the land into the sea. It's time to reunite with the humans worthy of our secret and work together to find balance between our two worlds. So tonight, under the light of the full moon that binds us to the ocean, I'm restoring the ocean magic into the sea stone rings. I hope you'll all agree to take one even if you choose not to go to land, but I want to encourage you to try. I want to encourage you to explore the world I grew up in and love. I want to encourage you to do what makes you the most happy."

With a twirl of my hands, I summon a small current between my palms, and it picks up the light of the moon and sets the chest of rings aglow.

Carter smiles at me when I meet his gaze, and the whole bay hums with excited voices. Because for some, this will be the first time they'll make it to land, even if it's only the Lost Cove, which I've renamed Celestiana Cove, to honor the queen who made this all possible.

Pale morning light trickles through the bay, and I spin in the water and transform into a human in front of everyone. Carter follows me a moment later, and we both kick to the surface together and gasp in the balmy sea air.

"Aves!" Giselle's voice rings out over the bay, and I wave my hand at the group of people waiting for us on the shore.

A few more people pop to the surface next to me, and I smile at Carter's—my—family. Luna surfaces next with the guard, Blue, and even Tide, Attilonious' old messenger, a merman I met during my first stay at Pearlestria, joins us.

We swim to the shore, and I exit the surf first and take a towel from Giselle. Darren and Sandra help the others from the water, providing them what they need to be on land, and everyone smiles and laughs. It feels so normal.

"Ava-babe! Carter," Matty says. "This is insane. It's the first time me and Logan both lost a bet. We were thinking marriage not mermaids."

Carter fist bumps Matty. It took a lot of consideration whether or not to tell my friends the truth about everything, but they deserved to know. We always shared everything between each other. And just like Celestiana said, only those worthy of my secret would know.

"So when are you going to find us mates?" Chloe says, standing next to Giselle.

I laugh, shaking my head. "Why don't you go introduce yourselves around?"

Giselle grins at me. "Don't mind if we do."

"Ava?" My parents stand together just outside the group of people. It's taken them some time, but they've finally accepted I'm not the same girl I was before I stepped aboard the Ocean Jewel. They've finally realized I'm so much more. And they love me for it. "This place is incredible."

I smile and hug them both. "It's a lot better now. I'm so glad you agreed to come."

"Of course we would."

"There are a few people I want you to meet."

I motion for Carter to bring his parents over to meet mine. It's something that hasn't happened in so long—blending a family of those from land and sea—and I'm so happy we can finally do it.

"Mom, Dad, this is Starla and Mateo Stevens, Carter's parents," I say. "Starla, meet my parents, Beatrice and Allen Adair."

Mateo ignores my dad's handshake and offers him a huge bear hug, making us all laugh. "Ava is the best thing to have come into our lives," he says. "I'm so happy to have her as a daughter."

My cheeks burn when my parents give me a strange look. "Merpeople relationships are a tad different," I say, answering their silent question.

Mom raises her eyebrows but instead of commenting, says, "We're just so relieved Ava has someone like your son watching out for her, and we're happy you've taken her under your care. We appreciate you looking after Ava."

"That's what family is for," Starla says. "And now we're all family. We look forward to getting to know you all and would love to visit Azure Waters. You are always welcome in San Francisco, too."

Our parents hit it off right away, and I turn to slide my arms around Carter's neck. He holds me against him, and I bask in the love and adoration radiating from his very essence.

"You're amazing," he whispers into my ear. "I never thought I'd ever see a day like this."

"It's great, isn't it?" I ask. "I don't think I've ever been so happy."

"I'll never get over that feeling washing through me. It's all I've ever wanted for us, you know. To be happy together no matter if we're on the land or in the sea." Carter slides his hand into his pocket and pulls out a set of rings, ones we no longer need to transform. He slides one onto my finger anyway.

I stare at the sea stone swirling with the magic of the ocean, and then I take his ring from him and slide it on his finger. "As long as we're together. I love you, Carter. More than the sea or the sand. More than anything. Forever."

"I like the sound of that." He pulls me into a kiss, sending me a dozen images showing me exactly how much he loves me, and I send even more right back to him.

I couldn't have asked for a more perfect merman to be my mate. I might be an accidental mermaid, and he might've given me his spark on a whim, but there's no doubt in my mind that this is how things were always supposed to be.

I've spent weeks fighting between my love of the land and the sea that lingers in my heart. Now, I get both. They share me equally. I get a future even better than one of my wildest dreams. I have the whole world in front of me. With it, I can do anything. I can face anything, especially with Carter by my side.

I finally get to live my life exactly how I want to on land and in the sea with the boy chosen just for me. Together, we'll always find happiness. Together, we'll change our world for the better. Because no matter how rough the water is or where life takes us, we'll always be able to swim. We'll always have our sparks to light our way.

~The End~

~THANK YOU!~

THANK YOU SO MUCH FOR following Ava and Carter's adventure to get the future together they desired. I do hope you enjoyed diving into the Spark of Life world as much as I did. As an independent author, I rely heavily on word of mouth to get my books out into the world. If you could please take a moment, I'd love for you to post a review online from the retailer you picked up your copy from. I'd appreciate it with my whole heart. Thanks again for taking a chance on me! I know it's a big book world out there.

To keep up-to-date with what comes next, please make sure to subscribe to my newsletter online at www.GinnaMoran.com. You can also follow me online on Facebook, Twitter, Instagram, and Snapchat.

ACKNOWLEDGEMENTS

THIS SERIES WAS SUCH A blast to write. It wouldn't have been possible without the invaluable help from some incredible people. As always, many thanks to the team who has provided me with amazing help—from plotting to blurb destroying, editing, proofreading, and even a listening ear—Sarah Collier, Katie Harder-Schauer, Jan Moran, Nikki Godwin, Jamie Hall, and Amy Holliday; you are all the best!

Thanks to the professional merpeople on Instagram—especially the Hawaiian Merman and Project Mermaids—who have given me such magical inspiration through sharing your journeys. I'm in awe of your passion and connection to the sea.

Lastly, many thanks to my family and friends, who have been so incredibly supportive of my writing journey. Much love!

 ABOUT GINNA MORAN

GINNA MORAN IS A WRITER from sunny Southern California. She started writing poetry as a teenager in a spiral notebook that she still has tucked away on her desk today. Her love of writing grew after she graduated high school, and she completed her first unpublished manuscript at age eighteen.

When she realized her love of writing was her life's passion, she studied literature at Mira Costa College in Northern San Diego. Besides writing novels, she was senior editor, content manager, and image coordinator for Crescent House Publishing Inc. for four years.

Aside from Ginna's professional life, she enjoys binge watching television shows, playing pretend with her daughter, and cuddling with her dogs. Some of her favorite things include chocolate, anything that glitters, cheesy jokes, and organizing her bookshelf.

Ginna Moran loves to hear from her readers so visit her online at www.GinnaMoran.com. You can also find her on Facebook, Twitter, Instagram, and Snapchat(@GinnaMoran). To stay up-to-date on new releases, sign up to her newsletter. You'll not only get a FREE story, but you'll be able to participate in monthly giveaways!

Ginna Moran is currently hard at work on her next novel.

Other Young Adult Novels by Ginna Moran

PARANORMAL
Destined for Dreams Series
Demon Within Series
Finding Nate Series
Going Ghostly Series
Spark of Life Series
When Souls Collide Series
Demon Watcher Series

CONTEMPORARY
Falling into Fame Series

STANDALONES
Life After Lila